NIGHT IN GLENGYLE

NIGHT IN GLENGYLE

John Ferguson

COACHWHIP PUBLICATIONS

Greenville, Ohio

Night in Glengyle, by John Ferguson
© 2018 Coachwhip Publications

Published 1933
No claims made on public domain material.
Cover image: Moon © Voraorn Ratanakorn

CoachwhipBooks.com

ISBN 1-61646-433-x
ISBN-13 978-1-61646-433-2

CHAPTER I

It was in the passage between Piccadilly and Jermyn Street, near St. James's, that I met Biddulph again. Though I recognized him first, I was unable to avoid him. He stopped and turned to stare just when it seemed I had got safely past.

"Maitland!" he cried.

I had to pull up and turn back.

"Hullo," I said.

"Thought you were touring in Australia," said he, offering his hand and shifting his gaze from my clothes to my face.

"Home three months back," I replied. "You still at the Whitehall office?"

"Oh yes," he laughed. "Still at my desk drudging away in the interests of our far-flung Empire, while you've been gallivanting among its palms and pines. The daily round, the common task for me, you know."

"You look pretty well on it," I declared.

Biddulph shook his head.

"But does it furnish all I ought to ask? No adventure comes to me, you know, no romance hovers over a desk in a Government office. Just safety, and one's bread and butter."

"They're not bad things—bread and butter and safety," I could not help remarking. Then, as his eyes began to stray over me again, I added: "I've got a much better suit than this at home."

That remark really pained him. His manner changed.

"You're out of a shop though, aren't you?" he asked.

"Yes, I am. The South African tour wasn't very successful. And things are pretty sticky in the theatre world just now. We came back at a bad time too. Not much chance for any of us till they begin to put on the new shows next autumn."

"You'll be all right then, of course," he nodded encouragingly. "By Jove, I still remember you in that comedy when you played Barker, the valet."

"Barker, the butler," I corrected. The mistake was natural. A stage butler invariably is a stout, comfortable, well-fed character; and at that moment I daresay to Biddulph's eye it must have seemed a part I never could have played.

"Well, you know," he went on, "I wasn't alone in expecting a great future for you in comedy character parts after that performance. At the time, wherever one went one heard people firing off the lines and tags you had made so gloriously funny."

Of course Biddulph meant well. But he didn't know how short lived an actor's repute can be. I had been away in East Africa with a touring company for two years, and two years in the theatre is a lifetime outside it. After two years even a star would come back to find all his blazing glory dimmed down to a faint sunset monochrome.

He detained me a few minutes longer, interjecting news about former friends, between more questions about myself. Finally as we shook hands he asked me where he could find me. When I gave the address he did not lift his eyebrows, but he did tell me the number of his Jermyn Street flat, saying I must look him up. So that was that!

But he knew I didn't want him to look me up. And he suspected, to judge by the way he kept reiterating the invitation, that I had no intention of going to see him in his flat. But things weren't nearly so bad with me as they had been. Charley Biddulph thought I was lying when I blurted out the assertion that I had a much better suit at home. He made sure that if I did own better clothes I wouldn't be wearing the things he saw me in at four o'clock in the afternoon in the West End where I might run into old friends like himself. There he was wrong. Hanging in the cupboard of my room above the newspaper shop in Soho I had a suit good enough to take me anywhere a blue lounge suit could fittingly go. But I only wore it when I tried to interview managers and visited agents, before whom one dare not appear in a down-at-heel or out-at-elbow condition.

In the last week or so, however, when funds had sunk to zero, I had got a little evening job on which I was compelled to dress decently. This job had come to me at the moment when I had begun to wonder how I could keep body and soul together till the autumn. Going back to my lodgings one night I stopped at a photographer's window in an alley leading into Dean Street. It was quite a little shop, but some business was done, as the exhibits and specimens showed me, with members of my profession, and half idly I scanned the faces to see if there were any I recognized. There were not, and I was about to turn away when my eye lighted on an enlarged photograph of a girl made obviously from a very small snap which was displayed beside it. At the foot of the big picture was a notice:

ENLARGEMENTS DONE
CANVASSERS WANTED

I walked straight in. At the sound of the latch click a small and dirty little old man wearing gold spectacles looked up at me. He was engaged in pasting brown paper on the back of a picture, but stopped on my entry and came forward wiping his hands on his trousers.

"You want a canvasser?" I began.

"As many as we can get, provided they're the right sort," he replied.

"Would I do?"

He looked me up and down, the red rimmed, watery blue eyes peering through the gold-rimmed spectacles. Then he said the unexpected thing.

"Belong to the profession, don't you?"

This I admitted.

"Out of a shop, of course?"

"That's it."

"Expecting to get one?"

"Yes, in September."

He grunted.

"Well, it wouldn't pay me to fit you out."

Not divining what he meant exactly, I asked him mildly to be more explicit. He was half angry that I had forced him to it; he pointed his unclean forefinger at me.

"People'd suppose you was only cadging a crust if you approached them in those clothes," he declared. "It'd let down the value of my work besides, for it to be seen in your hands."

"But you wouldn't need to fit me out. I've got an excellent suit at home," I protested hopefully.

"Well, if you have, boy, why not go 'ome and put 'em on and show yourself?"

It was clear from his tone and the way he turned aside to resume his work that he didn't believe me. But I did go and put 'em on and show myself all inside the next fifteen minutes. Mr. Lucius' crafty little face at the sight revealed surprise and approval. He even waived the deposit of two pounds he usually required on the specimens when I told him I hadn't the money, agreeing to deduct it from my first earnings instead.

The outfit he supplied consisted of some half dozen portrait enlargements, to each of which was attached the small photograph from which the enlargement had been made. These were carried in a leather cloth portfolio and I was also given a notebook in which to enter orders. But it was only after Mr. Lucius had handed me the agreement whereby he was to pay me five per cent of the net profits on my orders, that he really unbent.

"You're just the man I wanted," he said, "to work the West End."

"Really?" I said, delighted.

He nodded.

"You've got what we call a good address, which don't mean the place you live at but the way you speak to people. Gentlemanly, you understand, but not too free and easy. Now these dagoes around here"— he waved a hand to indicate Soho—"I could get loads of them, only they're too cheeky, especially with the women, and you can't trust them with the money neither."

Lucius, however, pulled at his lip when I asked how much he thought I might count on making.

"Well," he said finally, "you've got a good address, a good honest face and good work to show, and you'll have a good neighborhood to work in. I don't see why you shouldn't sometimes make as much as ten bob a night."

I left the shop overjoyed. But I had not been long at the work before discovering that Lucius had either overestimated the value of my address or the goodness of his own work, for at no time did I earn more than half the amount he had mentioned, and very frequently I got nothing at all. Nothing at all? As I write these three words I recognize how essentially untrue they are to the facts. In the limited sense of getting a few shillings out of the work they are true; but in the deepest sense the words are untrue. For I can now see that but for that night on which I stood with my nose glued to Mr. Lucius' window and as a result became a photographer's tout, I never could have got as much as my nose into Glengyle Castle. In the real sense, then, I got everything out of those nights when I carried my portfolio of photographs from door to door. This is how it happened.

About a week after my meeting with Biddulph I got back one night to find a note from him in my rooms. That night I had left off earlier than usual, for though I got some fun as well as snubs out of the work, that night the snubs had been much more numerous and, some of them, vitriolic enough to burn through my skin, thickened though it had become. Though it was torn up afterwards, this is the note as I remember it:

> 6 The Burlington,
> Jermyn Street.
>
> Dear Maitland,
> If you are still without an engagement and care to consider one, will you come round to see me as soon as you get this? The man who may offer you the job is to be here at about eight, and I understand you usually get home about then. I had hoped to see you before you meet him. I told him you were just the man we needed. But he's the sort who must always judge for himself.
>
> Yours,
> C. B.

Diving downstairs into the newspaper shop, I learned from Mrs. Peters, my landlady, that the note had been written there half an hour earlier and put in my room by her husband. Mr. Peters, in shirt sleeves, was engrossed in a detective novel, cheap reprints of detective fiction being one of the shop's side lines, I myself as a lodger being another. So, as I had not yet changed into my old suit I was able to make for Jermyn Street right away. And before I'd had time to speculate as to what the engagement could be, I was at the door of Biddulph's flat.

In the study, however, into which his man put me to wait till his master finished dinner, I had ample time for speculation. If it wasn't for some new show coming on about which I had not heard, it must be to take the part of some actor who had fallen ill. In that case it would be a very minor part, since no understudy had been assigned. And having settled in my own mind that I'd gladly take the part, no matter how small, I sat on patiently waiting for Biddulph to finish his dinner. The chair was luxurious and I was tired, my feet a little sore and heavy with the hot feel of hard pavements yet in them.

It was a beautiful room, a harmony in greys, with here and there in the silk cushions, lampshade and curtains, vivid splashes of orange and black. The rich carpet was a pale grey with a black and orange border, and seemed made for the room. The same grey was repeated in the wallpaper, on which a set of black framed etchings made a straight line from door to window. I remember as I looked round that richly appointed room, with the evidence of a first-rate taste and the means to indulge it everywhere displayed, thinking how absurd it was to call a man in Biddulph's position a clerk. When people spoke of a clerk they didn't have the War Office or the Foreign or Home Office officials in their minds, but some poor chap in a seedy black coat who slaved all day in the city and slept in a bed-sitting-room in Shepherd's Bush. And the absurdity struck me still more when Biddulph's man entered to set down a silver coffee equipage on the small table which he drew up before the regal-looking divan.

Then Biddulph entered, looking so clean and creaseless in his perfect clothes.

"Well," he said as we shook hands. "What are you laughing at now?"

He spoke as if I were notorious for my hilarity.

"Nothing much. I was just thinking of a man who sleeps with aspidestras and antimacassars in Shepherd's Bush."

"How awful. Black or white?"

"Black, please."

"Cognac?"

While I hesitated he splashed a liberal allowance into my cup and then pushed over the cigar box.

"Better smoke, Maitland," he laughed. "I'll have most of the talking to do."

At that, somehow or other I suddenly divined it was not to offer me a part in any play he had called me to Jermyn Street: it was for something much more important—ever so much more important—to himself.

CHAPTER II

This conviction flashing into my mind, sent my eyes to Biddulph's face. And as I waited for him to get on with the business, I was mildly startled to observe the change his face showed since our previous meeting. Then he had been the same careless, elegant, debonair man about town with the roving eye, I had always known. Now there were lines that were almost furrows on the forehead, and shadows under the bright, the over-bright eyes, and now and then an involuntary twitching about the mouth that told of worry, of sleepless nights perhaps, and apprehension. And perceiving this, I now understood the irritability with which he had questioned me on the cause of my amusement when he entered. Biddulph, in short, had aged more in the few days since our last meeting than in all the years of our acquaintance. Suddenly he lifted his eyes, and surprising my intent gaze, nodded like a man who has found the right way in which to begin a difficult speech.

"Yes, we are very worried just now."

"We?" I queried.

"Down at the Office, I mean."

"Oh, it isn't a personal worry, then?"

"Dear me, no—purely departmental."

With a mind relieved I now selected a cigar from the box he had set before me, and as I lit it a new respect for our Government services was burnt into my mind: for here, indeed, was an official who took his responsibilities with adequate seriousness! At the same instant, however, the perception that he intended to bring me into the thing, stimulated my curiosity.

"Go on," I urged; "you want me to do something about it."

Biddulph sat forward alertly.

"Oh, there's a job for you in it, if you care. That's what my note meant. You'd be surprised," he went on more quickly, "if you knew how often we have to employ outside agents on confidential matters connected with the work of our office. As often as not our trouble is to get men of exactly the type needed for the particular work entrusted to them. For we cannot employ them more than once or twice: they soon get known, you understand. And of course they must, whatever their class, be men of discretion, and honor, whom we can trust absolutely, men whom no one can buy, and who, in fact, undertake their work as much from a sense of patriotic duty to their country as for the sake of the big money we offer for success."

Biddulph must have noticed the glow of satisfaction this implied testimonial to myself and this prospect—so much better than hawking photographic enlargements—brought, for he smiled momentarily and shook his head.

"Oh," he said, "remember the money we pay is in strict proportion to the difficulty or the danger of the work done."

This rather dashed my satisfaction.

"You mean that this job is to be a soft and easy affair?"

Again Biddulph smiled.

"No job of this sort is ever soft and easy. It's a question of degree. The amount of danger or difficulty varies."

"All right," I said, my curiosity whetted to its keenest edge. "Just tell me what the job is."

Biddulph had his cup of coffee at his lips as I said this, and I watched him impatiently till he set it down. He set it down slowly and looked at me reproachfully.

"Maitland," he said, "that request is below your standard of intelligence, my boy. Where is the note I left for you?"

His tone was a little acid. He was disappointed with me. When I produced the note he took it from me and indicated its last two lines: "I told him you were just the man we needed. But he's the sort who must always judge for himself."

Of course I saw what the cautious Biddulph meant. Till his superior had seen and judged for himself, Biddulph would tell me nothing.

I sat back, somewhat damped and crestfallen, aware that, after all, there was yet no certainty the job would be given me. Biddulph began to tear the note into little pieces while I sat in silence wondering about the man who would come in presently to judge whether I was fit or not to be trusted. I wanted to ask about him, if only to prepare myself for the coming ordeal, but I feared to be again indiscreet.

Then Biddulph did a funny thing. He rose, and dropping the fragments of the note into a waste paper basket, pulled out a drawer in his bureau. A rustling of paper followed, and then having apparently found what he sought, he crossed over to the fireplace and took down a large silver frame which, as I had already observed, held the photograph of a very pretty woman. This he extracted, replacing in the frame another photograph which he had taken from the drawer. But when he gave the frame a place to itself on the top of the baby grand piano, I saw that he must have divined my unspoken question. For the massive frame now held the photograph of a man—a man whose face was familiar to me, whose smooth, smiling, almost cherubic countenance would have been familiar to anyone.

"*Not*," I breathed, "Mr. Wynne Chatsworth?"

Charles Biddulph laughed at my horror.

"Never talked to a Cabinet Minister before?" he inquired. "Oh, he'll make you forget who he is inside five minutes."

Biddulph seemed in better spirits now. He regarded the photograph almost quizzically, head on one side, and then stooped over to readjust its position, to, I fancy, make it more prominent to anyone entering the room.

"In two minutes you'll see him in the flesh," he reverted. "Punctuality is one of his vices."

Awed as I was, I could not forbear a smile. This displayed photograph, then, was intended for the minister's own eye and not for mine.

Then out in the hall the telephone whirred and Biddulph went to take the call. He had left the door open and it was impossible not to overhear something of what passed.

"Yes, Biddulph speaking. . . . Oh! . . . No, sir, certainly not. . . . He's here now. . . . Well, sir, if you wish me to. . . . Oh, yes, absolutely reliable. . . . Yes, I am prepared to answer for him. . . . Yes, in all

respects, I should say—a first-rate man for the job. . . . But I wish
you could have seen him for yourself. . . . Good. I'll give him the facts
myself, then. . . . Yes, no time to be lost. Hope the division will go
right, sir. . . . Thank you. Good night."

The telephone rang off and Biddulph reappeared, smiling as he
shut the door. If, as I gathered, the Minister had left him to explain
the mission to me, Biddulph did not seem disappointed that the
great man would not see the place of honor given to his photograph
in his subordinate's room. For myself, I felt relieved, and grateful,
as well as touched, by the handsome way in which Biddulph had
spoken about me.

"He can't come," he said; "a critical division expected any moment in the House. So he's left it to me."

"To give me the job?" I was thrilled with excitement.

"And to explain what it is," he nodded.

"Luck for me. Get on with it, then," I implored.

Biddulph smiled a trifle ruefully.

"I'm not so sure about the luck," he remarked. "I haven't his gift
of lucid exposition, and you may find me tedious."

Tedious! Why, at that very moment, but for him, I would have
been hawking cheap photographic enlargements from door to door,
and getting most doors banged in my face. But I let his remark
pass. He had drawn his chair up to the low table, after removing the
coffee tray. Then from his pocket book he produced four newspaper
cuttings.

"It's quite a simple little story," he began, "but I'll probably bun-
gle over it. So if I become obscure, or you miss a point in it, stop me."

On my nod of assent he shot a question at me.

"Ever heard of Nerani?"

"Vaguely. Somewhere in Africa, isn't it?"

Biddulph smiled indulgently.

"It's a young British Crown Colony, bounded on the east by the
Portuguese Colonies, and roughly three hundred miles from the sea-
coast."

"Sounds rather hard to reach," I said doubtfully.

Biddulph's teeth gleamed over my dismay.

"We're not going to send you there," he reassured me. "But, as it happens, that remark of yours leads us to the very core of the matter. Nerani is hard to reach, and if you were interested in Colonial expansion, you would know that Nerani never will develop until the long-projected railway to connect the colony with the coast has been completed."

"Quite so," I assented, trying to look wise, while wondering to what all this could lead.

Biddulph tapped his forefinger on my knee.

"But you will ask *why* the railway has remained so long no more than a project."

"That is what I do want to know," I declared. "If Nerani needs a railway, and if the Government is still shilly-shallying with the project, every British taxpayer will demand to know—"

"Oh, cut that out," Biddulph cried in sharp disgust; "it sounds like cackle from the *Daily Record*. The answer to my question," he went on, "is that since the territory between Nerani and the sea is Portuguese, the railway can only be constructed through an agreement with the Portuguese. And all the shilly-shally is on their side. When one objection they raised was smoothed out, another was raised to replace it. But when the late Government went out of power and Chatsworth succeeded Sir Charles Wridgley as Secretary, he soon got his nose to the unsuspected cause of the delay. Now read this." He bent forward and picked up one of the four news cuttings he had previously laid on the little table. It was a cutting, just one line, from the Stock Exchange columns of some daily:

Katanganas yesterday touched 18/10.

"Katanganas," I repeated, not knowing what was expected of me, but forced to try and look wise.

"Quite so," Biddulph snapped his fingers. "Katanganas, which two months ago were quoted, when they got a quotation at all, at about one shilling, yesterday rose to 18/10."

"For no apparent reason?"

"For no reason that was apparent to anyone except Chatsworth. He saw it almost at once."

"Well?" I prompted him, more interested now that I saw this must have some direct bearing on the job to be entrusted to me.

"Chatsworth saw that this rise in the value of the Katangana shares must be due to the fact that some people knew something about the prospects of the company which has been kept secret from the general public. And I'm sure he is right. Otherwise there is nothing to account for this rise in the shares."

At this juncture I responded to his invitation to stop him if he became obscure.

"But what are Katanganas?" I inquired.

"Katanganas is the name given to the shares of the Katangana Syndicate. The syndicate was formed five years ago to exploit the rich mineral resources of the Katangana territory which lies about two hundred miles north of the Portuguese colonies. But though easy to work, the cost of transport was found to be too great to yield an adequate return on the capital invested. Now do you begin to see what Chatsworth suspects? His suspicion is that the railway may be diverted away from Nerani to Katangana."

Biddulph bent forward to strike the table with his clenched fist.

"More than that! He is convinced that an agreement is about to be signed for the construction of the railway between the Katangana Company and the Portuguese people which will leave the British colony stranded, high and dry, beyond the hope of future development. More than that again! He believes that the Katangana Company has all along been able to go just one better than ourselves in their negotiations with the Portuguese, through being supplied with confidential information about our offers from our own Office. This is where you come in, Maitland. We want you to get possession of all documents, letters or notes which will enable us to ascertain who in our department has been betraying the interests of his own country. We've got to get that man!"

My heart sank. I still remember the sigh that came from me. For I was convinced that touting photographic enlargements was ever so much more hopeful a job than this. But Biddulph, raising his eyes, caught sight of my woe-begone face and burst into a laugh. It was amazing how his own spirits had mounted since our interview began. There was something reassuring in his mirth too: it witnessed to his belief that the job was not beyond my powers. Then just as I got a gleam of comfort from this he picked up the three remaining news cuttings and laid them down under my eyes. Each bore a date and a number. The first was as follows:

> Captain "Bob" Elliott, the big game hunter, was one of the passengers who landed from the *Batavia* yesterday at Plymouth, where he was met by his friend, Mr. Otto Rhand. Both, I hear, hope for some good sport together among the grouse when the season opens.

The second, in clearer type and on better paper, was a brief announcement:

> Mr. Allister Grant has let the Glengyle moors for this season to Sir Charles Wridgley.

The last was another of the personal gossip type:

> Count Pedro Fernandez, the celebrated African explorer, is, I understand, about to make his first visit to this country. His wife (portrait next column) who accompanies him, will be better remembered as Imogen Alessandra, the beautiful Spanish dancer.

While I was striving to connect up these apparently quite disconnected cuttings, Biddulph with a fingertip pushed the one I had previously read under my eyes once more:

> Katanganas yesterday touched 18/10.

Biddulph waited in silence while I racked my brains to connect up the four news cuttings. I wanted to be intelligent about them, and strove to recall anything I knew about the persons mentioned. Of the big game hunter I had never heard, but I had heard of the big financier, Otto Rhand, during our tour when we were in South Africa; and of course Sir Charles Wridgley had been Secretary till his government fell and he was supplanted by Mr. Chatsworth.

Biddulph stirred in his chair.

"Well?" he demanded.

"I see that each of these connects up with Africa," I replied, feeling that he must have expected me to see much more than that.

"You do? How do you see Africa in the first one?"

"Well, as the *Batavia* is a Hinton line boat, engaged in the East African trade, it suggested that this Captain Elliott does his big game hunting not in India but in Africa."

"Good, Maitland, quite good," Biddulph responded heartily. "Perhaps you can now connect the persons mentioned in the separate cuttings with each other?"

But that was beyond me and I said so. For Africa is a gigantic continent and Captain Bob Elliott and Count Pedro Fernandez might have been moving about Africa since the Creation and never met. As for Rhand and Wridgley, grouse moors in Scotland are numberless. When I indicated this, Biddulph nodded.

"Perhaps it was expecting too much of you," he conceded. "Possibly it's news to you that Elliott is Sir Charles' brother-in-law?"

"It's news to me, that he exists at all," I said.

I remember that Biddulph said nothing for about a minute. Then he looked round at me.

"You'd better keep yourself well aware of his existence," he said gravely. "Though Rhand is much more likely to suspect you than Elliott."

"And if he does?"

"Well, if he does, it won't be, let's say, very pleasant for you."

"Just how?" I asked. "Do you mean, it will be dangerous, then?"

"Oh, we'd not call this a dangerous job. Difficult, rather than dangerous, you know. But a lot would depend on how it is handled. A fool could make it dangerous enough; but I do think it would take a fool to do it. Listen!" Biddulph sat forward, laying his hand on my knee confidentially. "Elliott's sister married Wridgley about five years ago, and till lately she has financed her brother ever since her marriage. Till lately, I say, for last year we know Wridgley had losses which crippled him. But, real scamp as we know Elliott to be, it was news to us that he is a friend of Rhand's, and, for myself, I can believe it only on the friend-in-need basis. What I mean is that Elliott, ne'er-do-well as he always has been, is something of a snob, while Rhand is—" Biddulph's shrug implied more than contempt. "So the inference we make is that Elliott would never associate with Rhand unless the friendship were to his financial advantage. But on the other hand, Otto Rhand is the last person in the world to part with any money except for value received. That is beyond doubt. If Rhand is, as I gather, keeping Elliott in funds, it is not for nothing. There must be a *quid pro quo* somewhere," Biddulph reiterated, with an emphatic nod.

Now while he sat staring thoughtfully at his own carpet, I put a question, although in the act of putting it I guessed the answer.

"Is Rhand interested in the Katangana Company?"

"Of course he is—he founded it."

My eyes went to the four news cuttings on the table.

"Then," I suggested, "Elliott may have helped him with information obtained from Lady Wridgley."

"Ah," Biddulph laughed. "So you're beginning to see daylight. Well, there's your job, to get possession of those papers."

"But who has them?" I inquired.

"Rhand, almost certainly. We know for a fact he had them in a small black japanned box marked with two red and white stripes. Mind you," he ran on, "there's no time to lose. For it wouldn't surprise me if this Fernandez chap had come here to conclude the agreement. This rise in Katanganas indicates the barometric pressure. Rhand would not, as we suppose he is, be buying back the dirt-cheap shares unless he was fairly certain of Fernandez's signature. Once the Count lands in England, though, he won't find it easy to get to Glengyle as quickly as Rhand would like."

"You can't surely detain him in town by force," I suggested.

Biddulph smiled confidently.

"There are other ways. He'll get invitations from people who are too important to have their invitations declined. We can arrange all that. So you can count on a clear day or two before Fernandez turns up and after you yourself get into the house."

"Get into the house," I repeated, startled. "What house?"

"Why, Glengyle, of course. Don't you see the negotiations will take place or be concluded over that shooting party in Scotland? All so friendly, you know. Nothing draws people together like a shoot, in a remote place. That's an easy guess. What's harder is to guess how you are to get yourself included in the house party."

In that I agreed with him.

"Seems to me more like a burglar's job," I said.

"Oh, take a burglar with you if you like. That's your affair. We'll ask no questions so long as you bring us the goods. And above all, remember it's those papers that came from our department we want. We've got to know who sold us to Rhand. But if you can get the draft agreement between his company and the Portuguese, so much the better."

Biddulph got to his feet and stretched himself. Apparently he considered me ready for the good work. But that was far from my thought. I was, in fact, almost sure I would not touch the job. I didn't like the look of it at all. And possibly Biddulph, as he walked up and down, saw me eyeing it askance, as it were, for he stopped over me.

"Surely, Maitland," he said, "you aren't the man to funk such a duty."

"Duty," I echoed. "Is that what you call it?"

"Why yes. Surely it is the duty of every citizen to do what he can in the defense of his country's interests, even when he is not paid for it," he added in sudden heat. "And let me tell you, Maitland, there's damn few living or dead whose patriotism paid them so well."

I suppose he was indignant that I should hesitate over a job he'd taken so much trouble to put my way. But though I saw his point I wasn't going to be rushed even then. And the reason for my caution was this. At the very moment of Biddulph's scathing reproach there came a vague remembrance of a general election which had been won through the publication at the critical moment of a document, a mere letter, which must have been in the hands of the other political party for months before it was used with such devastating effect. Might not the astute Mr. Chatsworth wish to have this document up his sleeve for a similar political emergency? After all, he had taken care to remain in the background, leaving Biddulph to fix things up. I could not even swear to having heard his voice on the 'phone.

"Look here, Biddulph," I burst out, "isn't it the fact that there's a special branch at Scotland Yard for just this sort of job?"

"There is," he admitted. "What of it?"

"Why not employ them?"

"First because for a job like this in a remote quarter of Scotland we need a Scot. Less conspicuous, you know: nobody will ask why you are there."

"And are there no Scots at Scotland Yard?"

"Oh yes—there, as everywhere," he laughed, recovering his good humor. "Only, you see, if he got caught, his identity could hardly be concealed."

"And if I got caught?"

"Well, your identity would not matter—would not compromise us, I mean."

"But I might get six months for it?" I suggested.

"Very likely."

His coolness over the possibility was so superb that it amused me.

"You'd expect me to take my sentence and say nothing?"

"Certainly. Why else should we pay so much?"

"But," I objected, "circumstances, now unforeseen, might compel me to say why I was in the house and who sent me."

Biddulph, smilingly derisive, shook his head.

"Nobody would believe you. Such a cock and bull story would merely lead to an inquiry into your mental condition."

A moment's reflection showed me here his calculation was just. What an absurd story it would sound! I got to my feet.

"Well, what about it?" Biddulph, hands in pockets, inquired nonchalantly.

"I'll take it on," I said.

"Good for you," he nodded.

We talked over the affair more precisely after that, Biddulph unconcerned with the methods I was to employ, giving me a minute description of the wanted letters and possible documents. As a matter of fact, I had no notion as to how I would set about getting them, and while he talked I listened with care, my eyes on the photograph of the smiling Mr. Chatsworth. For, you see, I took that smiling face as an augury of success. Biddulph, perceiving my stare, also looked at Chatsworth.

"Have you noticed," he said, "he's never photographed without that smile? It's not always there, you know. He's not smiling just now, I can tell you. In fact, I've never known him so worried as he is over this affair. He's sworn to find the man who betrayed us to them. You'll start right on it tomorrow, of course."

"Of course."

We shook hands at the door.

"Thank you for putting this my way," I blurted out.

He patted me on the back. "Oh, that's all right. You looked so down on your luck that day we met, you know. Not much of a smile on your face, eh? And after all you're just the type of man we needed."

We shook hands once more. He was not to see or hear from me till I brought him the papers. That was the final stipulation Biddulph made. Whatever happened, the Whitehall Office must not be compromised.

Then the door closed.

CHAPTER III

Of course I hadn't walked a hundred yards before the stiffest part of my job stood staring me in the face. It was this. Biddulph had suggested a burglar as my assistant, and had hinted that no questions would be asked as to the methods I adopted so long as I brought in the goods. Not that I anticipated any difficulty in getting into touch with an expert cracksman. Even while still discussing things with Biddulph I had a shrewd notion of how and where to get my assistant. I have already mentioned that Peters, who ran the little shop in Soho, had several other strings to his bow besides tobacco and periodicals. The shop also served as an accommodation address to which, for a fee, letters could be sent and collected by the sort of people who did not, for reasons good or bad, desire their real address to be known. I had seen some of these clients in the act of collecting their letters, and—well—I thought it would not be hard for Peters to put me into touch with the skilled assistant I needed.

But now I perceived this wasn't a burglar's job at all. For how was I to know the precise moment at which the document of agreement would be ready for signature? Without that knowledge, all the odds were that a forced entry into Glengyle would be either too soon or too late. To have any chance of success the burglarious entry would have to be timed almost to a minute. Hard on the heels of this disconcerting thought there came a vision of myself stealing along dark corridors, trying innumerable doors, and rummaging in numberless rooms all in the few hours of darkness afforded by the brief Northern summer night. The thing was impossible! I did not even know

when any of the persons named in Biddulph's news cuttings would
be setting out for Glengyle.

But I saw that was what I must first know, and then suddenly, as
in a flash of light, I perceived how I might easily get that essential
knowledge. And it sent me darting across the Piccadilly traffic, over
Regent Street and up Shaftesbury Avenue for my lodgings in Soho.
I knew now that my real assistant was not one of Peters' customers,
but Peters himself.

At my question, Mrs. Peters, busy attending to a couple of customers, indicated Peters, seated on a stool behind the other counter,
deep in a detective novel. He looked up only when my shadow fell
across the page of his book as I bent over the counter.

"Come up to my room," I whispered.

He stared at the unusual invitation as if he were examining it.

"You want me?"

I tapped my finger on his book meaningly.

"Yes, for something of that sort," I whispered.

It was pretty quick of him to catch my meaning, but understand
he did. His eye brightened and he put down the book with a nod.
While Mrs. Peters' back was turned, I whisked up the telephone directory, got it out of sight under my jacket and carried it upstairs.
By the time Peters arrived I had ascertained Sir Charles Wridgley's
town address. Since there was little enough time to spare, I took the
shortest road, as I judged, to stimulate Peters' interest.

"I was wondering if you would care to do a little detective work,"
I said, waving him to a chair.

"Yes?" he replied, in a tone of question rather than assent.

"It will be new to you, that sort of work, of course, but you may
find it interesting."

And when this was met by a curious sort of incredulous smile I
added: "More interesting, anyhow, than merely reading those detective stories of yours."

"Go ahead, Mr. Maitland," he replied, at last taking the chair to
which I had been impatiently waving him.

When I began by saying I wanted him to go to Sir Charles Wridgley's house, 5 Elswick Square, to get me some information, the little

man was shrewd enough to see he wasn't expected to go up to the front door and ring the bell.

"From some maid in the area," he interjected.

"That's it. A maid or the cook or footman or chauffeur."

"Women's best for talking, especially in the evening when they've little else to do. Still, I was just wondering—"

"What?"

"Well, y'know it ain't so easy as it used to be. What with all them cat burglars about, domestics are warned not to talk to strangers."

"But do they obey?"

"Up to a point they do. Of course nothing can stop a girl talking to a man if she wants to, only they do seem to be more careful what they say, besides being quicker to get suspicious like. What's more, you can't hope to get much out of them at a first meeting. You have to have patience and cultivate them, as it were."

Hearing Peters speak with such assurance, I began to wonder if an occasional burglary was not another of his little side lines. It would account too for his interest in detective fiction.

"But surely," I objected, "it would depend on the kind of information you wanted from them."

Peters sat forward, alertly nodding.

"Oh yes, a lot depends on that. If, let's say, I want to find out the total value of the mistress's jewelry and where they are kept, that would take me, nowadays, three meetings and a cinema to do it."

"But it's not jewelry I'm after; it's something much easier."

"Oh," Peters hastily cut in, "I only put it as jewelry in a manner of speaking. But whatever it is, you've got to establish contact first. That's the hardest, to stop 'em from shutting the door in yer face. But after you've established contact, I've never found the rest of it hard."

This interested me as being akin to my own experiences with the photographic enlargements.

"What do you do next?" I inquired of this expert.

"Oh, I ask 'em no direc' questions, Mr. Maitland. I just talk about myself, and I usually find they don't listen long before wanting to tell me about themselves and their mistresses. Now what d'ye want me to find out?"

"Merely the day on which Sir Charles is leaving for Scotland."
Then a sudden thought made me add: "Perhaps you could find out
also whether there's any sort of a job going for a man who'd like to
get back to Scotland. That ought to be easy for you."

"Very likely it will be, provided I establish contact, which is not
so easy as you might think."

This was where I sailed in with my great idea. Going to my chest
of drawers I pulled out the canvas case in which I carried my enlarged portraits.

"Here's something to make that easy," I announced with pride,
handing him the case.

He was taken aback. "What's in it?" he asked in surprise.

"A new side line for you, Peters. Open it and see."

He extracted the enlargement of a coquettish, Marceled beauty
to which the original snapshot was pinned. Peters' jaw dropped as
he stared at the smirking girl; but the next moment he was slapping
his leg with delight.

"I get the idea," he cried. "You show 'em this and offer to do one
of themselves. Oh, it's great, it's great! For even if they don't mean
to give you an order they'll still want to look at the photos, which
provides time for talk. Just the thing for the women, that is, there
being no woman that isn't ready to examine another woman's face,
even if it is a total stranger to her."

So great was Jim Peters' enthusiasm that he wanted to start out
at once for Elswick Square. This was exactly what I wanted myself,
but I was doubtful whether the hour wasn't too late. He, however,
scouted this fear.

"Not a bit of it," he declared. "Why, in these hard times lots take
up evening jobs like this as a side line."

So I let him go off on his mission, confident of his discretion,
since he had neither asked me why I didn't go myself nor for what
purpose I wanted to know when Sir Charles Wridgley was to leave
London.

As soon as he was on the stairs, however, I turned again to the
telephone directory to get a move on with my second idea. Then,
slipping out, I made for the telephone box at the corner of Wentworth Street, and having got on to the office of the *Daily Record*, I

had to wait while they put me through to the department I wanted. But it was good to feel that things were moving, and I reflected with some complacency that though warned by Biddulph that speed was necessary and that I had better start in tomorrow, I had, as a matter of fact, got off the mark that first night. The man on the *Record* I wanted to get hold of was an ingenuous young fellow to whom I had given an interview when I made my great hit as the butler at the *Lyric.*

"Hullo!" the voice sounded in my ear.

"That Mr. Chance?"

"Mr. Chance it is."

"Alec Maitland speaking."

He hadn't quite forgotten me. After a hasty interchange of news which I cut as short as I decently could, I got in with my question.

"Where can I get a photograph of Otto Rhand?"

The question did not seem to surprise him. I suppose newspaper men are familiar with the unexpected.

"Otto Rhand of Rhand and Wynberg, the financiers?"

"That's the man."

A laugh came through.

"Is it for a new comedy part? You'll find it hard to make up like him," he said. "However, if you come round I'll take you to the mortuary and exhume him for you."

"The what?" I gasped.

"Oh," he laughed, "it's all right. Every paper has a department where the photographs of outstanding personalities are stored, for instant use when required."

Although aware of this fact, I was unaware of the gruesome name given to the store-room. Acting on sudden impulse I said there were several other outstanding personalities whose faces I wanted to study, but when I named them there was quite a long pause. Thinking he had not heard me I repeated the names.

"Oh, I heard you," he said in a subdued tone. "Yes, I expect we have them all. Come round right away." But when I explained this was impossible and that I hoped he'd let me send for the photographs, he was silent again. With my ear glued to the receiver, and feeling sure I had made a blunder of some sort, I waited.

"Lady Wridgley," I overheard his thoughtful murmur. "Now what on earth—" he cut himself short. "Well, Mr. Maitland, I'll risk parting with them for a couple of hours; I'll do more: I'll send them round on one condition," he went on briskly, "that you give the *Record* an exclusive story at the earliest possible moment."

"Of what?" I cried.

"Of anything of news value connected with Lady Wridgley."

It was my turn to be silent.

"Right. I'll tell you all I can," I said, perceiving that this bound me to no more than Biddulph would allow me to say. But Chance, of course, did not see that, and thanking me so warmly that I might have blushed, took down my address. So, assured that the photographs would be awaiting my return in an hour or so, the way was clear for the next step, which was to learn the exact position the Wridgley house occupied in the square. I had employed Peters because I could not go myself without risk of being identified by some domestic when I appeared afterwards at Glengyle, but I thought it would be quite safe to have a look at the house and if I could not glean anything helpful from that I might at least keep an eye on Peters.

Elswick Square, when I turned into it, seemed after the roar and glitter of Piccadilly like a place asleep. I had not, however, gone far up one side before becoming aware that not all of its inhabitants had gone off to the theatre or were dining out that night. From the far side of the square, penetrating the trees in the garden, came the sound of a piano and then a woman's voice in song. A little farther up I came on a young policeman, balancing himself on the pavement's edge, while, hands behind back, he listened to the girlish singing which came so distinctly across the gardens on the still night air.

I passed on, glancing at the numbers on the houses, though I already knew that No. 5 must stand on the further side. Having crossed the upper end I was sauntering down towards the Wridgley mansion when I saw a figure step through an area gate on to the pavement. His small size as well as the familiar canvas case under his arm, showed me it was Peters. I pulled up and waited for him. He seemed dejected. He passed me with head down and I let him go till he had reached the corner of the empty square. There I overtook him and caught his arm.

"Any luck?" I breathed.

Peters, as soon as he recovered himself, shifted the case from under one arm to the other.

"Well, I got these orders for you," he replied.

"But was that the right house you came out of just now?"

"No, that was No. 6, where the cook give me a order to enlarge her mother." He looked round. "You see, I approached No. 5 tactfully, beginning at No. 1 so's to get my hand in at doing the patter and making it sound natural like. In fact I'd got two orders before I reached No. 5, and that made me feel good. So I went to No. 5 feeling just like I was Hainly doing 'Amlet."

But I was too impatient to endure comparisons.

"What happened?" I diverted.

Peters sighed.

"Nothing. I just failed to establish contact. When the girl came to the area door I had my specimens ready. But when she began to shut the door in my face I stuck out my foot. Couldn't help myself, it was such a shock, after my previous success. She hollers out, and a chauffeur that was inside came bounding along, anxious to be gallant. I wasn't willing to be beaten like that, you know, not so easy as that. So I tried to get him to look at my specimens, offering, with the girl looking on, to enlarge any girl friend of his at a moderate price. But all I got was an order to 'op it and an offer to enlarge my own nose for nothing."

Here was my first check! All the more disappointing since things had been moving so well. But I was consoling myself with the thought that it was just a bit of bad luck that Peters should have called at the moment the chauffeur was flirting with the girl, when the little man continued his complaints.

"Called me a Nosey Parker, he did, following me up the area steps. That's why I went to six, to put him off suspecting I'd been to his place for some other reason."

This sounded just a little ominous. Why Nosey Parker? It looked as if they expected people to come prying about the house on any

sort of pretext. On the other hand it might only be the chauffeur's
natural indignation with Peters for interrupting some happy moment. Still, Peters' forethought in following up his call with another
at the next house was admirable, and I was telling the disconsolate
little man this when the sound of a piano came through an open
window further back and then a woman's voice joined in joyously.

Peters spat noisily on to the pavement.

"That's from No. 5," he said. "They're having a sort of 'do' on
there tonight—a lot of people."

I was about to follow as he moved away in disgust when my eye
caught something white at the top of the area steps. Instinctively
I stepped back into the shadows against the railings. The radiance
of the intervening street lamp made it hard for me to see with any
distinctness, but the white apron, cap and cuffs were quite visible.
It was a girl carrying something. When she put her load down I saw
it was a little dog on a lead. I could see him pulling hard in his anxiety to explore the railings. After a little of this pulling I saw the
girl stoop and let the dog free, with the result that he immediately
doubled across the pavement and made for the larger and evidently much more interesting railings across the road which encircled
the gardens. In the stillness I heard him snuffling along while the
maid on the pavement moved on opposite him watchfully. Suddenly
an idea came. I slipped on to where Peters stood waiting for me,
gripped his arm hard and shook him to waken him out of his despon-
dent lethargy.

"There's a dog there," I whispered.

"A dog, what of it?" Peters grunted in disgust. "Do ee want me to
cadge 'im for 'is photo?"

"It came from the house and I'm going to steal it."

"What for?"

"For you to rescue."

Peters leapt to life.

"I get you," he whispered eagerly. "That'll establish contact all
right. Go ahead."

I darted across the road and then along to where the Pekinese
was snuffing under the garden railings. The sudden yelp of fear or
protest that came as I snatched the animal, was followed by a cry

from the pavement. The dog I stuffed under my jacket, held it tight and ran. The girl ran too, out into the road, to intercept me. But, head down, I swerved past her as she made a wild clutch. It was not till I reached the further corner of the square that I heard the rapid patter of Peters' feet. Once round the corner, I slackened the pace and allowed him to overhaul me. Jim Peters, in his enthusiasm, however, rather overdid his part. Perhaps he did not see me, but he came into me with a crash, just as I made a grab at his collar to provide him as quickly as possible with visible traces of his gallantry. The dog got badly bumped and my own arm too, as I went sprawling to earth, Peters on top.

"I got you," he yelled, gripping my free arm. "Give it up, will you?"

That I was only too eager to do, for with the tail of my eye I saw light across the way as a door opened. But Peters, in his anxiety to do the thing well, pinned me so tight that it was impossible to release the dog, which all this time had never relaxed from his ear-piercing, high-pitched yelping. But when I saw the white cap and apron and waving cuffs explaining to the man who had emerged from the lighted door the meaning of the scuffle over in the road, I visualized capture, a month's imprisonment for myself and an end to my job before it had well begun. . .

As the slow-witted man began to run across to where we lay struggling together, I became desperate, and struck out with my left for Peters' jaw. The blow had considerable annoyance behind it, and Peters, clinging to the dog, rolled over on his back. I scrambled to my feet just as the newcomer made a grab at my collar. He would have got me too, as I tripped over my prostrate assistant; but just as he recovered his lost balance after missing his tackle, and was darting after me, Peters thrust out a foot and brought him down heavily. That gave me time to get a start. But it was a narrow squeak. A yard less and there would have been no story to tell.

Half an hour later I was sitting in my room, waiting for Peters to return and report. I passed the time examining the rather queer faces depicted on the photographs Mr. Chance had sent round from the *Record* mortuary.

CHAPTER IV

Peters got back shortly before eleven, looking mighty well pleased with himself. My anxiety vanished on seeing his smirk of self-satisfaction, for I knew that since that self-conscious grin could not come from any pride in his personal appearance, it must be due to his success. In fact I was shocked to see how much damage I had done to Peters' face and clothes during that scuffle on the road. His left cheek had a strip of sticking plaster that extended over to the ear, his right wrist was swathed in bandages, and his neck enveloped in a pinkish feminine-looking scarf. But Jim was too full of his triumph to be aware of his appearance. He sank into the chair with a sigh of content.

"Well?" I prompted him.

He slewed the chair round to face me on the bed. "If ever I saw gratitude on a human face it was that girl's," he said.

"You held on to the dog then?"

Jim lifted his bandaged hand.

"That wasn't so hard, not with him holding on to me the way he done. But that girl was so glad she kissed him when I handed him over after persuading him to leave go of my wrist. She looked ready to kiss me too, if only that other fellow hadn't been there. You see, she didn't ought to have let him off the lead. That were against her ladyship's orders, as she explained to me afterwards when we'd got rid of that other fellow."

"You mean the man who nearly got me?"

"Yes, nasty brute to get rid of, that flunkey was too. Seeing how pretty Grace was, he made the most of the knees he'd got barked on the kerb-stone when I tripped him up. But of course he couldn't decently show 'em off to the girl, whereas she could see for herself how I'd suffered." Jim grinned knowingly. "We're meeting tomorrow night, it being her night off. We're going to a cinema," he added quietly, as if this were his crowning achievement.

I was surprised.

"Quick work that, Jim."

"Oh, Mr. Maitland, she's full o' sympathy, that girl is. I knew what a kind heart she had as soon as she began to 'elp me along the road to look for the case o' photographs I'd risked the loss of to save Tutu. And then the way she 'elped me down those area steps, the very same which I'd been made to skip up not 'alf an hour earlier! No need to put my foot in the door this time. And the gentle way she 'andled my cuts and bruises, you'd never believe."

But I'd heard enough of this rhapsody.

"Well, and how did you handle her?" I inquired pointedly.

"Oh, I got what you wanted all right," he nodded proudly. "The staff are due to leave by the ten o'clock from Euston on Friday night and the family follows on the Monday. There's to be a big house party and as the house is an old rambling Scotch castle and thirty-five miles from a railway station at that, her ladyship is busy trying to get extra help."

"Trying—did you say trying?"

"Well, that's how the girl put it. It ain't so easy, she says, to get good class servants to go so far away from modern comforts. And I don't wonder at it myself. Most high-class London domestics never having been more than thirty-five yards from a 'bus stop, much less thirty-five miles from a railway station. Gracie herself didn't half like the idear, she says."

"Gracie?"

"That's the girl's name. Gracie Turton, she is. She don't half like the idear of going to this Glengyle. That's why it was so easy to get her to do a cinema with me. Said it would be just a last little peep at civilization."

"Jim," I said, "forget Gracie for a moment. Remember you have a wife. Did you tell her you had a friend who's looking out for a job?"

Peters, rather abashed, sat up eagerly.

"Of course I did. Soon as she told me about her ladyship looking for extra help for the shooting party, I sailed right in on that and said I'd got a brother-in-law who was on the look out for a situation."

"A brother-in-law?" I cried.

"A brother-in-law is what I put you down as being, to account for me asking her so many questions, if you'll excuse it, Mr. Maitland."

Jim's astuteness had been admirable.

"So you put me down as your wife's brother?"

"Well, no, not exactly. My sister's husband is what I really called you. You see," he went on hastily, "my little idear was just to open a way for you to establish contact with Gracie yourself if such should be desirable, and if you 'ad to see Gracie it would explain why we are so different in looks and build."

My spirits rose on seeing how promisingly things were now going. But I didn't spare Peters.

"All right, Jim, having made yourself out a bachelor and me a married man, prepared evidently to go anywhere to get away from my wife, what did Gracie say?"

"She just asked what you could do."

I asked what he had said to that.

"Well, Mr. Maitland, not knowing what you're up to, I just said you were ready to do anything."

"Did she notice that was no answer to her question?"

"Not as far as I could see she didn't. But I'd like to know myself just what the game is you're up to—if I'm to go any further, that is."

The decision of tone in Peters' last words surprised me.

"It isn't in the least bit dangerous," I assured him.

Peters hesitated a moment, shifted about in his chair and then blurted out:

"But is it . . . honest?"

"Honest?" I repeated, taken aback.

"On the right side of the law is what I meant. I wouldn't like to get Gracie into trouble, you know."

This sudden change in Peters' attitude astonished me. It was the first time a question of that sort had ever been put to me, and from him I took it as an impertinence.

"Squeamish, are you?" I retorted. "That strikes me as comic when I remember the sort of customers who get their letters left here."

Peters, however, kept cool.

"That's neither 'ere nor there, Mr. Maitland. Even the G.P.O. don't open letters to be sure everything in 'em is all fair and above board. And I can't neither. And anyway, I don't let any of that sort have a room in my house."

This was trouble I had not foreseen. And I needed Peters' help. He had opened up a possibility that thrilled me by his handling of the girl, Gracie Turton. The scheme I had conceived as I squatted on the bed was entirely built up on what he might do for me next night with that girl. A glance at Peters' face showed me that his determination not to go further till he knew more was even stronger than his words had revealed. And inwardly cursing this unexpected setback, I sat wondering how little I need tell him to make sure of his services. Before I could decide Peters spoke again.

"Look 'ere, Mr. Maitland, I only want your word that it's all on the square. If you are a crook you don't look like any crook I've come up against. I can't say no fairer than that." His tone was almost pleading. "You see, I do a little of this kind of scouting work for a professional detective, and if I got on the wrong side of the law—well—"

"There'd be an end to that side line," I concluded for him.

Now I understood not only Jim's devotion to the cheap detective fiction which made another side line to his little shop, but also why it was he knew so much about this sort of work. To be candid, when I had heard Peters talk so knowingly about how to handle servants and pump them for information, I had qualms about Peters' own honesty of much the same kind as he himself had about me. But now that I knew him to be honest as well as experienced, I was less than ever willing to fall out with him. Suddenly I thought of a way to reassure him. Getting off the bed I unwrapped the photographs from the *Record* office and handed Peters the one I had studied most, that of Otto Rhand. If Peters knew a crook when he saw one, here was the test.

"What do you make of him?" I asked.

Peters stared at it for a time in silence.

"Well," he said finally, "he's no beauty anyway. Kind o' dago, ain't he? Looks as much like a monkey as a man."

This was not quite just, and merely reflected all the lower-class Englishman's prejudice against dagos. Yet there was something simian about Rhand. The straight, lipless mouth, the deeply indented temples, the small round staring eyes, dark, with a hint of malice in them and the suggestion of malformation in the narrow shoulders, did raise the image of an ape in one's mind. But as I studied the face over Peters' shoulder, I saw there was a difference from the ape to which Peters was probably blind. Rhand's mouth, eyes, ears and the rest might suggest the ape; his forehead did not. The forehead did not slope back from the eye sockets. On the contrary it towered high and white above the alert little eyes, and the mental capacity revealed by the forehead, seen in combination with the watchful eyes and the determined mouth, gave me the first warning that my job might not be the easy thing it looked.

"This the man you're after?" Peters asked suddenly.

"One of them. Here's another," I added, handing over Captain Bob Elliott.

The big game hunter looked the part, facing the camera four square as it were, hands in pockets in a sort of off-duty attitude of careless ease. Not unlike his sister, Lady Wridgley, except that his eyes were closer together, he did not seem to have an ounce of soft flesh about him, and his air of quiet cool masterfulness, whether natural or acquired from his adventures among lions, was unmistakable.

"What do you make of him?" I asked with some curiosity.

"Officer in civvis," Peters promptly replied.

It was quite a good shot for Peters, though I knew that the straight, lithe pose was derived not from the barrack square but the jungle.

"What they been up to?" Peters asked, putting the pair of men together.

I hesitated.

"Does your—does the other man you work for tell you everything before you begin on a job?"

Peters laughed.

"Not much he don't. He just tells me what he wants done and I do it, blind. Still, a man's only human, you know, and I have my little curiosity, Mr. Maitland."

"Who's the man you work for?" I inquired.

"Ah, that 'ud be telling, wouldn't it?" he nodded, amused at me.

This refusal being exactly what I hoped for, I went on: "Well, you see, Jim, I'm on exactly the same kind of work as yourself. I'm only employed by someone else—a sort of side line for me too, you understand."

I believe it was the use of his Christian name more than anything else that melted him, clever as I thought my method of wriggling out of the need for explanations had been.

"Oh," he cried, "I'll stand in with you, of course. Why, I sometimes have to sub-contract part of a job myself, you know. There will be a little money in it, of course?" he added.

"A lot if we make a success. If not—well—I'm afraid there will be little, if any at all, Jim."

"Payment by results, is it?"

"That's it. I'm on that myself, you see."

There was a slight pause.

"Well," Peters said, "I like steady money as a rule, but also I like 'aving a bit on an 'orse now and then to add to the excitement. I'm ready to begin at once, so just say what you want done, Mr. Maitland."

Peters was not aware how much he had already done. As a matter of fact it was the information he had got out of the girl, Gracie Turton, which lay behind the scheme I had formulated.

"When you meet Gracie tomorrow night, find out what Agency Lady Wridgley uses, and what kind of servants she is seeking."

"That all?" he inquired.

"For the moment, but it's pressing. The staff goes North on Friday and that leaves us only three days."

Peters sat up.

"Look 'ere," he whispered, "what's to hinder me going round first thing in the morning? There's this 'ere scarf she lent me after you tore off my collar and tie. I got to take it back anyway. Do it up in a neat parcel as if it was something special, get myself up to the nines and ask for Miss Turton. 'Tain't as if I didn't know her name, you see."

"Splendid, Jim," I said, with real gratitude.

"And when I sees Gracie. I'll explain not waiting till the evening by telling her how anxious I am to help you to a job, which will likewise explain my question about the Agency and the kind o' servants her ladyship is wanting."

So we fixed it up. When we had discussed the details I found myself more than content with the progress made. Biddulph had expected me to begin tomorrow. I had done better than that. With luck I might have the free run of Glengyle inside the next few days.

But when we had settled our plans and Peters was about to leave, he hesitated at the door, and then turning, removed the pink silk scarf from his neck.

"Better leave this with you for the night," he said rather sheepishly, "the missus mightn't like the color."

CHAPTER V

It was close on half past ten next morning when Jim Peters got back from Elswick Square. He had only been away about an hour, but, up till then, I never knew how long an hour could be. At that stage in the affair there was just nothing for me to do but kick my heels and wait. For it had not taken long to decide what my next moves must be if Jim's were successful. Peters, on entering, shut the door carefully, and then planted his back to it as if to keep someone out. It was not hard to see which of his various side lines lay nearest his heart.

"The Albemarle Agency in Port Street," he announced. "That's the place her ladyship goes to. What she wants particular is a man to valet for the guests. Most of the other places have been filled, Gracie says, but not him."

"It doesn't sound as if it would be difficult to fill," I said, wondering.

Peters shook his head.

"Ah, but there's a catch in it. He's got to be up in guns and know about ammunition so's he can look after 'em as well."

Half an hour later I was mighty busy on the hunt for testimonials as to my character and abilities. This I expected to be the hardest part of the whole job. As things turned out it wasn't, but at first it looked like it. First I went to my theatre agents, Duckworth and Formby in Leicester Square. I went there because of the, as I thought then, brilliant idea that I could induce them to provide a testimonial on my capacity as a valet from the celebrated author of the comedy in which I had made my hit as a butler. They would have none of it. They didn't even ask what I wanted it for.

I left the office shaken. It was as if I'd taken a push in the face. Then I had an inspiration. Getting hold of a directory I rang up George Decies, the author, and was lucky enough to get him. Now I knew Decies—his real name was something much more Scriptural— was a sporting chap, and he somehow or other gave me more credit for making his play a success than I deserved. When I told him I was out of a shop and down on my luck he said, "O-h," in a way I'd heard before; but when he realized I wasn't proposing to borrow money but was in need of a testimonial to get a job which would tide me over the dead season, he was heartiness itself.

"Certainly, my boy," he chirruped, when I had provided the explanation I had prepared. "Certainly give my name. All credit to you. Oh yes, I'll be careful what I say. You leave it to me."

Then, actually as I was turning away, a still more promising name occurred to me. Wentworth! Why hadn't I thought of him first? I had been Jack Wentworth's fag at school. It was he, in fact, who first taught me how to press a pair of trousers and fold a coat without making it look like a concertina. Later on in life I had several times stayed at his father's place in Rutland for week-ends and shot rabbits on the Sundays. Now he had succeeded to the title and the place in Rutland. He was a personage. With care I might get him to testify to my skill in both clothes and guns.

I admit that for a moment I was dubious as to whether I was justified in hazarding other people's names by procuring the job in this way. If I got caught, there might be trouble for them. But I decided that since Biddulph had assured me this was a patriotic duty, I was fully justified in employing both Sir John Wentworth and George Decies in the same duty, although they might never discover the fact that they had been turned into patriots by me. After all, I argued, it makes all the difference whether an act is done in the public interest or in one's own. To kill a man in one's own interest is murder: to kill him in the interests of one's country is patriotism.

But I wasn't so lucky in getting into touch with Wentworth. At his house they told me he was out and might be found at his club. Rushing to the club I learned he had been there but had left a few minutes ago. On that I called up the house from the Piccadilly tube only to learn that he had just left to catch the one-ten from Victoria. That left me fifteen minutes. I took a taxi at Victoria and was set down with still seven minutes in hand, though I thought I'd need them all to find a man in that crowd whom I hadn't seen for seven years. The luck, however, swayed my way again, for I found him almost at once at the bookstall, getting periodicals, his man standing behind, obsequiously attendant. After a slight stare as I touched his arm, his face lit up.

"Maitland!" he exclaimed. "My dear chap."

It warmed me to see his spontaneous pleasure. After the exchange of small talk usual under such circumstances, he asked me if I was traveling by his train. When I said, with a glance at his man, that I had come there to see him, he handed the man his armful of papers and sent him off to keep his seat. Then I told my story, without any beating about the bush, for which there was no time anyhow. That is to say I told him about being out of a job, and to fill in the time till the autumn, and with a desire to see my native land and get some sport, I was after a job as a valet who could act as valet to the guns as well as to the guests. Wentworth's eyebrows lifted at the word "valet" and then he burst out laughing.

"Well," he said, "you always were a bit of an oddity, you know. Always doing something unexpected, like taking to the stage instead of the bar. Still, you ought to get more fun out of it than the nice girls who nowadays take on jobs as parlor-maids and nurses. Who are the people you'll be doing for?"

"Oh, one's Rhand, the financier, another's a Portuguese."

"Good Lord, a Portuguese! Mind you don't get shot. Is there anyone included who can shoot, or are you to act as instructor?"

"Captain Bob Elliott is in the house party, I believe."

"Ah well, you're not likely to get shot by him. Now what do you want me to do? Testify to your bad character?"

"No, merely to answer for it that I can crease trousers properly and know the difference between buckshot and rifle cartridges—that sort of thing."

We were walking up the platform by this time.

"Why yes," he said, "I can certainly answer for all that. Let me see, how long is it since you fagged for me at the old school?"

"Oh, you needn't mention that to them," I said, laughing but anxious all the same.

"All right, I won't if it would give the show away. Come round and see me when you can. I'll be back tonight." Then leaning out of the window he added, "Alec, I believe you're taking on this job to study for some character part in a comedy. No? Well, it ought to be rather a lark anyway."

That was exactly what I thought myself, then. But as I left the station it struck me that I'd had to put in a mighty lot of work since last night. Was it only last night that Biddulph had put the job into my hands? I seemed to have been on the go ever since. It surprised me, however, to see how laboriously one had to get to work, even to lay the foundations of success in such a case. No detective sleuthing after his quarry could, I thought, have to exercise more cunning thought and contrivance. But I was satisfied, perhaps too smugly satisfied with my scheming, above all in my handling of Wentworth. For with his name behind me, I considered my entrance to Glengyle Castle as good as already made, provided Lady Wridgley had not in the meantime found someone else.

That was a possibility that made me hurry back to my room and write a letter to the Albemarle Agency in which I stated the sort of position I desired and the sort of qualifications I had for it. Having got this letter off I went into the shop to have a word with Peters about the Valet Service shop round the corner where I wanted to do some work. He betrayed no surprise at my request. His favorite type of fiction must have made anything seem quite natural to him.

"Oh," he said, "that's all right, if you don't want to get paid. I know the man what runs it. We play darts together when things is slack."

He laid down his book and took me round to see Mr. Moscovitz. And the rest of that day I put in among steam, and hot irons and chemicals, learning how to clean and press gentlemen's clothes.

The night finished with a visit to Mr. Lucius. Having handed over my portfolio of enlargements and account books and got from him the money deducted as a guarantee, I found that, with what he owed me for commission added, the amount came to almost five pounds. The four notes I folded carefully and tucked them away in a pocket

I pinned up. Under no pressure would I part with them. They were reserved for the moment when I would have to bolt from Glengyle, supposing I was lucky enough to get there.

Next morning I entered the Albemarle Agency after watching from the opposite side of Port Street, the girl open the door. It was rather a trying moment when I faced that girl at the counter. For I had got myself up to look the part I was playing, and after the subtle little changes made in my personal appearance I wanted to see whether she could distinguish between one who came to seek a situation and one who came to seek a servant. She ought to be an expert at that, I felt. After a diffident cough intended to draw her attention from the pile of letters she was arranging, I said:

"Could I see the manager, miss?"

She shot me one glance through her horn spectacles and apparently took in all of me there was to see.

"Manageress," she corrected. "Not in for another twenty minutes. You may sit down if you like," she conceded with a vague wave of the hand.

Over by the window a table stood, loaded with the sort of periodicals one sees in a dentist's parlor. Very content with the effect made, I pulled out a chair and sat down to wait for the manageress. I'd rather it had been a manager. Men are not nearly so inquisitorial.

In about half an hour the door swung open and a tall woman in black marched in. She was not only tall but angular, and held her head high apparently to keep the pince nez on her thin nose in position. Clearly a woman born to be a manageress of something or somebody. Casting a wintry smile from her thin lips to the girl clerk and shooting an appraising glance at me, she passed through the inner door. The girl at the counter having called me up with her forefinger and got my name and business, disappeared through the same door. After another ten minutes she reappeared and I was summoned by the same forefinger and ushered into the presence of the manageress. She did not appear to be aware of my presence and left me standing while she ran through some letters.

It was quite easy for me to take all this lying down as it were, like the well-trained flunkey I was supposed to be. That was exactly how I wanted to be taken. It proved that I looked the part. But I owed it to that female that I began to feel the part. Presently her cold glasses glittered up at me.

"You have not been on our books before?"

"No, madam," I bowed, "I have not had that honor."

Flicking through the pile of letters, she pulled out the one that bore my signature and began to read it. Covertly and anxiously I watched her, for I knew that now I was face to face with another stiff hurdle. I thought her stiffness relaxed as she read. Remembering every line in that carefully constructed epistle, I saw that the process of thawing began when she read that I had also been accustomed to help with the guns. But I believe it was the mention of Sir John Wentworth that melted her. Lowering the letter to look at me, she said:

"D'you know, Maitland, I think we have a client who's looking for precisely such a man as you."

"Very fortunate for me, madam."

The excitement I was unable to keep out of my stammered words she took for something else.

"Oh, don't build on it. We have to verify your references, and of course our client will have to see you personally."

Just then the 'phone on her desk began to whirr, and after an exchange of words with the outer office a call was put through.

"Yes, the Albemarle speaking. . . . Yes. . . . Oh, will you tell her ladyship we have at last succeeded in finding *the* man who answers to the requirements. . . . Yes. . . . Yes . . . extremely good references. Twelve, you say. Oh, not at all. Thank you. . . . Yes, I'll see he is there punctually at twelve. Please inform Lady Wridgley."

As the manageress replaced the receiver I thought she must hear my heart thumping. But I admired her cheek in saying, with me standing there, that she had at last succeeded in finding *the* man who answered to the requirements. Still, that was nothing. The great thing was that I had topped another big hurdle. Only the interview now remained, and my thought was that if I had taken in this professional interviewer I could not have much to fear from Lady Wridgley.

While entering some note in a ledger the manageress said: "I hope you are a good sailor, Maitland."

This made me blink a bit.

"A good sailor? Is that a necessity?"

She unbent in a smile at my bewilderment.

"Oh no, not a necessity. But as Lord Billinghurst wants you for his yachting trip to the Canadian lakes it would be well if you are, don't you think?"

"Lord Billinghurst?" I cried.

She thought me, I suppose, stunned with delight at the social altitude of my prospective employer.

"Ah," she said almost archly, head on one side, "your surprise is not flattering to us, Maitland. You ought to know we have none but the best, the very best, people on our books."

The question about my sea-legs remained unanswered. But anyone who saw me, at that moment, struck on a heap if ever man was, and staggering, would have thought it hardly needed an answer. The next thing I remember is hearing her voice telling me Lord Billinghurst, now at the Ritz, was in a hurry to settle this business, and that I'd better see him at once, with a letter of introduction from herself. In a stupor of disappointment I watched her write the note I never intended to deliver. I was now only anxious to get away, to get away so that I might begin all over again the ghastly process of scheming for an entrance to Glengyle.

"This," she said, as she closed the envelope, "will explain you to his lordship. I've told him we are verifying your excellent references and will ring him up later."

I turned away. In the outer office a young man, sitting where I had sat, idly turning over the same journal, looked up at me with a smile. My face of blank despair must have led him to suppose I now had lost all hope of getting a job.

"Ah, Martin," the manageress addressed him from the door, "come this way. Lady Wridgley has just 'phoned about your interview."

I did not return Martin's smile. If he was going to Glengyle this meeting with him had doubled my difficulties. For this young man would almost certainly remember me, in whatever capacity I afterwards turned up at Glengyle. And to realize that was just the last straw to a bad morning's work.

Half-way along the street I pulled up. Somehow or other this young fellow must be prevented from going to Glengyle. I turned back towards the office, determined to head him off, but not seeing how it could be done.

CHAPTER VI

Almost despairingly I saw it must be now or never. If that man went to Lady Wridgley's it was goodbye to my chance of success. That conviction gripped me in that moment of sudden crisis. It was bitter to recall the care I had taken to employ Peters and so avoid all chance of future recognition at Glengyle and then to have that recognition made almost certain by a chance encounter like this. But life could be like that. Martin simply must be stopped. But how?

From a position in which I could intercept him on his way to Elswick Square I kept watch on the Albemarle. Several people entered and left, and the minutes ticked off till there was left not more than three quarters of an hour before he was due at Lady Wridgley's. But at last he appeared, walking in leisurely fashion, for, after all, he had ample time to reach his destination before the appointed hour. Not knowing what I meant to do next I went up to him and greeted him with a hearty "Hullo!" He stared blankly, looking almost scared for a moment and then, remembering me, smiled.

"Forgotten something, have you?" he said with a nod towards the Albemarle.

"Oh no, just passing the time till I'm due for my interview," I explained.

"Why, that's what I'm doing too," he grinned.

"Let's have a drink on it then," I suggested, "for luck."

I watched him turn over the proposal in his mind.

"I'd like to. Hanging about like this is thirsty work." He hesitated. "No, I'd better not risk it, before that interview, anyhow."

Of course after the interview was no use to me. And he did look as if he wished he could risk it. Yet I dare not press him too much or he might suspect something.

"Yes, of course," I agreed. "And yours is with a lady too, and the ladies have such sharp noses, eh? I'm going to a master, you know, who wouldn't mind if he did smell it. But what about a coffee, though? No harm in that."

At the mention of coffee Mr. Martin made a wry mouth which indicated plainly enough where his preference lay. All the same he followed me round the corner and into the snack-lunch bar.

"Who's your boss then?" he inquired, casting an envious eye at my whisky.

"Lord Billinghurst," I said.

"Not him they call the sporting peer?"

"The same."

"Well, well, it's no wonder you're having a drink on it. And it's himself would be the last man to mind, by all accounts."

"I'm engaged for a yachting trip to Canada and the great lakes," I announced.

He eyed me enviously while stirring his coffee.

"Ah," he said, "that's life now. Change of scene every day and jollity all the time. I'll be thinking of you when I'd drying wet duds every night after being squatted all day in a damp bog, loading guns and waiting for the birds to fly over. Isn't it yourself is the lucky dog! And isn't it myself would be handing you all I have in the world to be changing places with you!"

In the stress of his emotional envy his Irish accent and idiom came into play. I shoved my cigarette case across the table.

"It's hard to content some people," I remarked. "I'd much rather have your job than my own."

Martin shook his head with a sigh.

"Oh, you mean that kindly," he said, stretching for the matches, "but well I know it isn't true."

"You're Irish, aren't you?"

"I am that, though how you knew it—"

"Well, I'm a Scot. I've done a lot of wandering lately, and what I wanted was a look at my old country."

"Is that why you looked like a man who'd met with a great disaster just now?"

"It was," I admitted.

He laughed.

"Why, I thought you were just getting booted out," he declared.

"I've wandered the world quite enough."

"Well, well, and isn't it a great pity we neither of us can get what the other wants?"

"Oh," I said, trying to keep the excitement out of my voice, "we could quite easily."

Martin arrested the cup on its way to his lips. "What are you meaning?" he demanded.

"What I say."

"No!"

On this I produced my letter of introduction to Lord Billinghurst.

"So far as I'm concerned," I said, "nothing could be simpler. Lord Billinghurst has never seen me."

He stared round-eyed at the letter. A glance at the clock showed me time was running short.

"And Lady Wridgley hasn't seen you either," I suggested.

"She has not. I'm on my way to let her see me now."

"Well, you see how easy it would be. We've only to change names. Nothing else, not even our shirts, for your name is Martin and mine is Maitland. You go to see Lord Billinghurst and I go to Lady Wridgley's. Result: you get what you want and I get what I want. Then, both jobs being temporary, we resume our real names at the end of our trip and go on where we left off. Think it over."

He scratched his head thoughtfully for a moment.

"Sure," he said at last, "it's you are the great schemer, and if it wasn't that I was always the one for a bit of adventure, I'd be feeding the pigs in Ballymeena yet. But what if you don't bring it off with her ladyship—that would mean I'm out of a place again."

"No, no, of course not. If I don't bring it off with her there's an end to it. I stand aside and you sail away to see the world with Lord Billinghurst."

I observed that he seemed in no doubt as to his own ability to satisfy Lord Billinghurst. But it was lucky for me he was a harum-

scarum Irishman. He was attracted by the picture I drew and, seeing that only a taxi could now get me to Elswick Square by twelve, I
rushed him off his feet. Ordering and paying for a large whisky and
soda, I said: "You stay here and have a drink till I come back. Then
we'll fix up everything over a bit of lunch."

And if he was rather doubtful, as well he might be, to see me
so eager, the approach of the whisky diverted his thoughts just as I
made for the door.

I don't pretend I was as cool as ice when I rang the bell at the
Elswick Square mansion. Yet the incident with Martin gave me confidence, for by getting the Irishman to exchange his place for mine
I had not only found a way into Glengyle and escaped the danger of
being identified by him if I turned up there later, I had also by my
change of name eliminated any possible embarrassment to Wentworth and Decies if I got caught. And it did fortify me to feel that I
had made a success out of what looked like a hopeless position when
Martin got the job I was after.

All the same, as I waited in the room into which I had been
shown, I was distinctly uneasy. It was awkward to know so little of
the man I was supposed to be. If questions came about my past experience I could only refer to "my late employer," and trust to pick
up the name from Lady Wridgley herself. Risky as it was, I had to
carry it off somehow. So waiting for the door to open which would
bring me face to face with Lady Wridgley, I braced myself for the ordeal, well aware that in coming to the house I had burned my boats,
for a failure now meant total failure, since, after the close scrutiny
she would naturally make, she would know me again. Then the door
opened and, rising, I found myself facing, not Lady Wridgley but
Captain Elliott.

"Morning," he greeted me with a sharp little nod, his eyes going
all over me in a single glance. "Lady Wridgley is very busy and in any
case is satisfied as to your character."

"Thank you, sir," I murmured.

He half seated himself against the table.

"Oh, that's all right, but I've got to satisfy myself about your
efficiency, you know."

"Quite so, sir," I said, wondering how he could doubt Wentworth's guarantee till I remembered that I wasn't there on Wentworth's testimonial at all.

"This is the only testimonial that matters to me." He had a letter in his hand, which he began to read over, with little nods as he did so. It was quite a lengthy document, and I tried to read the address heading when he laid one sheet down on the table, only unluckily it was wrong side up. "Yes," he said in a murmur to himself, "yes, he ought to know, Ridgway ought to know about guns."

He looked up at me as he folded the letter.

"I suppose you would have a well-furnished gun room at a place like Brookfield?"

"Well, sir, we had a good selection. I don't say I have never seen better, but Mr. Ridgway—"

Elliott looked up to stare at me. At once I knew something was wrong.

"Mr. Ridgway," he cut in. "Don't you mean Colonel Ridgway?"

I had run my head up against it! For a moment I must have looked pretty foolish.

"He didn't call himself Mister Ridgway, did he?"

"Oh no, sir."

"Then why should you?"

"Well, sir, it was like this. About the house we got into the habit of dropping his military title."

"Why?" he demanded curtly.

I struggled desperately, almost despairingly, to find a reason.

"Well, sir, it was on account of the colonel's aunt. An eccentric old lady, sir, who was such a strong what they call pacifist who could not endure military titles. It was the colonel's instructions that we should drop his rank while she was staying there, and as she was so often there we got used to doing it even when she wasn't there. But the colonel didn't mind, sir."

Elliott, in the act of lighting a cigarette when I began, had stopped the operation while he listened. When I had finished he applied the match and after a puff or two burst into loud laughter. It startled me horribly for I was myself full of anxiety at the moment.

"Well, that's damn funny," he cried. "I bet Colonel Ridgway had big expectations from that old aunt."

At this pleasantry I forced up a momentary smile of assent, and he then went on to question me rather closely about my experience in the gun room. Finally, to my surprise and joy he informed me that I would suit them quite well. In fact I left the house with instructions to join the other members of the household staff at Euston to catch the ten p.m. on the following Friday.

On entering the bar in which I had left Martin I got an unexpectedly warm welcome.

"Thanks be to God, there you are at last," he whispered, a great relief showing on his face. "Is it all right?"

I had thought my face might have made such a question superfluous, but when I told him the news in so many words he slapped his leg and cried that he was as good as half-way to Canada already. So great, in fact, was his delight over my success, that he insisted on paying for the drink we had as well as for the snack lunch which followed. This touched me, for of the two of us, I considered I had made much the better of the deal, since he could not possibly desire my job so much as I wanted his. So, as we fixed up the details necessary for a complete change of identity, I took an oath with myself to do my utmost to get him the trip on the yacht that had so caught his adventurous fancy.

To be candid, it was not long before I discovered that the best service I could do him was to keep him from drinking too much that afternoon. Every detail we agreed upon to conceal our real identity, he made an excuse for a fresh call to the waiter, and as we had a good deal to fix up, I was in the end compelled to call a halt. Of course I was myself in a rather exalted frame of mind. Up till then I had been all the time poised, as it were, on a razor edge between failure and success, for at any moment disaster might have come, as it nearly did in the matter of Colonel Ridgway. But now, having with luck kept clear of all the rocks, I felt full of confidence: the rest of my job now seemed simple. But I saw to it that Martin did not get himself full of drink. Alas! if I had only taken equal care to prevent my recent achievements from filling myself with pride!

CHAPTER VII

There was nothing wrong, however, with the plan we contrived to exchange our identities. Martin had been occupying a room in Guildford Street, and at about four in the afternoon I sent him there to collect his things. It was, I saw, essential to our scheme that we both should change our place of residence. So while he went to Guildford Street I dropped in on Peters to tell him I'd got the job and collect my own things.

Peters came up to my room just after I'd changed into my old suit, and while I was stuffing my case, he told me about his evening out with the girl Gracie at the cinema. He had got little out of her, except gossip about a beautiful Spanish lady who with her husband was coming to Glengyle as one of the house party on the Tuesday after they arrived. Of course that made me prick up my ears. The husband must be the Portuguese Count Pedro Fernandez, and for him to be at Glengyle next Tuesday meant that the nefarious agreement would be signed next week. When Jim, then, asked when I might be coming back, the answer was easy.

"About the end of next week," I said. "And if there's anything for you to do at this end you'll hear from me."

Martin and I met as arranged on an island refuge in Regent Street. Among a crowd who waited for the policeman to hold up the traffic we put down our baggage together, and when the white gloved arm arrested the stream we each took up what the other had put down. That was all. No need to change labels or initials. We even went together to the Soho café where he was to put up. It was quite

57

a small place, kept by an Italian, with only a few rooms for letting purposes, the ground floor being used as a restaurant.

Having calmly registered under the name of Maitland and getting his room, he went up to have a wash and in ten minutes returned, wearing my good suit and looking pretty smart in it too. In fact I thought my suit fitted him much better than the one he'd been wearing. Then the patron offered me his other vacant room, but that I refused. I had another place in view, not far off; for it was better on all accounts that Martin and I should not have the same address, not even each have one in the same street. That is why I went to the place in Greek Street. But I took Martin with me, for I had no mind to see him further increase his high spirits by more drinks. Conspiracy seems to exhilarate all Irishmen, and Martin was no exception, to judge by the way he entered into this one. For while I saw no real reason why we should exchange clothes, he insisted on it, asserting that in these affairs one could not be too careful. But when I got on his own suit I saw that one reason at least for his insistence on the exchange might very well be that in making the exchange he had got rather the better of the bargain. It was not that the suit was poorer in quality or in condition, but that it fitted me rather badly. And this I put down to the inexpert Irish tailor, for looking at the way in which my own clothes fitted Martin, I could hardly believe that the suit I had on was ever made for him. However, I was far too well content with the way things were going to be worried by a detail like that, and I should probably have thought no more of it but for an incident that happened soon after the moment came to take Martin to the Ritz for that crucial interview with Lord Billinghurst.

The fact is I had forgotten the tightness of the jacket under my arms, and elsewhere, till we were turning out of Dean Street into Shaftesbury Avenue, when I saw a man who was sauntering into Dean Street stare oddly at us as he passed. Feeling a little self-conscious I took a glance back as we rounded the corner and just saw that he had turned round and was smiling broadly. That made me take a look at myself at the first convenient window we passed, but from that reflection and also from the fact that nobody else took any special note of my appearance, I came to the conclusion that the man was either a very superior tailor or at least had been smiling at something else than my appearance. Anyway, I soon had other things to think about.

Martin, I saw, grew more nervous the nearer we got to the hotel, and this did not tend to allay my own anxiety. I had spent the previous two hours in coaching him up to meet any questions he might have to face, and I'm bound to say he seemed an apt pupil. He had a quick wit and foresaw for himself the awkward corners, so that when I had pumped him up with all the facts, I knew he was going to enter for his interview far better prepared for it than I had been for mine.

Martin's nervousness I put down to much the same cause as my own: he was as desperately eager to get this trip to Canada as I was to get to Glengyle. That was all. So as I saw him enter the hotel and turned away to pace up and down while waiting for his return, I did not see how he could come a cropper. After all, I told myself, he has been for years in just this sort of employment. There isn't anything he doesn't know about the work. Unlike me he had nothing to be frightened about, for he had only changed his name, which was a change anybody might make. And Billinghurst, having put the matter of character and qualifications into the hands of the agency, no doubt only wanted to be satisfied with his appearance, I did not see how anything could go wrong.

For half an hour I paced back and forward waiting, and then when Martin emerged at last I perceived that nothing had gone wrong. Triumph was written all over his face. He hurried up to slap me on the back.

"Sure," he cried, "it was as easy as fallin' into a ditch, it was."

Only under excitement did his Irish accent and idiom become pronounced.

"You're engaged then?"

"I am that. He took to me at once, you understand. I hadn't any trouble."

"No trouble?" I repeated with relief, and anxious to hear him say it again.

"No trouble at all, except for the matter of my name."

That pulled me up.

"What about the name?" I asked, startled.

"Why, when I told him my name was Francis he told me it wouldn't do at all since his wife's maid had that name too."

Then just as I began to laugh again in renewed relief, my eye lighted on something that shut my mouth. We were by this time walking along the railings outside the Green Park, and in the act of lifting my head and turning away, as one does, to laugh at a companion's drollery, I noticed a man walking parallel to us on the opposite pavement. Of course there were many on the opposite pavement going and coming, but this man somehow seemed to be going step for step with us. That I might not have observed but for one other thing: that man had taken my eye already. He was in fact the same rather red-faced man who had turned, as I thought, to stare at my ill-fitting suit at the corner of Dean Street. But now I did not think it was the suit that had made him stare. Had I been clad in armor, or pyjamas, he would hardly have followed me from Dean Street to watch me. It was something else. But what? Had the Albemarle Agency, in its super-efficient way, got wind of the change of parts we had agreed on? I could not see how. Not so soon anyhow.

My mind turned to Peters. Had he become doubtful after my departure and consulted the detective for whom he scouted? It was true I had been rather reticent with Peters, my going had been hurried, and I had not been able to pay him anything for the work he had done. Or was it Captain Elliott? Had my mistake over Colonel Ridgway and my invention of the pacifist aunt not been so convincing as I had supposed? I remembered the long pause before Elliott began to laugh at my story. Or was it just coincidence that the man was there? One does sometimes chance to see the same person twice in an afternoon, even in London. I had no answer to any of these questions and was becoming correspondingly uneasy when Martin's voice came, almost querulous.

"Why are ye so quiet all of a sudden? What is it you're thinking about?"

"A drink," I replied, "to celebrate our success."

"It's a good thought that," he cried, "for it's my own too. Where shall we go?"

We were now abreast of the Park taxi rank, and I saw a way that would show me at least whether the man's presence was due to coincidence or not. I took Martin by the arm and almost shoved him into the nearest taxicab. The driver, surprised at the sudden move, stepped over from the two others with whom he was chatting.

"Where to?" he asked.

"Britannia, Dean Street," I said, almost mechanically naming the first pub that came to mind, for with the corner of my eye I was watching the man on the opposite pavement. This would show whether the fellow was there by coincidence or not. At first I saw him continue his leisurely promenade. This was a good sign. My sudden move into the taxi ought to have made him pull up, if he was dogging me. When we pulled out and turned back along Piccadilly I kept my watch on him through the little back window and, though he still kept sauntering on, there came an instant just before the traffic became too thick for me to see him any longer, when I thought I saw him pull up. But by then the distance was too great and I could not be certain. Indeed, I felt much more certain that it must have been another figure that turned round, since if he had been watching us, that is what he would have done before we got so far away. And he certainly could not overhaul us now even if he wanted to. The weight lifted from my mind. I took Martin's arm.

"We'll make a night of it," I said.

"We will so," he replied. "I've got a few pounds on me yet and there won't be any way of spending them on that yacht before others are due to me," he added with a grand air.

This touched me, for a good slice of the apprehension I felt had been on Martin's account. If my trickery led to any trouble the entire responsibility for leading this innocent Irishman into it would have been mine. But I knew well enough that that fact would not save him once the imposture was discovered. It was this that made me stick to Martin that night. But it was a harder job than I bargained for.

As soon as we reached the Britannia he let me see that he was going to make up for the forced abstention of the afternoon. The pub, for all its name, numbered fewer Britons among its clientele than foreigners. Around us we could hear much talk in a variety of tongues; and as most of the habitués, either from national habit or more probably from want of funds, made their different drinks spin out and last for a long time, Martin's repeated orders soon won him the attention of our neighbors. Of course it was soon seen he was paying for all my drinks, and I fancy their thought was that the Irishman was a bird I was in the process of plucking. Their sympathies, of course, lay with me, and more than one pair of eyes, glittering with malicious amusement, met mine knowingly or with an offer of assistance in their look. The fact that I took care to let them see that if Martin paid for my drinks I had on an average only about one to his four, told them nothing, unless indeed they thought I was keeping my wits clear for my own purposes while letting my companion drown his own. If so, they must have been moved to admiration by the strength of Martin's head, for the only perceptible effects made on him by the drinks were a slight rise in color and a more boisterous and bragging note that came into his voice and bearing as the evening wore on.

There was one thing, however, that kept me content. For all his wild talking not a word fell from his lips which might have betrayed our plot. Indeed, it secretly amazed me to hear him calling me Martin while I myself had to be continually on guard to remember to address him as Maitland. In my time as an actor I had played a good many parts and so had practice in thinking myself into other people's skins; but never apparently had I done this half so thoroughly as this half-tipsy Irishman, inspired by the natural genius of his race for conspiracy.

The trouble came near closing time. Up till then things went quite well, and I was thinking that in no time now I would be shepherding him back to his hotel, and that tomorrow he'd be getting up with a steadying headache, ready to take the train for Southampton to report to the yacht lying in the Solent. Already, in fact, I reckoned that my anxieties, so far, that is, as these related to Martin, were over. For once he was away on the high seas, no matter what he did or said, I would have ample time in which to get my own job over and done with one way or the other, without fear of discovery through him.

Then the trouble began. It came when Martin's roving eye caught sight of a group of men playing darts at the upper end of the bar. There was a good deal of clamor going on, and some disputing over the game, challenge and counter-challenge coming rapidly, for it was a game in which the loser paid for the drinks, and closing time drew very near. Before I could stop him, Martin rose and stalked over, offering to take anyone on for drinks all round. I tried to get him back to the table. That upset the entire company. The astute gentleman he had challenged patted him on the back indulgently and nodded at me.

"No, no," he said. "You go back with your keeper."

"Keeper be damned," Martin cried. "He's no keeper of mine."

The other appeared surprised.

"Ain't he? Why, we all thought he was from the way he's been ordering you about and treating you like a kid."

That was enough. Martin shook off my hand and turning savagely, told me to go to the devil.

Of course he lost. Even had he been an expert at the silly game, in his half-fuddled condition he could hardly have hit the target at all. And his opponent got most of his darts on the bull's-eye. Then Martin, as if to show how little he needed to care, made a display of his bundle of notes while paying for the drinks. Being offered his "revenge," he had another try with the darts. This time he lost again, but they let him come so near to winning that he was encouraged to go on. I saw their game, of course, but a second effort to get him away was still more violently resented, not only by him but also by the onlookers who, to a man, flamed up against me for selfishly attempting to rob them of free drinks.

"Plenty more where that came from," the Irishman cried as he threw a fiver on to the tray. Then they cheered him. I suppose they took every note in his bundle to be a fiver, but I knew this was not the fact, though I doubt if he would have been left with enough to pay for his room in the morning had not the clock struck the hour of closing and the inexorable bar man turned us into the street.

But that only made things take a new turn. An altogether unspeakable little dago in a blue shirt and pink tie with a flower in his

buttonhole, sidled up to Martin with the offer of an introduction to a
night club round the corner. Irritated at this and seeing my troubles
with Martin were not, as I had supposed, over, I almost kicked the
fellow out of our way. But the other loafers weren't to be so easily
robbed of one they already considered as an easy victim, and an
attempt was made to trip me up from behind.

Martin, perhaps sobered a little by coming out into the fresh night
air, came to his senses as he saw me stumble, and turning, promptly
knocked the man into the gutter. That caused all of them except five
to stand back and assume the attitude of interested spectators. But
the five undoubtedly meant business. They knew the pocket in which
Martin stowed his money, and that money they beyond question intended to get. This sort of rough and tumble, if new to us was not
new to them; and unluckily for us they were in the right place for the
job. For just before Martin knocked this man into the gutter we had
passed out of Dean Street and were against the blank brick wall of
the connecting alley I had taken as a short cut back to Martin's hotel.
It was against this wall we stood, hemmed in and screened off by the
ominously silent knot of spectators who had left the business in the
hands of the five experts.

The affair lasted no more than a few seconds, but I remember
thinking as I stood with my back against that wall, that this was
hardly the sort of thing I had anticipated when I took on my job in
Biddulph's luxurious room in Jermyn Street. Then they came at us
with a rush. I was horribly afraid for more reasons than one. At the
very least we should both get so marked and knocked about that it
might be impossible for either of us to show our faces tomorrow.
And just as little did I want to be saved by the arrival of the police,
since a court case might lead to all sorts of questions and complications for me. No such fears troubled Martin. As the men came at us
he roared aloud when he struck out, his Irish soul apparently thrilling to the joy of battle.

I heard his fist go home on naked flesh with a terrific smack,
but I was at once too busy to see or hear more. Only two of them
came at me, and these the smallest of the five, either because the
Irishman was the real game or because he had shown himself to be
a real bruiser. And at first, obsessed as I was with the thought of my

appearance and the sedate employment on which I hoped so soon to enter at Glengyle Castle, I merely attempted to protect myself by keeping the pair off. This was a mistake. Martin they only wanted to hold up in order to get at his pocket, but me they did want to damage as a spoil sport, and a light duty they clearly took this to be, since up till then I had shown no sort of fight at all.

But when they proceeded to lighten their job by getting me down with a kick on the shins, I came to my senses. For the kick failing in its effect, the other man, an undersized creature whose eyes suggested a Levantine birthplace, drew back his leg to try his luck on my stomach. But just as he did so I stepped forward from the wall to give my arm a good draw back and, catching him poised on one leg, sent him, both legs up, slap to the feet of his friends.

A cry from Martin let me see him being pinned against the wall, both hands held high over his head by one fellow while the other two were getting busy with his pockets. He was equal to the situation, however, for with a quick upward jerk of his knee he doubled up the man, holding his hands as I got the nearest fellow by the back of his collar and swung him tottering sideways to the pavement. Then, just as I was feeling strung up to go on with the good work, the shindy which had lasted no more than a minute altogether, came to a sudden end.

Without a word our assailants simply melted away, as if they had been no more than shadows cast against the dingy brick wall. I think we both felt flattered as soon as we realized the fact. But a glance in the direction of Dean Street lowered my complacency, for I saw there the lamplight glancing on the bright buttons of a policeman's tunic. Someone must have given a signal, unheard or not understood by me, before the officer rounded the corner, for he advanced without haste, walking in the manner of a constable patrolling his beat. So, being probably almost as unwilling as any just then to be interrogated by the police, I seized Martin's arm and got him on the move. We made back towards Dean Street, of course, having no mind for any more short cuts through dark bye streets, passing the officer arm in arm so that I might keep Martin going if he were tempted to stop and make a complaint. But the Irishman was sober enough now and had no inclination to speak to the officer, almost, indeed, slinking past him as if he were just as nervous as myself. This belated evidence

of good sense on his part did not mollify me much, however. I was
much too angry with him over his behavior in the pub. And now that
I had escaped complete disaster as by a hair's breadth, it only irritated me the more to see not only from the way he remembered our
change of names but also from his avoidance of the policeman, that
he was capable of sound common-sense.

As soon as we were safely back in the well-lit street
I stopped to inspect my clothes and feel the spot on my leg where
the little dago's kick had landed.

"Something biting you?" he inquired, jocosely.

Then I rounded on him.

"I'd like to give you the same kind of bite in another place."

He was taken aback by the fierce rush of my words, and not having seen the dago's kick, did not comprehend what I meant, which
was perhaps fortunate for me.

"And what might you mean by that, Mr. Martin?" he asked, with
stiff coolness.

"You very nearly wrecked our whole scheme," I declared. And
then indicating the torn seam of the over-tight sleeve which had
burst when I struck out, I said, "Look at that. How can I present
myself for my new job in this rig-out?"

"Sure, that's nothing," he replied, putting his hand to his breast
pocket. "Here's the price of a new suit. I owe you much more for getting me the fine sail to Canada."

"You haven't got it yet," I retorted.

He stopped short with the notes in his hand.

"What do you mean by that?" he demanded with a snap, all the
brogue gone from his voice.

"You were nearer the dock in Bow Street than Southampton
Dock tonight," I said.

It was a surprise to see that I really had frightened him. His jaw
dropped comically and he even glanced around swiftly this way and
that as he gripped my arm.

"Did you see anyone following us at all?" he whispered.

Remembering the crowd of riff-raff who had followed us from
the pub I began to laugh. But suddenly an earlier memory stopped
that laugh abruptly. He was quick to notice this.

"What is it? What's come to you?" he repeated.

"Well," I said, "I did think a man was watching us earlier in the evening."

"What was he like?"

"A big red-faced man in a blue serge suit. Looked as if he might have been an ex-policeman doing private inquiry work," I added, glad to see how I had sobered him. There would be no more trouble from Martin now, I felt sure. But to make quite sure of that I did not tell him that I no longer thought the man had been dogging us, neither did I tell him that even if he had, our dash in the taxi to the Britannia had shaken him off. But I did point out to the silly Irishman the danger we should both have run into had we got involved in a court case through his behavior in the pub or in the brawl that followed our exit.

The consequence was that Martin, almost, as I thought, childishly frightened now at the risk he had run of losing that yacht trip to Canada, wanted to get back to his room in the little Italian café at once. And as that was exactly where I wanted to see him, we set off for the café at once. No, there would be no more trouble from Martin that night. "And tomorrow," I kept repeating to myself, "tomorrow he'll be safe on the yacht and too far away to do any more harm."

On the pavement opposite the Café Sorrento we shook hands and I waited till I saw him disappear through the doorway, noting that he had not turned into the restaurant, but must have gone straight upstairs, when I saw the light go up in a front room on the second floor. Then I turned away contentedly. Somewhere in the distance a clock began to strike eleven. It had been a hard day. But it was over now. "And tomorrow," I said to myself as I walked back to my little hotel, "tomorrow by this time you'll be on the road to Glengyle." It was a cheering thought, after all the scheming and anxieties of the day, but I felt that having so carefully and laboriously laid my plan on a sound foundation, the rest would be little more than child's play.

But at the hotel a shock awaited me. The proprietor, Papini, a rotund little Italian in white shirt sleeves, with blue-black hair very much *brossé*, stopped me as I was making for the stairs.

"Mistaire Martin, is not it?" he addressed me.

At my assent he said a gentleman had come asking for me, about half an hour earlier. This was the unexpected with a vengeance. When I inquired what he was like Papini laughed merrily, explaining that the caller had himself asked the same question about me.

"A big man with a red face," Papini said he was. "It wass when I tell him you take the room onlee for one night he ask what you was like becos he is not certain you was the Mistaire Martin what is his friend."

When I asked him what he said I was like he explained that not having previously seen me himself he had called his little Francesca who had shown me to my room.

"She touch you off for him," he laughed. "Oh yes, ver' nice. Quite buttering you up, as they say."

That was all very well; but what Papini could not explain to me was how this stranger came to know there was anyone called Martin at his hostelry at all. Further questions as to the man's appearance only revealed the need for the little Francesca's descriptive talents, for Papini described him as a tall, well-dressed man about thirty-five, which fitted too many. Unfortunately the sharp-eyed little Francesca had gone to bed.

In my room I had a look at myself in the glass. If Papini's daughter had described me adequately I never could be mistaken for the real Mr. Martin by anyone who knew him. I sat on my bed to think it out. It was all very well to say Martins were as plentiful in Ireland as Smiths in England. That might or might not be true. I didn't know. The trouble was that that did not explain how this man came to know there was one of that name in this hotel within a few hours of his taking a room there. And had he been looking for the real Martin or myself, the sham one? If he were making inquiries on behalf of the Albemarle it might be that he was after both of us. This possibility got me to my feet. The sooner I saw Martin the better. I slipped downstairs and made for the Café Sorrento as quickly as I could walk. And the nearer I got the more sure I became that I should hear of someone who had called there to ask for a Mr. Maitland.

The Café Sorrento, as I have said, was a small house with the door at one side, the ground floor being used as a restaurant. On entering you found the door to the restaurant on your right, with the flight of stairs to the bedrooms facing you. There was practically no hall, the foot of the steep narrow stairs finishing just short of the glass door into the restaurant. The café, in fact, was typical of the Soho *quartier*: it seemed to sleep throughout the day and to make up for it by a feverish activity at night.

As I approached I could hear the babble of commingled voices inside. Stepping into the dimly lit passage I peeped through the half-screened glass door and saw the place crowded with men and women, mostly young and strikingly dressed, seated round their little tables smoking, chatting, laughing while the padrone moved among his guests serving cups of coffee from the large tray he carried balanced high on the extended fingers and thumb of one hand.

For a moment or two I watched the colorful interior, uncertain what next to do to get unobtrusively at Martin. For I did not see myself plunging in there to ask for him, and bell there seemed to be none. Then I remembered having seen that room on the second floor lit up soon after his entrance, and I thought it would be easy to find. There were only three windows facing the street on that floor, I remembered, I fancied it was in the middle one I had seen the light go up. Anyhow, I quickly resolved to chance it. The shoes outside the doors would probably help me. And it was as well if I could see him without being seen by anyone else.

The only illumination I found on the upper landing came from the fanlight over one-bedroom door. Outside this door stood a pair of very feminine shoes, and a pause by the door allowed me to hear someone moving about as if in preparation for bed. The next door had no shoes outside, nor could I hear any sound from within. As this was the room I had supposed to be Martin's, I held my own breath in the effort to overhear his breathing. The absence of the shoes bothered me. For Martin, due to join Lord Billinghurst's yacht tomorrow, wasn't likely to join up with dirty shoes. His whole training and occupation would make such a neglect impossible. As easily could I suppose him to have gone to bed in them. But he might, very well, after the night's excitements, have forgotten to put out his shoes.

After a little hesitation I stole along to the furthest door, to examine another pair of shoes I saw standing on the mat. Picking one up I tiptoed back to the lady's door, and under her fanlight judged that it might be of the size that fitted Martin. Closer inspection showed me a small oblong silk label inside, with the maker or vendor's name, on which I made out the word Edinburgh. That left me doubtful. Martin had come from Ireland and I could not see him going to the Scottish capital to buy his shoes. Still, it wasn't conclusive, since this pair might have been passed on to him either by his former employer, Colonel Ridgway, or one of his guests. I didn't know what to do. But aware that I had better act now before someone came, I replaced the shoe and got my ear to the keyhole. While stooping to listen it struck me that this was probably just exactly the sort of thing I'd be doing at Glengyle next week. Of course here, if a door did open unexpectedly, or if anyone should corner me by coming upstairs, I could explain that I was merely looking for my friend, Mr. Maitland, having failed to discover any bell below.

Then I saw the best thing to do was to try that middle door which had no boots or shoes outside to show that it was occupied. If it were empty, why then this one must be Martin's room, since the only other room fronting the street was that occupied by the lady.

I tapped gently on the door. Getting no response to a quiet tapping I tried the handle. The door was not locked. Almost certainly it must be unoccupied. I pushed it open a little and tried to see inside. A dim radiance from the street lamps shone on the ceiling, but that only served to make the lower levels of the room rather more impenetrable. As I hesitated uncertainly the silence was suddenly broken by voices, and then the stairs creaked as men in laughing talk came swarming up.

Almost involuntarily I stepped into the room and shut the door. Then, before recalling that the room was empty and that they might be coming here, I felt for the key, found it and turned the lock. The next moment my heart began to thump on seeing how very awkward it would be if they were coming to this room. Undoubtedly I was getting fine practice for the work before me at Glengyle, but, I said to myself as I waited, *if* this is their room and an arrest follows, I'll have little chance of profiting by this practice.

When I heard them come along the passage I had a presentiment I should never see Glengyle: the difficulties to be surmounted were altogether too numerous. When the footsteps stopped outside the door my heart stopped also. I could hear the light chatter of the voices. This, then, was the room assigned to one of them. Presently he would be saying good-night to his friend and then his hand would go out to open the door and find it locked. After that, what? But the next moment both passed on, and I knew they had merely paused momentarily, as arguing men do to make or emphasize a point in their discussion. I breathed again, relaxing when the voices died away, knowing that the two men must be ascending to another floor.

Of course, subconsciously, this alarm had suggested to me I was in an empty room. The mere expectation that one of these men was about to enter had planted that idea in my mind. And, quite irrationally, it remained there even after the men passed on. That must have been why the sound that came from behind was so startling. It was quite a small sound, lasting not so long as a breath. But in the silence and darkness its unexpectedness made me jump round as if I had been shot, leaving me rigid, with ears straining for its repetition. When no repetition came I called myself all kinds of things: a nervous ninny, a coward, a fool to be so startled, and telling myself, but without conviction, that it came from the street. There could be no one in the room. In that stillness while I listened so intently the lightest breathing must have been audible.

At last the sound came again. It was exactly the same sound lasting but an instant. I hung on, waiting to hear it repeated, this time determined to locate it. And after a shorter interval it came, to be followed immediately by a quick succession of identical sounds. I knew now exactly what it was like. It was like a very rapid succession of light hammer strokes, heard at a great distance. But it was in that room all right, over in the far corner that looked just a wedge of blackness in contrast to the faint up-thrown radiance from the street lamp. My hand went hunting on the wall for the switch, only to come in contact with the polished surface of a wardrobe or chest of drawers that stood close up to the side of the door. The switch must have been in some unusual place, for I could not find it. But as I groped about the queer sound which had gone on now all the time changed in the quality of its note. My ear instantly noted that. It was no longer like a distant rain of little hammer-blows: it had become liquid in quality.

And suddenly realizing what it was, I stood back against the door and laughed. Laughed aloud, quite forgetful in my reaction that I might be overheard. Of course that was what it was—water falling on the floor and then forming a puddle. Water spilt on a washstand does act like that, first slowly finding its way over the dry surface and then dropping with increasing rapidity to the floor. This empty room was probably used as a dressing room for the café's female guests, and probably several of them had used the washstand just before I reached the place. Very likely there would be hats and cloaks lying on the bed now.

Again my hand sought for the switch to verify this by a momentary flash of the light. But once more I failed to come on the switch. Still, this was a fact that could be verified by touch, and thinking I'd better, in view of the job that lay before me at Glengyle, school myself to work in darkness, I went over to feel for the washstand. But it was the bed I found first.

I walked into it before I was aware, and would have overbalanced on to it if I had not thrown out my hands when my knees came against the edge. As it was I stumbled forward awkwardly, half falling on something that told me the bed was not unoccupied, something too that made my hands both wet and warm.

I suppose I must have known as I jumped back instinctively who lay there and what had happened to him. Now that I knew I felt no fear of anything inside that room. For a moment or two I stood considering what I must do. The door was locked, no one could come in. For the time I had the room to myself. But I must know beyond doubt who the occupant was. Not that I doubted for an instant. Still, I must know. The first thing to do was to make sure. There might be a switch on the wall at the top of the bed. As I took a step in that direction I came against a table at the head of the bed, and groping on it, touched a box of matches. I must know for certain who it was. One match would be enough. As deliberately as I could, I opened the box, and striking a match, held it high above my head.

CHAPTER VIII

In the bed Martin lay on his back, his eyes staring as if transfixed in sudden terror, his mouth agape as if shaped for a cry he had not time to make. So much I saw before the match went out or fell from my hand.

But I did not need to see any more to know he was dead. My ear confirmed what my eyes had seen; for the same sound that had first startled me when it began, still went on, the drip, drip, drip of his blood on the floor beneath the bed. There was no need to strike another match to make sure that that wound in his chest was mortal. His features, set and fixed in the last emotion he had felt, proved it. And that abrupt, terrifying end must have come to him but a few minutes before I reached the café. It would not take long for so much blood to percolate through the bedding; and it had not begun to sound on the floor till I had been some time in the room.

An almost irresistible impulse to flee came to me. But before I reached the door I saw the danger in which a mad rush down those stairs might lead me. I had to keep my nerve, get a grip on the situation and the possible consequences of my next act while there was time. By an effort of the will I felt about for a chair, found it and sat down to think things out.

What was the right thing to do? Give the alarm, while there was a chance of getting the murderer? But who was I, and what was I doing in that room? Would anyone dream of looking further than myself for the assassin? Then the thought came that I had seen no knife in the wound. This would make a difference. After the police arrived they would look for a weapon, and not finding one, it would be clear that I, who had come to my companion's room and had not left it, could not be the man. But though no knife had been left in the body, how did I know it was not somewhere in the room? Those toughs from the Britannia were not the sort to leave such a good clue as a knife behind them. That got me to my feet again. I must see if the knife had been dropped on the floor.

Another match revealed the light switch on the right of the door, and, after switching on, my search ended as soon as it began: a long-bladed, horn-handled sheath knife was lying beneath the chair on which I had been sitting. In stooping to pick it up I saw my hand was red. And as if that were not enough, there was the torn sleeve of my coat as evidence of a struggle.

That settled the matter. Switching off the light I went back to my chair to consider how I could escape unseen. I do not pretend that I was quite collected and calm. And now that the first shock of horror had passed, I was shaken by the thought that it was I who had, however unintentionally, led Francis Martin to his death. By a foolish display of money he had brought on the attempt in the alley. Were we wrong in supposing them to be finally shaken off when the first attempt failed? The likelihood of this brought me some comfort, for I was feeling pretty bad about my responsibility just then.

That this murder was real dago work I felt more and more certain. They knew he had money, and from the boastful way he had talked about it in the pub they would suppose he had heaps of it. That, in short, was why they had gone after him and left me alone. From the perception that I had done my utmost to shield him, I at once drew courage to make my own get-away. There were still people about, but they were leaving more frequently. The voices and laughter of men and women leaving the café came from the street, and several times footsteps sounded in the passage.

I saw where my chance lay. I must change into the clothes in which Martin had been seen, clothes which after all were my own, put my hat on with the brim well down, and walk out.

So I boldly switched on the light and proceeded to wash my hands. Yes, on all accounts, I saw it was desirable that I should resume possession of that blue suit. If I left it behind I might be traced by it. But the one I took off, with its torn sleeve and blood stains on the right cuff, would make a mighty sore problem for the police.

As I dried my hands I noticed my own suit neatly arranged on a chair, the coat suspended on the back, the trousers carefully folded on the seat, just as Martin would have put them before retiring. The murderer must have been hidden in the room at the time. Then when he had done his work, he had unlocked the door and walked out, exactly as I intended to do, though probably with twice my coolness.

Stripping quickly, I dropped the ill-fitting clothes I had worn all day in a heap on the floor, and put on the other suit. Running my hands through the pockets to make sure I took nothing away that belonged to Martin, I got a disconcerting surprise. For in the breast pocket I touched his wallet, and on withdrawing it discovered it to be full of notes. So, the assassin could hardly have been one of the dagos from the Britannia. And the next moment I saw it was impossible he could be, since these men could only have learned where Martin was staying by following him, and therefore could not have got into his room ahead of him to wait for him to get into bed, as the folded clothes suggested.

That set my mind seething once more over the motive behind this murder. And in the position in which I then stood it was far from helpful to feel oneself in a mental fog. For I had a conviction that if I got caught in the act of leaving that room, nothing short of a miracle could save me from the gallows. Some blind instinct prompting me, then made me, after restoring the money to Martin's clothes, go through his pockets and remove the papers and letters I had handed over for the interview with Lord Billinghurst.

Then I stole to the door, switched off the light and listened. Hearing nothing, I carefully turned the key and opened the door just sufficiently to get a slit through which I could peep into the passage. Seeing nothing, I slipped out, and, closing the door behind me, made for the top of the stairs. All went well till my foot got to the first step. Then voices rose from below with abrupt loudness as the restaurant door swung open, and the next moment I saw the white shirt-sleeved proprietor carrying a suit-case, ushering a man upstairs. I saw the man, evidently a late arrival, glance up at me as the padrone half turned to lock the front door. It was the click of the lock that roused me out of my paralysis.

I turned and made for the room again, uncertain as to whether the proprietor had seen me or not, but quite sure that if he had, my wish to avoid meeting them on the stairs must be evident. Behind the door, which in my panic, I had re-locked, I waited to see what would happen. If the man had seen me and from my clothes taken me for Martin, he might knock at the door to see if I had wanted any-thing. On the other hand, if he knew I was not one of his guests, he would certainly at once begin to investigate. And the strain was not eased when their voices fell to a whisper as they reached the top of the stairs. That was, of course, out of consideration for the sleepers around them, but I did not think so then. The next sound I heard was the sharp creak of a door opening on the other side of the passage.

Reassured so far, though it sounded as if it might be a door ex-actly opposite, I got my own door opened and peeped out. The light from a room between me and the stairs streamed into the passage. Quickly I stepped out, gently shut the door, and in crossing that beam of light saw both men standing in the room, the landlord with his back towards me, in the act of bidding his guest good-night. So fortunate for me he was an Italian! An Englishman in his position would not have been so flowery and long-winded in offering his good wishes for a restful and refreshing night.

As I slipped nimbly down the stairs, however, I was aware my anxieties were not yet ended; for I did not know whether the land-lord had removed the key when he locked the front door. If he had, the game was up; for it was almost certain that there would be some-one, a yawning wife or a waitress, in the one big room at the foot of the stairs; and the man himself would be at my back in another second. To avoid the chance of being seen I ducked low in passing the glass-topped door below, and then found myself up against the locked door almost before I knew it. The key had not been removed. One turn of the wrist and I was free. I stepped into the street and the next moment was running away from the Café Sorrento as hard as if I had a thousand Italian waiters shouting at my heels.

It was the maddest thing I could have done, but the impulse was uncontrollable; and luckily no policeman chanced to meet me till

I had rounded a corner and sobered down to a walk. Ten minutes later, having taken a slightly circuitous route to regain my nerve, I was at the door of my own hotel. And here another bit of luck befell me. Luck for me in this affair was long overdue. At least so I had begun to think; for certainly up till now I had to work and scheme hard for my success so far achieved. The luck lay in the fact that in Papini's establishment, which had much more floor space than the small Café Sorrento, the clients could dance. In consequence, it remained open to a much later hour, attracting clients from the earlier closing cafés by the blatant music which penetrated to the street through its open door. Life at Papini's had, in fact, hardly begun when I left for the Sorrento, and as I stood on the opposite pavement the sounds of revelry from within let me understand why sleeping accommodation at Papini's was so easily obtainable at such a moderate charge.

What I now desired was to slip up to my room without being seen by Papini himself or any of his small staff who could recognize me. It only took a few minutes' watch to let me see how this might be done. For I observed that while Papini, who stood in the entrance to welcome his clients, allowed some to pass with a smile and an exchange of familiar badinage, others he conducted with much empressement into the dance room in the back premises. And it was easy to see why he discriminated. Some were regular and known habitués, others were obviously strangers. So I bided my time and presently a small knot of these strangers, unmistakably up from the country and wandering around in the conviction that they were "seeing life," entered the place with noisy self-assertiveness. Then when Papini's back was turned in the act of conducting his guests towards the *salle*, I slipped in close behind the group, only to detach myself when we reached the foot of the stairs. The rest was easy. I skimmed up to my room ready to swear that not an eye had seen me leave the one café or enter the other.

But next morning I found that I was mistaken.

It was well after ten when I came down to breakfast. Sleep had not come easily, and when it did, had not been very restful. The house, however, even at that hour, had the air and aspect of the very early morning about it, and the pale-faced waiter who eventually brought me my coffee, yawned unrestrainedly and looked as if he had slept in his clothes. Outside someone was sluicing down the window with a bucket of water, and the occasional knocking of a broom, mingled with the noises from the street. But inside, a frowsty stillness pervaded the place; the only fresh-looking thing which had so far penetrated into it being the morning newspaper which lay unfolded on a table by the door.

After a little while I rose and took possession of the paper, not of course, expecting to find any reference to the murder in it, since poor Martin's body would not be discovered till long after the daily newspapers had gone to press. But as I propped it up against the milk jug the badly printed stop press square on the front page caught my eye:

MURDER IN SOHO: Early this morning the body of
a man stabbed to the heart was found in a Soho café.

That was all, but it put me out of taste for the rest of the news. It took me by surprise that the discovery had been made so soon. Indeed, it made me very uneasy. What more would come to light presently? I could not imagine how the tragedy could have been discovered till the late forenoon, when someone went to knock at Martin's door and got no reply. For I felt sure that if I had been murdered in Papini's house, my nonappearance even later than eleven o'clock would not have made them knock at my door. And I had no reason to believe that people got up earlier at the Café Sorrento. How then had the murder there been discovered in time to get into the newspaper?

My knowledge of news offices was limited, but I had a vague idea that they went to press somewhere about two or just a little later. If that were so, then something suspicious must have sent someone to look into Martin's room. But what? Had I after all been seen? That indeed would account for the early discovery. Possibly the padrone, descending the stairs a moment or so after I got away, saw the door had been unlocked. And he would know that all his customers had left before he himself locked the door. Did he suspect a burglar and go round the house trying all the bedroom doors?

There was, too, that late comer he had taken up to his room. He had a chance of seeing me as I went past his door. At the time I had thought there was little risk in his suspecting anything wrong, since he would naturally take me for a fellow guest if he did see me pass.

But it was futile to speculate on how the tragedy had been so quickly discovered. So, seeing the waiter's lackluster eyes fixed on me over the top of the toothpick he was manipulating, I tried to get on with my breakfast. All the same, that feeling of queer restless uneasiness would not be banished, and I toyed with the other items of news in the paper, as I toyed with my breakfast, longing to learn more about the murder.

Up to the moment when I entered Martin's room at the Café Sorrento I had looked on the whole business as more or less a game. A game of wits, and sporting in so far as in case of detection I stood a first-rate chance of finding myself in the dock with no defense to offer. Never for an instant had I dreamed of its bringing me into contact with death. It left me shaken, horrified and strangely awed to feel that, since this brutal murder could not be the work of the Britannia toughs, it might have a connection with the job on which Biddulph had sent me. For I could not forget that Martin had died while bearing the name of Maitland, and if he had been murdered because he was supposed to be me, then he had died on my account. It was this last thought that fell with such shattering force on my mind, and not the thought that if our connection with each other could be traced I had a first-rate chance of being hanged for his murder.

It was about twelve o'clock when I heard the distant cry of the newsboy in the street. Here was the forenoon edition of the papers: there would certainly be fuller details now. The waiter was still engrossed with his toothpick and his thoughts. He had heard nothing. I got up before he should hear, and nonchalantly filling my pipe, strolled out to meet the oncoming newsboy. From afar I was able to read the bill hanging from his armful of papers:

MURDER IN GREEK STREET

FULLEST DETAILS

People were eagerly buying his papers. This was after all a Soho concern. With the paper in my hands I strolled back to Papini's and under the pretense of having forgotten my matches, took it up to my room. This is what I read:

MURDER IN SOHO

Last night a murder of a peculiarly brutal nature was perpetrated in a little café in Greek Street, Soho. So far little more is known of the victim except that his name is Maitland and that he took a room from Mr. Luigi Donati, the proprietor of the Café Sorrento which was the scene of the crime about three o'clock on the afternoon of yesterday. After registering as a British subject with a Sheffield address, he went out, explaining that he had to keep an appointment, and no more was seen of him till he returned shortly before eleven, when he went straight to his room. The discovery of the murder came about in a strangely dramatic way which must be almost unique in the annals of crime. It appears that the café, though a small place, does a quite considerable business in serving coffee to theatre goers, and last night while the murder was taking place, Mr. Donati and his staff were fully occupied in attending to the orders of an unusually large complement of guests, the last contingent of whom did not leave till shortly before midnight. At that hour, as Mr. Donati explained to our representative, he himself locked the door while showing one of his guests who was staying for the night up to his room.

On descending a few moments later Mr. Donati found that the door was unlocked and ajar, but thinking this must have been done by some guest whose presence he had overlooked, attached no importance to the fact, such an occurrence being not altogether unusual. Mr. Donati relocked his door, therefore, and went into the restaurant where, the work of the day being over, it was his custom to partake of supper with the members of his staff before retiring for the night. Yet it is now beyond question that in the brief interval between the locking and relocking of his front door the murderer made good his escape from the house.

A second or two before the proprietor ushered his guest upstairs the murder had been done, and while Luigi Donati stood for a moment in the room to say good-night, the watching criminal seized his chance to escape. The time has been established almost to a second, for Mr. Val Smith, the guest in question, remembers that while winding up his watch he observed that the hands showed six minutes after midnight. Not, however, till a late hour of today might the crime have been discovered but for the strange and surely unique incident which next occurred.

It was, as has been said, Mr. Donati's custom to partake of his supper with the members of his establishment in quietness after all his guests had left and the labors of the day were ended. The little party, consisting of the proprietor himself, two women and Guiseppe, the waiter, had almost finished when Mr. Donati surprised a look of extreme horror on Guiseppe's face. Following the direction of the waiter's horrified gaze he saw something in the center of the table: a small red stain. Thinking it to be a wine stain for which the waiter was responsible, he was about to rebuke him for carelessness when he noticed that the stain had increased in size and that the waiter had suddenly shifted his gaze from the wet tablecloth to the ceiling. Then he knew that the stain was not wine but blood, blood which was beginning to drip through the floor from the room above.

On entering the room thus indicated, Mr. Donati and the waiter, Guiseppe Fillipo, found Maitland dead in bed, stabbed through the heart. The police were on the scene within a few minutes after the discovery of the crime, and investigations are proceeding. We understand that though the case possesses several unusual features, the police are in possession of clues which they regard as of first-rate value, including a description of the murderer supplied to them by Mr. Val Smith, who was conducted to his room by Mr. Donati himself. Mr. Smith, seen by our representative, explained that he had no idea when he caught sight of the man in question that he was looking at the murderer. He states that when Mr. Donati was showing him to his room he looked up the stairs before he began the ascent and saw a tall, clean shaven, rather pale, youngish man, in a blue suit and grey Trilby hat, apparently about to descend. This man drew hastily back, but Mr. Smith thought nothing of the act at the time, as the stairs are narrow, meaning to thank him for his act of courtesy when he himself reached the top. Even when the ascent had been made and he saw no one there he thought that the man had merely forgotten something and gone to his room.

Subsequent conference with Mr. Donati, however, proved that no one answering to his description was then resident in the house. The authorities have requested Mr. Smith not to disclose the full details of the description he supplied nor the nature of the important clues left in their hands since it is from the prompt use now being made of these means of identification that an early arrest is anticipated.

I laid aside the paper, feeling both anger and dread. Anger at the cocksure way in which it was taken for granted that I was the murderer, and dread when I perceived that they could hardly come to any other conclusion. Then I lit my pipe and lay back on my bed to think the situation out.

CHAPTER IX

No great astuteness is needed to recognize the chief danger to which I lay exposed. I did quite a lot of thinking before it dawned on me. What the clues might be on which the police relied for an early arrest I could not guess, but eventually I did see how I could be tracked down. It was all quite simple. They had merely to establish a connection between a man calling himself Maitland and a man calling himself Martin, and it was all up with me. Indeed, if the name Martin came to be mentioned in connection with the case, I was as good as lost, since even Papini himself could tell them where to find me. But would my assumed name come out?

My first thought went to the Britannia where we had spent the night together. Yet though Martin had addressed me, as if enjoying the conspiracy, as Martin, frequently I had not remembered to call him Maitland. Consequently the report of the murder of a man named Maitland would tell the Britannia people nothing. But what about the Albemarle? We had both procured situations on the same day through that agency. Yet very likely others had also done so; and so far as I knew no one in that office had seen us exchange a word together. Billinghurst, when he went aboard his yacht that afternoon, would certainly discover that his new valet had not turned up; but I doubted whether he would delay his voyage on that account, or even go ashore to wire a complaint to the Albemarle. And he would have left town before the papers came out with the news that the name of the murdered man was Maitland. True, the manageress of the Albemarle would doubtless see the papers, but, even if she were not too genteel personally to read murder reports, I felt fairly sure that

short of compulsion she would not endanger the high-class reputa-
tion of her agency by coming forward to connect it with such a case.
And, even if she were willing, so long as the name of Martin did not
come into the report, there was nothing to suggest to her that the
"Maitland" who was murdered was the "Maitland" on her books.

But there was one man who undoubtedly did read murder reports, and who would certainly act on reading of the murder of a
man named Maitland—Jim Peters. And it was certain that if Biddulph would take no action under any circumstances, as indeed he
had told me, Peters at least would come forward. What then? They
would show him the body, with the result that Peters could only
say it was not that of the Maitland he knew. No, I thought, I may
be quite safe so long as the name Martin does not come in. Then
I stopped, suddenly in one paralyzing flash remembering the man
who had come to Papini's the night before, asking for me under that
very name! Foolishly, I had dismissed his visit from my thoughts
after reaching the comforting conclusion that his call was merely a
coincidence. How idiotic that now seemed! Who was this man who
came seeking me just before Martin met his death? I seemed forced
to the conclusion that he could only have known I was staying at
Papini's by following me there. Just as whoever killed Martin must
have followed him there *in the afternoon* when I first took Martin
to the café.

Suddenly it struck me that there was no need to presuppose two
different men in the affair: the one man had followed us both in the
afternoon and knew where we had each put up. He would be the
man whom I had noticed loitering in Dean Street, who had followed
us to the Ritz. We had thrown him off when we picked up that taxi
afterwards. But he knew where we had put up, and later had gone to
Papini's to ascertain if I had returned.

Then another significant fact came back to my mind. He had
asked them at Papini's to describe me. Why? If he had seen us both,
he did not need a description. Unless—here was the significant feature—unless he was uncertain which of us was which! That difficulty
would be solved at Papini's: he would then know which of us was
Maitland and which Martin. Or rather he would suppose he did and
then go off to wait in the Café Sorrento, as he thought, for my return.

My thoughts for a time went back to that evening in Biddulph's flat in an attempt to find a motive. For as yet I could not see why anyone should want to put me out of the way. Was the Glengyle job Biddulph had given me far more dangerous than he knew?

For an hour I lay puzzling over this possibility, and then just when I was saying to myself that in any case I must now abandon that job, a sudden burst of light, like a physical shock almost, made me sit up and send my dead pipe rolling on the floor. Why had I assumed that the man was after me and not Martin himself? What, after all, did I know of Martin? Now that I thought of it; he had more than met me half-way when I suggested the exchange. His delight at the chance of getting away to Canada had even amused me in its exaggeration. And was it not my very own suggestion that we should exchange names? If he had anything to hide or fear, no escape could be easier than one made on a private yacht under another person's name. And, after all, what reason had I to suppose that the man who had dogged us had made a mistake in our identities and killed Martin for me? Such evidence as I had went to show that he had been at pains to make sure which of us really was Martin and which Maitland. That was precisely what he would do if he were sent as the agent of some Irish political organization which Martin had offended. Such political murders were not uncommon just then, and this would put a motive behind a crime which, had I been the intended victim, would have been altogether motiveless.

The relief which this conclusion brought was amazing. But it showed me how much I had been depressed by the feeling that I had been in some measure responsible for Francis Martin's death. Besides that, it was a relief to be convinced that this was no hidden hand stuff, striking at me on account of the Glengyle business. I felt rather ashamed now that I had ever been so melodramatic as to think such a thing possible. Biddulph had described the work as difficult but not dangerous. He would know what he was talking about, for such a mission as he had given me, quite often had to be undertaken by his department. Difficult but not dangerous; I pondered these words. For when I recalled all my planning and scheming, I wondered whether I had not made it much more difficult than it need have been. Of one thing, however, I was quite certain, and that was that I had contrived to bring real danger into it through getting myself mixed up with Martin. For the police were looking not for the real murderer, who probably was now far away, but for me, whose description they had, whose finger prints were all over that room, on chair and match box, light switch, even on the knife handle itself.

And I thought I had been so clever! As I stood at the window looking over a desolation of roof tops, I asked myself whether I could in fairness to Biddulph go on with the job. Biddulph had vouched for my capacity when the Minister was prevented by stress of work from seeing me and judging for himself. His responsibility was all the greater on that account. And it reduced me to despair to see how I had mishandled the business, introducing all sorts of needless complications, and even finding myself in danger of arrest for murder—all inside three days. Did this not prove that I had better get back to my old job of hawking photographic enlargements from one area door to another?

The next half hour I passed sitting on the edge of my bed, kicking my heels in self-disparagement. Above all it was from the way in which I had been used by the Irishman Martin that I found good cause for my loss of self-confidence. As the event had shown, he had even a better reason than myself for wishing to exchange our identities and get safely out of the country. Yet he never let his real eagerness reveal itself, had even offered objections after he had led me on to make the proposal, and I had plumed myself on my astuteness in persuading him to do the one thing in the world he must then have most wanted to do.

Then after I had touched the lowest depths of self-contempt, there came a rebound to my thoughts, and my heels ceased their aimless kicking.

"After all," I murmured to myself, "what has he made of it? He's dead. I'm still alive. His bluff has been called. Mine? Not yet at least, whatever may happen today or tomorrow."

On that, something new came to me, something not at all like the old self-confidence that had been so badly shattered, but something that might serve me to better effect: a grim determination not only not to give up, but not to bring censure on Biddulph by failing in the patriotic work for which he had selected me.

"After all," I repeated to myself once more, "after all, the way now lies clear and open. Tonight, when you join the Glengyle staff at the railway station, you will find them prepared to receive you as one of themselves. The only danger left is the very remote chance you must run on your way to Euston of being stopped by the police for the murder in the Café Sorrento."

So all that day I lay low, never going outside, and, though during the day Papini's had few guests, only descending for meals. About eight, when the place began to fill up and I was taking my last meal, a newsboy stuck his head inquiringly through the door. I nodded to him and he brought me the "final extra special" *Record*. Up till then I had denied myself a sight of the evening papers, knowing that the surest way to rouse suspicion would be to yield to the impulse to buy each edition as it came along. The "final extra special," beyond a recapitulation of the story given in the noon edition, contained little that was new about the case. The London police, it appeared, were in communication with the Sheffield police, and although nothing definite regarding Maitland was known in Sheffield, this went to establish the belief held by London that the deceased had lately been resident in South Africa. It made me smile to see from what that belief was derived—the labels on the old suit case which I had exchanged with Martin. But I found no cause for amusement in the paragraph which followed:

> The police have meantime circularized all hotels and lodging houses with the very precise description of the wanted man which Mr. Val Smith supplied. It will be recalled that Mr. Smith (portrait on left) is the guest at the Café Sorrento (picture on right) who saw the murderer in the act of leaving the house. His description will be of immense value to the officers now watching the various ports and termini.

This was distinctly nasty. I breathed quiet curses on Mr. Val Smith while examining his smiling, self-complacent face. It was bad enough to know that a full description of me lay somewhere in Papini's at that very moment. But that was not the worst. Papini would not suspect me, for he thought I had not been out of his house after he saw me go up to bed about eleven the night before. Besides, Papini's knowledge of English seemed restricted to the phrases essential to his profession, and I guessed that the printed description with its official police jargon would be altogether beyond his comprehension. But what did put me in a funk was to learn, just half an hour before I must leave for Euston, that my full description was in the hands of sharp-eyed men accustomed to make full use of such things.

What was I to do? I toyed with my coffee over the problem; as I suppose many an actual murderer must have sat in a room, safe for the moment, though feeling himself hemmed in on all sides, but faced with a terrible risk he must take inside another hour.

The first solution to suggest itself was that I should give up—abandon this Glengyle job altogether. And though I told myself that this was a temptation rather than a solution, I wasn't sure that it was not a temptation to which I had better yield. For I had no doubt that the evidence against me was quite strong enough to get me convicted of murder. Once in custody, the fact that I was caught masquerading under the dead man's name was bound to come out, and this would bring in the Albemarle and the Elswick Square people, and even the Britannia toughs who had seen us together, and I was sure the smug Mr. Val Smith would promptly identify me as the man he had seen slipping from the house. If caught at the railway station, I had not a dog's chance for my life.

But was my chance improved if I stayed on in town? My resources were at an end. All I had left beyond the money reserved for my escape from Glengyle would only cover Papini's bill. True, I might go back to Peters, to admit failure, and try to get taken on again as a hawker of photographic enlargements. But that meant I must be out and about, open to arrest all the time. Whereas if I could only get away to remote Glengyle on Sir Charles Wridgley's staff, I should be not only beyond suspicion, but above it. Surely it was better to take one big risk at the station than to expose oneself to a life that would be full of risks for months to come if I stayed on.

And then there came the thought of Biddulph's reliance on me, and how galling it would be to give up now when, after so much painstaking labor, the way to success at Glengyle had been made smooth and easy. No! I must go. And having perceived that I must take the one big risk, the question of how to lessen that risk arose at once. Of course I was an actor, doing character parts at that, accustomed to the use of "make-up." And I had not overlooked my talents in the art just now. For the thought had come to me to do up my face and put a nice scar on my cheek, since a scar on the face would be one of the first items set down on the description of a wanted man, if he had one. Only, I had no make-up, and though I might have contrived a passable birth-mark with stain from the beetroot, touched off with charcoal from a burnt match, I did not forget that I would have to face the keen scrutiny not only of the police, but also that of my fellow employees when, as arranged, we met for the first time in the booking-hall at Euston. And it would hardly do to make any radical alterations in my appearance afterwards.

It was nine-fifteen when I paid my bill and sent the boy to get a taxi. When it arrived, Papini himself with exaggerated courtesy, handed up the suit case, while the expectant boy held open the door.

"Where to?" the driver inquired.

"Liverpool Street Station," I promptly replied, glancing around.

Nobody seemed to take any notice, however. There were no loungers on the pavement, and in the streets itself only another taxi which had drawn up behind, waiting to deposit someone when we moved away. As soon, however, as we got to Gray's Inn Road, I got my head out of the window and told my driver to take me to Euston. Unfortunately, he was either a little deaf or more probably in the noise of the traffic my order was misunderstood. Anyhow, he was over the crossing before a louder order from me made him pull up so sharply that a following taxi almost hit us. After an interchange of rapid vitriolic pleasantries between the two drivers, we wheeled round and the other passed on. At first I thought the other taxi was empty, but I almost laughed—even with that ordeal at the station drawing so near—to see the shadowy figure of his fare, who had evidently been thrown to the floor by the cab's sudden twist to avoid us, rise into sight and with frenzied gesticulations obviously start cursing his driver.

Then in looking through the back window I saw the cab make a detour, swing round and come on after us. That at least killed any inclination to smile. I was being followed. It was the taxi which had drawn up behind us at Papini's door. I sat back in the deepening dusk and tried to think. In that cab there was an officer who had come to Papini's to tell me I answered the description of a man wanted by the police, and that he proposed to take me to the police station for further inquiries. At least that was how I thought they put it. What could I do or say?

Before I found an answer we were held up at the top of Gray's Inn Road by the volume of traffic making for the three great termini, and when the block formation compelled the other taxi to draw up almost alongside, I got a glimpse of my pursuer's face before he could draw back. One glimpse only in the light of a street lamp. But it was enough. He was no police officer. He was the man the police ought to have been after—the man who had followed Martin and myself from Dean Street to the Ritz Hotel.

But why did he follow me? He had got Martin. What could he have against me? I felt irritated more than angry. Irritated and exasperated that the police should be after me and be missing such a fool as this man was showing himself to be. But then two questions quickly presented themselves: had he after all, been misled by the name Maitland into killing the wrong man? Or did he believe Martin had me as an ally and confederate in the dark business, whatever it was, for which he had forfeited his life? This of the two was the more likely, for while I could see no reason why anyone should want to murder me, I could understand that if Martin had been guilty of some disloyalty or treason against some secret Irish political society, my association with him would look very suspicious. As the hold-up came to an end and we began to move again, I cursed the fellow! The proper place for crude melodrama like this was the stage, not life.

All the same, if he followed me to Euston and I became the center of a scene at the railway station, this would double my danger. I could not hope to escape detection. Then the wild thought suddenly came that it might be his very purpose to get me detected by the police stationed there. For he must know from the papers that they were after me, not him. But what was I to do? As we passed the clock at King's Cross it showed me it was nine-forty already; and we were drawing near to the station.

In hopeless desperation I knocked on the glass and shouted to the driver to go into St. Pancras. He must have thought me cracked, and at every opportunity kept glancing round uneasily as if to see what new whimsy had taken me. But the oncoming traffic prevented him from getting across and he had to pull up with the nose of the taxi pointing towards the station entrance. Glancing behind, I saw the following taxi was for the moment blanketed by a big trades van which intervened. It was a moment I dared not miss. Seeing my driver's attention concentrated on finding a break in the off-side traffic, I opened the on-side door and, hopping on to the road, joined the stream of pedestrians on the footway.

Fortunately it was now too dark for anyone to see much, and if any did and thought I was bilking the taxi, the wave of my hand as I paused for a moment to see if my action had been observed from the other cab, must have corrected that notion. But nobody seemed to notice anything, least of all I think, the pursuer behind the trades van, who must have been watching the off-side so as not to miss the chance of getting across when my own taxi found its passage free.

After walking quite sedately for about a hundred yards, I crossed the road and then taking to the almost empty side streets, ran like the wind for Euston. I had lost my suit case, of course, but that loss was unavoidable, and I hoped it would console that taximan for the loss of his fare.

On entering the station yard I saw I had just ten minutes to spare, and I fancy I was sufficiently white and breathless for the part I meant to play. The booking hall was crowded, but I had no trouble in finding the Glengyle staff among the various groups slowly edging for the train. The Glengyle party, standing apart, I identified at once, not only from remembering the young man who had ushered me in when I went for my interview with Captain Elliott, but because they were all obviously watching for the arrival of a late comer, interested as it were in his race against time. Except for two men they were all chattering girls. The younger man was quick to remember me.

"Here he is," he cried as I approached. The chattering ceased.

"Name of Martin?" the elder man, whom I judged to be the butler, inquired.

I nodded assent and said what I thought would be considered the right thing.

"That's me. Please to meet you, Mr—"

"You very nearly didn't," he snapped sourly, ignoring my extended hand. "And you wouldn't neither, if it 'adn't been for that Café Sorrento murder."

To say I was taken aback is to say nothing. I stood speechless and terrified. And I must have looked quite funny too, for the young man burst into a hearty guffaw.

"Oh, Mr. Barker, what a thing to say!" one of the girls exclaimed.

Mr. Barker turned to the girls.

"You follow me," he commanded. "We've no more time to lose."

As I stood thus rebuked, the young man held out his hand.

"My name's Darby," he said. "Pleased to meet you, Mr. Martin."

One of the three girls who stayed with us nudged the young man.

"George, he ain't got his luggage yet."

That woke me up, and I explained that my taxi having broken down, I had to leave my luggage and make a dash for the station on foot.

George whistled his dismay.

"I'd sooner 'ave lost the train," he declared.

"You will if we don't get a move on," came acidly from a tall young woman in a red leather coat. "You 'eard what Mr. Barker said."

I took Darby by the arm.

"What did he mean by that?" I asked as he stooped to pick up a heavy bag.

"By what?" he inquired.

"About the murder at the Café Sorrento. What's that got to do with us?"

Darby laughed.

"Oh, he meant it was good luck for you, that murder. What I mean to say is, if it 'adn't been that the police being out there at the barriers holding up the passengers looking for the murderer, we'd been in our places now and you'd got left."

We moved on after Mr. Barker and the others. On the platform I slipped a suit case from the hand of one of the girls, and Darby,

catching her pretty smile of thanks, shook his head in mock seriousness to me.

"Beware of her, Martin, beware of her. Gracie's what the French
call an ardent cocotte, you know."

"George!" Grade protested with a giggle. "I never did know your
like."

But I was too conscious of the police at the barrier just ahead to
share in their light-heartedness. And though I had now made myself
less conspicuous by having possession of some luggage, I dreaded
the moment when watchful eyes would light on the blue suit which
the murdered man had been wearing. For though it was my own
and though there were doubtless others like it in that crowd, yet the
fact that it had been worn by Martin, somehow seemed to give it a
character of its own and made me feel more conspicuous. Then an
idea came. But I had to be quick now, for the barrier was very near.
Getting behind the overburdened Darby, I put my foot on the rain-
coat which he carried on his arm as it was sliding to the ground, and
brought it down. When he turned I had picked it up.

"All right," he said, "you carry it."

The next step was easier. The tall girl in the red coat carried two
cases. Going after her I slipped the heavier out of her hand with a
word of entreaty. And when she surrendered the case I promptly
dropped George's coat.

"Mind if I put it on?" I asked as carelessly as I could.

"All right, perhaps it would be safer," George replied, eyeing his
property.

In that I agreed with him. But I contrived in putting on the coat
to get it on with the collar turned up. Then the supreme moment
came. I could see a couple of policemen, one at each side of the gate,
and between them the two ticket collectors. Some good-natured
chaff seemed to be addressed to the imperturbable constables by a
few of the travelers, most of whom looked like members of household staffs sent in advance, as was the custom, a day or two before
the shooting season opened.

But I knew the real danger was to be expected not from the two
policemen but from the two men not in any uniform who stood one

outside and the other inside on the left of the barrier, men who looked as if they were merely waiting there for the arrival of an expected friend.

"Ain't you got him yet?" a querulous voice demanded.

"He's coming on behind us," another whispered confidentially. "You keep your eyes skinned."

It was poor enough chaff, but it brought some laughter. Suddenly Darby took me under the arm and shoving me before the policeman, to my horror cried: "Here's your man, officer. He's just coming rushing in to catch this train."

The statuesque constable unbent in the faintest possible smile. I was conscious of other eyes fixed on me, and got my hand up to pull my collar down, exposing my face more fully. It was not meant to be an act of bravado. I simply did not know what I was doing. Perhaps I pulled the collar down from a vague feeling of uneasiness in my throat. But this rash show of innocence did not appear to have saved me. Out of the corner of my eye I saw a huge hand rise on its way to my shoulder just as the pompous Mr. Barker, in passing the ticket collector, loudly called attention to our presence as he presented the tickets:

"Sir Charles Wridgley's party—eleven."

Never, surely, did an exhibition of vanity come more opportunely. The lifting hand was withdrawn as if it had been suddenly stung. The ticket collector counted us and, as we were passed in like sheep in single file, no heavy hand descended on my shoulder. But all the same I walked up the platform bathed in a cold sweat, fairly shivering at the narrowness of my escape. For many hours afterwards, indeed, a certain sensitive feeling, like a blister on the top of my left shoulder, persisted.

And it was not till three o'clock on the following afternoon, when we left the train at Keppoch Bridge for the thirty-six-mile drive to Glengyle, that all my apprehension faded away.

CHAPTER X

I was glad to have that breathing space of three days before the family and the house party arrived and my big job began. It gave my shaken nerves time to settle down. And a better place for that process could not be imagined. In all the miles between Keppoch Bridge and Glengyle we had passed but one house on the roadside, and that was the little white inn which stands by the bridge over the Quoish river and seemed to be used only by anglers.

Glengyle Castle stood terraced on the north side of the glen, high above the river, facing the pine-clad slopes on the south side, and backed by similar pine-clad heights behind. It was not an old building as Scottish castles go, having been begun in the late eighteenth century and added to as its owner's wealth increased, just when hill sheep farming began, and later when grouse and deer made the land still more valuable.

The ancient castle of Glengyle, now a ruin, stood on the island in Loch Garre, a mile to the west of its modern successor. Except for Forsyth the gamekeeper's cottage by the loch side and the forester's cottage near the bridge, there were no other houses in the glen. A remote place, indeed, it was, and outside the wooded little valley in which the castle and the loch seemed to nestle, nothing but the bare heather-clad hills for miles and miles, with here and there the blue top of a distant mountain showing above the purple slopes.

On the evening before the big folk were due to arrive, I was sitting out on the low wall that guarded the terrace in front of the castle. It was a pleasant evening and my labors in the gun-room were over for the day. From where I sat I overlooked not only the river which wound its way through the valley towards Loch Garre on my right, but also the pine-clad slopes on the south and a section of the road from Keppoch Bridge at the top of the glen on my left. It was that bit of road that interested me. I was watching for the post-man, and the postman was due about eight. But already I was aware that his times were very highly variable.

Postie left Duich, the fishing village seven miles further on, each morning with the one outward mail of the day, returning at night with the one inward mail. And as he sometimes had to tramp a mile or two over the heather to some outlying cottage, leaving his motor cycle and the red box combination attached, by the roadside, it was the custom, Forsyth told me, to expect Postie only when one saw him.

My anxiety to see him arose from the loss of all my kit when I bilked the taximan outside St. Pancras. As soon as we got to Glen-gyle I had written off to an Edinburgh firm for a new outfit, believing they would be sufficiently impressed with my address to let me have what I needed on credit. As I sat watching, a step sounded on the gravel behind me and turning, I saw Forsyth approaching. Forsyth, a big, loose-limbed man about forty, looked in his rough tweed knick-er suit, his keen eyes and his wind-blown face, exactly what he was. We were already on friendly relations, for the others hardly under-stood his speech and indeed he lived in a different world from theirs. Mr. Barker considered him, too, off-hand and familiar. But that was after Barker, deceived by the gamekeeper's likeness to a sporting gentleman, had addressed him as "Sir" in front of Darby too, who had reported the fact to me with great delight. Forsyth seated him-self beside me and took out his pipe.

"Waiting for Postie," he announced.

I told him that also was why I was there.

"Expecting some physic for two o' my dogs," he explained.

I did not tell him what I was expecting, but I took the tobacco pouch he offered. My pipe had lain long empty in my pocket. Darby smoked cigarettes only and Barker did not approve of pipes.

"How are the birds?" I asked.

"Fine, man. Full grown and strong on the wing."

"You had a fine late spring then," I remarked, lighting up.

"Aye, did we. The tenants will have nothing to complain o' this year."

"You mean the Castle shooting tenants?" I asked.

He turned his regard from the river.

"What na' Castle?"

"Why, this Castle—Glengyle Castle," I said, nodding at the big pile of buildings.

Forsyth withdrew his pipe to smile.

"Och, I see! Well, ye see naebody here abouts calls that a castle. That down there"—he indicated the ruined battlements peering through the trees on the island—"is the Castle. This house is only called the Castle in the advertisements in the English papers, ye ken. It looks better, and the English folk like the notion of living in a castle. Forbye," he added, his eyes going back to the river again, "it assists the laird to ask for a bigger rent than he otherwise could. What do ye make of them?" he asked, pointing to the field between the river and the forest.

Knowing gamekeepers and their ways, I knew he could not be referring to the aesthetic qualities of the scenery or indeed to anything except game.

"Wild duck," I said, after watching the birds till they settled in the field.

"That's good for you," Forsyth nodded. "I doubt none o' your freends in by would be able to tell a wild duck from a turtle dove."

Now it was no great achievement to distinguish between a turtle dove and a wild duck, but Forsyth's approbation flattered me and I turned from watching for Postie to display my knowledge.

"Going there to hunt for snails, I suppose. That looks like rain coming."

But instead of being impressed, the gamekeeper laughed.

"*Oh ho!* So ye've got that kind of lore, have ye? Weel, it does not hold good up here. For here the dew is so heavy that it brings out the snails like rain in the south, ye see." His eyes narrowed. "What's that?" he asked, his gaze now on the road.

Turning back I saw a small dark moving object on the little stretch of road visible at the upper end of the glen.

"Postie," I hazarded.

"No, too slow, unless of course that bicycle o' his has broken down again. We'll have to wait," he added, when the moving object dropped out of sight in a dip of the road. And as the road itself, screened by the trees, did not come into sight again till it reached the bridge down below the castle, we had some time to wait. Forsyth saw my impatience.

"You have to allow Postie some latitude, you know," he said. "It's no' many postmen that have over forty miles to deliver in, not counting the diversions to the shepherds' cottages on the hills."

So for another half hour or so I listened to Forsyth's talk on the countryside in the depths of winter, postmen, poachers, the ways of wild animals, and a variety of other matters more or less connected with life in Glengyle. The talk of men who have the observant eye is seldom tedious, and probably no such being as an unobservant gamekeeper ever existed. Suddenly in the midst of a deer stalking story on Ben Macdui he stopped to listen. Of course his ear was better than mine: I could hear nothing except the rustle of the tumbling river below us. Then he began to laugh.

"Och," he said, "it's the McPhees come back."

"The McPhees?" I asked.

"Aye. Listen! You surely can hear the rumble o' their cart. See, yonder they are."

Following his pointing finger I saw a dilapidated cart, heavily laden, and drawn by a pony many sizes too small for the vehicle, emerge from among the trees on the road below us. Two men and a woman walked by the cart, and on top of the loaded cart two children were perched as if to keep the load in position.

"Tinkers," I said.

"Aye, tinklers. They're making for the quarry along the road where they pitch their tent. You don't see it from here; it's hid by the trees, it's there they got the stones to build this house."

While we watched the little procession I remarked that it must be mighty hard for them to pick up a living in such a lonely countryside.

"Och, they do pretty well," the gamekeeper said. "There may be few customers, but what work there is they get it all, and all the mending of all pots and pans and dishes broken in a year is kept for a year, waiting for them to come round. Forbye that Murdo makes money as a piper and we take him and his father on as beaters too when beaters are scarce."

Then the detonations of a motor cycle engine sounded in a rapidly increasing crescendo, and presently we got off the wall as Postie, surmounting the ascent, wheeled round and came to a halt at the front door. Forsyth got his dog physic and I was able to claim my parcel before Barker emerged. By way of the gun room I reached my quarters in the back wing and there soon satisfied myself that the Edinburgh outfitter had not let me down. To get out of that old blue suit made me feel that at last all possible connection with the sordid Soho crime had been destroyed.

Mr. Barker was enjoying an after supper cigar on the terrace when I strolled out to give my new things an airing. At first sight of me he removed his cigar to stare, but he said nothing. Sauntering to the edge of the terrace and looking down, I saw a thin column of blue wood smoke ascending from the spot Forsyth had pointed out, and judged that the McPhees had taken up their quarters in the quarry. For a little I debated whether I would go down and have a look at them or wander round to the kennels to see Forsyth and his dogs.

But before I had decided a loud skirl of groaning bagpipe tuning came from the drive, and presently the piper, head thrown back and with cheeks like apples in shape as well as in color, marched proudly on to the terrace. He was in full Highland dress, tartan kilt, green doublet with bright metal buttons and glengarry with a cock's feather; all complete but all rather the worse for wear. As he stalked past, Mr. Barker stared, his cigar poised in the air, almost defensively, as if he had seen an apparition. The place reverberated with sound. Some maids at work in the upper floors came to hang out at the different windows, and George Darby skipped down the steps to join me by the wall. Mr. Barker, too taken aback to do anything, just stood and gaped. At the end of the terrace McPhee wheeled grandly and then came back, his eyes a-gleam, kilt a-swing, fingers dancing.

"First home-like touch since I left home," Darby remarked. "Sounds just like a hundred cats in the back garden."

McPhee came to a halt before Mr. Barker, finished his march tune, slung his pipes deftly under his left arm, and clicking his heels, swept his right hand up to his Glengarry in a very smart salute.

Mr. Barker, unaccustomed to being saluted, took it for mockery. His face turned scarlet.

"What is the meaning of this—this—this unwarrantable intrusion—this offensive noise?" he demanded.

The piper seemed greatly astonished.

"Oh, no offence at all," McPhee said with quick earnestness. "Sure, I was only giving your honor the Highland welcome. It is the custom hereaway," he added deprecatingly.

His obvious seriousness and the respect with which he spoke should have mollified Mr. Barker; instead this deference in tone and bearing seemed to increase his sense of self-importance.

"We don't like it," he declared.

McPhee, hesitating, glanced at Darby and myself and then turned to the butler.

"Am I speaking to Sir Charles Wridgley Bart?" he inquired.

George gasped with horror and made a clutch at my arm as if for support. But Mr. Barker was enormously flattered. No mistake could have pleased him more. He melted instantly.

"Well, no," he said. "Not—er—quite, you aren't. But I am—er—Sir Charles' . . . factotum, you understand. Here in advance to arrange everything, you know."

The shadow of disappointment passed from McPhee's face.

"It's hoping to be taken on as your piper I am," he explained.

"As piper?" Barker echoed.

"Yes. To the castle—for the season only, you understand."

"For the season—as piper?"

"Yes, sir. It is the custom to have a piper here. For three years I have been piper here to all the shooting gentry."

Mr. Baker seemed nonplussed by the proud announcement.

"Really," he said, "really I don't know what to say. What did you do exactly?"

"Well, when the gentry are eating their dinners, you see, I walk up and down out here, playing. And early every morning it was my duty to walk round and round the castle to play them awake."

Here at Mr. Barker's look of intense incredulity I stepped forward to explain that to play a house awake was an ancient Highland custom. And, I added, being much taken with young McPhee, that, little as he might think so, to hear the rising and falling of the piping as the piper walked round the house was the pleasantest way of being awakened he could imagine.

"Sort of perambulating alarm clock," Darby murmured.

"Well," Mr. Barker finally said, "I'll mention the matter to Sir Charles when he arrives."

"Thank you, sir," McPhee beamed.

"But I promise nothing, you understand," Barker added, with a gesture of dismissal.

I walked down the drive and over the bridge on to the road, talking with McPhee. He was grateful to me for my intervention, but kindled up much more when he perceived I was interested in pipe music. When we reached the narrow entrance to the quarry I saw the tent pitched before a fire on which a pot was suspended on a tripod. The old man, squatting on a stone, fed the fire while he smoked; the mother was busy skinning a rabbit for their supper.

The lad begged me to come in, and having introduced me, went away to the cart to change out of his finery. When he returned I sat and listened to their talk, liking the sound of the soft West Highland voices, so much more easy to understand than Forsyth's broad lowland dialect. A mighty snug place that quarry would have been, even in rough weather, for cut as it was deep into the hill, its precipitous sides overhung with trees and undergrowth sheltered one from all winds, and it afforded ample room not only for themselves but also provided enough grazing for their old grey pony.

Though I had entered more from curiosity than any real kindliness, the time came when I was to be glad I had made friends for myself in that quarry. Like most of the race who could neither read nor write, the elder McPhee had a mind filled with stories and was a great hand at telling them. So till darkness fell, and there was nothing else to be heard on that still night but the occasional hooting of an owl and the regular sound of the pony cropping the grass, we listened to Donald McPhee talking of his travels and adventures, his animated, weather-beaten face on which the firelight danced, strikingly vivid against the blackness of the night beyond him.

It sticks in my memory, that night, because it was so unlike the nights that now lay ahead.

CHAPTER XI

I was busy in the gun room alone, sorting out the cartload of ammunition which had come in earlier in the afternoon, when I heard our party arrive. I stood up to listen to all the bustle and banging of doors that followed, suddenly aware that at any moment now I might be face to face with the chance of getting my hands on that black japanned box with the two red and white stripes. How often I had seen it in my imagination. And how far away it seemed that afternoon when I had to lie low in Papini's! And now it must be somewhere among the baggage out there on the terrace. Would George come in presently to call for my help with the luggage? But even if he did and I got my hands on it, I could not walk off with it. To get away with it I needed an interval of hours before the loss could be discovered. And in any event the small black box would certainly be out of sight in some larger piece of luggage.

No, to cover the miles and reach Keppoch Bridge before the papers were missed, I would need a whole night's freedom at least. So I bent down to my work again and presently the door opened and Captain Elliott strolled in.

"Ah—er—Martin, isn't it?" he greeted me with a nod, his sharp eyes at once going to the guns in their racks, the cartridges in their various boxes and the game books on the table.

"Quite comfortable, I hope. Settling down and all that, eh?" he went on, picking up a rifle and throwing open the breach.

"Yes, sir, quite comfortable, thank you," I responded, watching him peer down into the breach and barrel.

"I rather like that way of numbering the shot," he said, coming up behind me.

"Yes, sir. That was how Colonel Ridgway liked it done," I said.

"Not a bad idea, Martin. Well, you'd better go now and get my things unpacked. You'll find them in my room."

"And the other gentlemen, sir?"

He stared for a moment.

"Oh, I see. Well, Count Fernandez doesn't come till tomorrow, and Mr. Rhand has brought his own man with him after all. Yes, everything seems fairly straight here, so I'll go and have a look at the kennels."

It was rather a damper to hear that Rhand had brought his own man. It meant that I certainly would not have the free run of Rhand's quarters I had counted on having. And Biddulph had said it was almost beyond doubt that the wanted papers would be in Rhand's keeping. However as I mounted the stairs my thought was that this difficulty might be overcome if I could get on good terms with Rhand's man. If we became such friends that I could, when free, drop in on him at odd moments for a chat, it would not seem odd if I were found in his master's rooms even when nobody happened to be there. And, as I had already discovered, the rooms allotted to my master and his were in the same corridor, separated only by a bathroom. I was passing the room when the door was flung open and a man whom I instantly recognized as Rhand appeared.

"Bantok!" he cried, looking up and down the corridor. "Bantok!"

He was not as small as I had judged him to be from his photograph. Perhaps Jim Peters' suggestion of his likeness to a monkey had unconsciously influenced my judgment on his size.

"Bantok," he shouted again. "Where the devil have you got to?"

"Coming, ba'as," another voice boomed out. From the stairs a huge negro was advancing, carrying a heavy valise with as much apparent ease as a lady carries a dainty vanity bag. I had to step aside to let him pass and avoid a knock from the swinging valise. He passed with neither word nor glance.

After that I went about my work in the Captain's room more or less mechanically. I was able now to understand why Elliott had said that Rhand had *after all* brought his own man. There would be objections to Bantok. Probably from Lady Wridgley, who would dread trouble from the other servants. But these objections had apparently been over-ruled. By Rhand? That told me something more about Rhand. Well, anyway, Bantok was not one with whom I could be on terms of friendly intimacy. That way was closed. I must think again.

I had finished in Elliott's room, being in the act of kneeling to put away some odds and ends in a drawer when a slight sound like a whisper behind, caught my ear. The door of the wardrobe partly hid me, but when I got to my feet I saw someone was there—a woman, and a very pretty one too, with dark red hair and nice eyes, who stared at me blankly, as if I had been a burglar or a ghost.

"O-h," she stammered, "I—I—thought—"

But by then I had assumed the attitude and the wooden face of the well-trained flunkey which explained me to her.

"Captain Elliott is round at the kennels, madam."

"Oh," she said, "I thought this was Mr. Rhand's room."

With a nod and a gracious little smile she opened the door which I noticed she had closed behind her on entering, and was gone, leaving me—well—wondering. And my wonder did not quite cease when later on I discovered she was Mrs. Rhand. For though she might easily have made a mistake about the room on the first evening of their arrival, I did not see why she should have slipped into it so softly, or call to her husband in a whisper. That little incident, however, was banished from my mind by another of quite a different character which happened later on that evening.

As soon as the dinner bell sounded I went to the Captain's room to tidy up. Already I had discovered that it is one thing to play the part of a stage valet and quite another to seem so efficient in actual life. And the lion hunter scattered his things about the room much as the lion itself might have done had it got into the room.

Just as I reached the top of the stairs I heard a smothered feminine shriek which appeared to come from somewhere down the corridor which opened out of the wing opposite to that for which I was making. Turning, I saw the negro Bantok standing in front of one of the maids. He was playfully refusing to let her pass, barring the entire width of the corridor with his outstretched arms. Seeing me coming, she made a dive to get under one of his arms, but he caught her, swung her up into the air, holding her high above his own back-bent head. She seemed too terrified even to cry out, and Bantok laughed softly up at her.

I knew that I couldn't treat my black brother exactly as I wanted to treat him, since Gracie would undoubtedly have suffered most in the tumble. But before I reached him he lowered the helpless girl, till her face was at the level of his own, and then slowly drawing her towards him, so that she could see his intention, planted a kiss on her mouth. The grinning devil had just released her when I reached him. He had not heard me and I got him in a relaxed attitude, unexpectedly, with all the impetus gathered in that rush and final jump which planted my bent knees in the small of his back. He went down with a thud that seemed to shake the flooring. I pitched right over him myself, of course. But for that I was prepared, and got quickly to my feet again.

Bantok was up as quick. In a second he had rounded on me, his face almost ashen with rage or pain, his flabby lips so indrawn that his teeth flashed white like the teeth of a snarling dog. There was murder in his eyes as he stepped towards me. But when I drew back and slipped a hand to my hip as if I had a weapon there, he hesitated. His hand went round to his waist and I called myself a fool, thinking my last hour had come. A fleeting glance showed me the girl leaning against the wall, rubbing her mouth with her apron. The apron was very white and so starchy that in that quiet moment I heard it crackle in her hands. But Bantok drew no weapon. As we faced each other I saw the fire go from his eyes.

Whether it was fear of Rhand and the consequences, or if something else held him back I do not know, but Bantok was cowed—for the moment at least. He turned, and simply slunk away down the corridor. As I watched him go with surprise and relief I noticed he still kept his hand to his back. It pleased me well to see I had hurt him. I watched till he passed out of sight.

"Nasty brute, ain't he?" said Gracie.

It was the first word spoken since I had heard her cry.

"I'll tell Mr. Barker about this," she declared.

When I said nothing she looked up at me over her dainty uplifted apron.

"Don't suppose any nice man will ever want to kiss me again," she said.

Her eyes were very bright and her lips, from the scrubbing with the well-starched apron, were very red.

"He won't know anything about it, unless you tell," I said.

Gracie hesitated, and looked into her apron.

"Yes, but you know he done it," she murmured.

"Well, I won't tell," I assured her.

Gracie abruptly dropped her apron and with a toss of her head went off to finish her interrupted duties. So did I, wondering whether my defense of Miss Turton had been worth the bad blood it had created between Bantok and myself.

My last duty that night was to act as billiard marker for any of the guests who might want a game. The billiard room must have been one of the latest additions, a large room that looked out on the drive up to the main door. It had obviously been designed to improve the general aspect of the house as one approached it, for its four windows were high and deeply mullioned, like the windows of a church. Like the hall its walls were now adorned with the usual trophies of the chase: a stag's head with a couple of ancient muskets crossed beneath, adorning the space above the huge fireplace. The fireplace itself was flanked by two of the largest highbacked settees I have ever seen. As I entered George was engaged in placing his coffee equipage on the table that stood between the settees. He looked up to stare at me.

"Well, George, how do I look?"

George had been kind to me in the matter of sharing his wardrobe with me when my luggage got lost. In consequence George now regarded my new dress suit very critically, for quite a time, from head to toe. Then he gave me a shock.

"You ain't ever been mistaken for a gentleman, 'ave you?"

I knew this was not chaff for he was always mighty serious in whatever touched his calling.

"No, George. I don't think I've ever been mistaken for one."

"Well, you take care. I'm not sure but you might be. That suit will pass, but only just. You don't look quite a gentleman."

I was slow to take his meaning and asked him what he meant. The question seemed to surprise him.

"Well," he said, "you don't want to be took for a guest, do you? I once was by an old lady, and I ain't forgot the rowing I 'ad for it. A really first-class man don't need to wear a striped waistcoat nor a bit of color down his trousers to convey the fact that he ain't one of the guests, do 'e?"

"No, of course not," I agreed.

George went to touch up the fire which had been lit for the sake of the billiard table.

"Funny you not knowing a thing like that," he remarked. He turned quickly. "You didn't 'ave to wear bright buttons or colored trousers in your last place, did you?"

"Certainly not," I asserted.

"There you are," he flourished the poker at me. "It's only in third-rate 'ouses where they 'ave only third-rate men-servants that such a warning as colored breeches is necessary."

A clatter of voices sounded as the dining-room door opened and George stopped, quite obviously concerned about me, as he passed, to whisper earnestly: "Martin, you take care now. This ain't Ireland, you know. You've got to convey without words that you're not a gentleman. You got to be a lot stiffer in your movements, you know. You've got to suggest that you've not got too many *joints*, as it were."

When Rhand and Elliott strolled in I had the green-shaded lamps lit and was at my place by the marking board at the far end of the room, trying to look as stiff as a wooden god. The anxious George's admonition had not been lost on me. And from the free way they presently began to talk, I must have suggested to their minds that it was only a robot who stood there in the shadows, a robot who was capable of lifting a mechanical arm to the old-fashioned marking board and registering the score each player made. I divined, however, a certain excitement between the two men, and though the slight flush on their faces might have been due to the port, a certain vibrant note in their voices suggested something else. And from the way they played they seemed to have escaped from the others to be free to talk. I guessed that this was their first chance of being alone since leaving town. It was Elliott who began while chalking his cue.

"Somebody's been selling heavily," he said.

"Because somebody else had been too greedily buying," Rhand replied with a snap, running his eye along the cue he had selected.

Elliott played a miss in baulk. Rhand replied with a shot at the top cushion, his ball coming back off the side to touch red and slip on with a click at Elliott's ball as it passed.

"Got you!" Rhand grinned.

Elliott said nothing as the other moved round the table. Rhand had long fingers, with short black hairs between the knuckles.

"And it was to *get* me you are selling out?" Elliott said.

Rhand did not reply till he had made the cannon, a deft shot, his own ball seeming just to breathe a caress on the other two in passing to an improved position.

"Yes," he said, straightening himself.

"What for?"

Rhand's next shot took him back to where Elliott was standing. He had not forgotten my presence. But a swift glance at my impassive face probably reassured him.

"To teach you a lesson you damn well needed," he muttered quietly. "You broke our agreement in buying as you have. Where did you get the money? You must have sold your shirt to do it."

Elliott, with his back to me, said something I could not catch. Rhand, about to make his next shot, stopped and turned.

"You are insane," he said quietly, leaning against the table. "Even now you don't appear to realize your blunder. Your heavy buying of the shares had two evil results. First, it forced up the price and set outsiders, who knew nothing, buying too, which forced up the price still more. The enhanced value of our shares will make a big difference to the terms the Portuguese will now demand, as you'll find out from Fernandez tomorrow. But bad as that is, the worst, far the worst is that all this has put Chatsworth on the scent—"

"What?" the other cried. "Chatsworth! You mean—"

"Softly. We needn't lose our heads about it, bad as it is. After all, we know how the Office usually goes to work, and can be on our

guard. In fact I was, when I fixed on Glengyle for our negotiations,"
he added complacently.

"Rhand, I've been a fool."

"You have—the greedy kind of fool who cannot wait. It's an expensive form of folly too. You forced me to sell a huge block to reduce the value and so avert official suspicion. But for that, as for other things, you will have to compensate me later."

Then Rhand turned, and missing an easy shot at the red, revealed the fact that he was not quite as calm as he looked. Neither was I, though I did just remember to put the miss to Elliott's credit. Not that Elliott would have noticed the omission. Indeed, he seemed to have forgotten he was playing. Rhand prodded him with his cue. The quiet touch brought him to life.

"Chatsworth!" he whispered. "If he's got wind of it—"

"Oh, for Heaven's sake keep your head," Rhand cut in impatiently. "Nobody can get in on us here. If any of his infernal secret service spies turned up in a place like this we'd spot him at once. Come and have a drink."

"That's true, we would—at once," Elliott said, following him towards the table by the fireplace. I don't think they touched the coffee; but I heard the tinkle of the liqueur glasses while they talked on the hearthrug. But nothing of their talk reached me, and it is possible that Rhand had drawn Elliott away to avoid being overheard. Had I been the man Rhand supposed me to be, this precaution would not have been too late. But I did wish I could have heard what passed between them on the hearthrug; for, after all, what I had heard told me nothing more than I already knew from Biddulph. On one point, however, on which Biddulph himself had not been certain, I was able to make a safe deduction: the papers must be in Rhand's possession. He would never have entrusted them to his friend Elliott. But I wanted to learn much more than that.

However, when they returned to resume their game it at once appeared that the chance would be denied me.

"You needn't wait, Martin," Elliott said in an offhand way. "We're only knocking the balls about."

"Very good, sir," I said, laying down the cue-rest.

"Table's a bit slow, isn't it?" he remarked.

"Yes, sir. Cushion's still a little hard in spite of all the ironing we gave it, sir," I said, trying to linger. I lingered just long enough to let me see they were waiting for me to go. Then the door opened and Lady Wridgley and Mrs. Rhand entered.

"Ah, here you are," Mrs. Rhand exclaimed. "We thought we'd look you up as Sir Charles has deserted us."

"Gone off to bed. He's rather tired," Lady Wridgley explained as they moved over to the fireplace.

The Captain promptly challenged Mrs. Rhand to a hundred up, on which Rhand himself promptly called me back to my post, laughingly explaining to them that he wanted no wrangling about the scores while Lady Wridgley was talking to him.

Mrs. Rhand played quite a good game. I daresay she had played quite a lot, for she must have known it was a game that permitted her to show herself in various attitudes which she knew how to make very graceful. The line of her body when she stretched forward over the table in her backless dress of black velvet, two long slender arms held widely apart when making a stroke that needed the cue-rest, the poise of her head under the bright light when she stooped to consider an awkward shot, were all exhibitions of studied grace rather than of billiards. Not that she played badly. In fact, I judged that Elliott would have been better pleased had she played badly enough to give him more chances of moving close to her, and taking her hand to bend and to adjust her arm to the right angle for some shot she had just muffed. I am bound to admit she might have manufactured more of these chances had she liked. But whether she refrained from fear of being seen by her husband, or through dislike of Elliott's handling, I could not at first decide.

Of Rhand and Lady Wridgley I could see little because of the six low-hung, green-shaded lamps which intervened, but Rhand's white shirt front I could discern in the distance, and from it I knew he was more or less facing us all the time. Towards the end of the game, however, I had proof of Rhand's assertion that Elliott was one of those greedy fools who cannot wait. The two players were at my end of the table, with all the light between themselves and the others. Elliott either lost his head or thought it safe.

"Christine," he whispered in her ear, slipping an arm around her as she stood back to make way for him to play. I took it as a tribute to me that he had forgotten my presence behind them. But the woman had not forgotten me.

"*Prenez garde, mon cher,*" she murmured, deftly releasing herself. No, she had not overlooked my presence, that the French told me; but she had overlooked the fact that a man acting as billiard marker might know some French. In a queer way I felt sorry for Rhand. Of course when she had slipped into the room in the afternoon it was not true that she had mistaken the room. Both men were blackguards, of course, but of the two Elliott was the worse. And somehow that made me sorriest of all for the woman.

A few minutes later the game ended and I got my release. Closing the door behind me I ran up the stairs and then moved quietly along the corridor towards Rhand's bedroom. I reckoned nobody would leave the billiard room for the next ten minutes at least. They would have a drink on the hearth-rug, and probably talk of things upon which they could not very well gossip while I was there. They might, in fact, be there for another hour. But I could not count on more than ten minutes. Still, I might not need more to find out what I wanted to know about that room.

The real danger was Bantok. Had he been an English servant I could have counted on his being down in the staff room. But I doubted whether Bantok had been able to fit himself in with the other servants. He would probably be in his room at the top of the house. I must make sure. Outside the bedroom I listened for a full minute. Inside there was not a sound. But the very stillness and silence somehow so affected me that I shirked entering till I had taken some precaution against being caught unawares inside that room.

The service staircase from the upper floors opened into the corridor at the far end. That way Bantok must descend if he came at all. The chances were he would not, at least until summoned, since none could tell at what time it would please Rhand to leave the billiard room. But I must be safe against surprise. Half suspecting I was a fool to begin my hunt until I learned more of the habits of those concerned, I moved hastily along to the foot of the service staircase, and stretching up to the lamp which there served both the corridor and the staircase, I removed the bulb with the result that the staircase was reduced to darkness. Then, feeling about in the housemaid's cupboard for something noisy to place near the stair foot, I found a small tin bucket. This I placed on the edge of the third step so that it would topple into the corridor at the slightest touch. Had I been sure that the only person likely to descend would be Bantok, I would have set it much higher, but I did not wish to break anyone else's neck.

Rhand's room was not hard to ransack. It was so neat and orderly, with everything already just where it ought to be, all the traveling cases evidently already stowed away in the box room. Anyhow, there was no sign of a black japanned case with red and white stripes. Not that I supposed that to have been stored away in the box-room. I tried the drawers. Every one in the wardrobe was open, but in the dressing table I found one locked. That satisfied me for the moment. The little black case must be there, if anywhere. I could make a collection of keys from other rooms and probably find one to fit. If not, the lock must be forced when the right moment came. But that could not be till I knew for a certainty that the little black box could be nowhere else.

After a glance round to make sure I had disturbed nothing that would suggest a visitor had been in the room, I went back to the staircase, replaced the lamp, and was in the act of putting the bucket back in the housemaid's cupboard just as Bantok himself came down the stairs. In fact, he would have passed me unheard if I hadn't, as if feeling his presence, chanced to look round. He had a habit of going about the house barefoot—another of his South African habits which was not liked by the other members of the staff. If he saw me he gave no evidence of it. I stood still till he passed like a moving shadow along the corridor and into his master's room.

So far so good. It took but a minute to get back to the hall and mount the service way to my own room. In passing through the hall, however, I picked from the table a newspaper which I carried up with me. It was the first paper I had seen for several days, since Postie only carried newspapers when specially ordered from the old woman who kept the shop in Keppoch Bridge, and who herself only ordered them when ordered by a customer.

When I saw that the paper I had snatched up was the Glasgow *Bulletin* I thought it unlikely that a Scottish paper would make much

of a feature with a Soho murder nearly a week old. But on turning
its pages I discovered my mistake. There were, it appeared, points of
unusual interest in this Soho murder. This is what I read:

HUNT FOR THE SOHO MURDERER
Victim Not Yet Identified

The verdict of "willful murder by some person or persons unknown" returned at the inquest on the victim of the Café Sorrento murder, has been followed
by days and nights of intensified activity at Scotland
Yard. Unfortunately, however, up till now the criminal still remains at large. The feature which the authorities admit to be the most baffling is one which
relates to the identity of the victim. It may now be
revealed that the police got into touch with several
persons, two in particular, who knew an A. Maitland,
who disappeared a day before the crime was commit-
ted, one being a photographer for whom the man in
question had worked, and the other the occupier of
the house in which he lodged. Both, however, not only
failed to identify the body but positively affirmed that
it bore no resemblance to the man known to them.
And neither could see any resemblance between the
signature in Mr. Donati's register and that of the man
known to them, a conclusion with which the police
experts were forced to concur when the photographer produced a specimen of the other's signature for
comparison.

Of the several other peculiar features this case
presents, the only one we are permitted to divulge is
the strange fact that despite the widespread publicity
given to it in the press, no one has come forward to report anyone of the name of Maitland as even missing.
This is the more peculiar as, the victim's underwear
being marked with the initial "M," the police have no
reason to believe him to have given an assumed name
when he booked his room in Luigi Donati's café.

So I had been right about the Albemarle Agency. The manageress must have assumed that the Maitland murdered in the Soho Café could not be the Maitland who had gone to Canada in Lord Billinghurst's yacht. Her natural repugnance against getting her high-class agency mixed up with such a sordid affair would bias her in favor of that belief. And by the time she got, as she no doubt would, a letter of complaint from his lordship when the yacht reached the other side—well, it would be too late then for her or anyone else to view the body in the mortuary.

My next emotion was that of gratitude to Jim Peters, coupled with an increased respect for his mental perspicacity. I could see what had happened as clearly as if I had been there. Jim, in his shirt-sleeves, reading the report of the murder at the very time I was in hiding up in that back bedroom of Papini's two streets away. He thinks my business has miscarried. But he is cautious. He will give nothing away till he has verified the fact by a sight of my body. Then, when he is satisfied I have not been done in, he keeps his mouth shut. Mr. Lucius, of course, told all he knew, which could amount to nothing of any value to the police. But Jim could so easily have put them on the track!

I laid aside the paper fairly satisfied with the way things were going. Even the knowledge that Rhand now knew that Mr. Wynne Chatsworth's suspicions had been aroused, did not greatly trouble me. For Rhand's own suspicions would now be concentrated on any strangers who might turn up presently in the glen. He did not dream that the Secret Service agent was already not only in the glen but in the house before he himself arrived.

CHAPTER XII

All next morning I was possessed by the feeling of being on the edge of big events. A sort of zero hour it felt like. For I learned that the Portuguese Count was expected that afternoon, and I knew his appearance on the scene would bring the business to a head just before I was ready. But I discerned the same feeling of tension pervading the house—a sort of restlessness that kept them all moving about as if they could not settle down. My own disquiet was entirely due to the news that the Portuguese man was expected that afternoon. Biddulph had assured me that they would find a means of detaining him in London so that I might have more time in which to do my work. Had they been outwitted? It looked like it. Still, I thought I now knew where to lay my hands on the papers when the chance came. And if I failed to get away with the draft agreement, after all, they wanted the incriminating departmental letters most. Probably because these papers would be enough to get the agreement annulled or dropped even after it had been signed.

While I was ironing the billiard table I observed Rhand and Elliott fretfully moving about on the terrace. Then Sir Charles wandered in to stand awhile gazing moodily out of the window. I doubt if he was even aware of my presence. Up till then I had hardly seen him, but of course his features, the long nose and pointed moustache especially, had been made quite familiar by press cartoonists. He seemed restless enough too, now nervously clasping and unclasping the hands he held behind his back, and staring out of the window exactly like a man caged in an uncongenial house on a rainy day.

After lunch, while I was busy in the gun room, Darby put his head inside the door to tell me I was to get a couple of rods ready as some of the party wanted to fish.

"Fish for what?" I asked in disgust.

"They didn't say, but it wouldn't surprise me if it's for fish," he replied with affected seriousness.

"There's not enough water in the river," I said. "It's waste of time, they'll catch nothing."

George sniffed.

"Nobody I've watched ever does; but it don't seem to keep them from trying. Anyway, it's the loch, not the river you've to go to."

As I got the tackle together I had a bet with myself that I knew the two who were going out on the loch. But on going round to the front with the rods I found myself mistaken, at least about one of the couple. Mrs. Rhand was there, but the other was not Elliott but Sir Charles.

Following behind them with the rods, I was once more struck by his aspect of moodiness. Mrs. Rhand, looking very attractive in her tweeds, was most vivacious, and seemed to be doing all she could to brighten things for him. But I could see he had very little to say in reply to her chatter, and was blind to all coquettish charms. As they passed the quarry, the sight of the McPhees' encampment within brought forth a little cry of delight from her, and as if involuntarily she took his arm to stop him. I drew up behind.

"I haven't seen anything like that since I left the veldt," she was saying. "How thrilling. What do they do—hunt?"

"Poach," said Sir Charles. "Poach and beg."

He moved on, taking Mrs. Rhand with him, as her hand was still holding his arm. As I passed I had a glimpse of both the McPhees busy with soldering irons over the fire.

But when I got the boat out of the boat-house and they both took their places, Sir Charles did brighten up a little. Apparently the lady had begged him to teach her how to fish for trout, and we had not gone far before he began to react to that itch for playing the schoolmaster to others from which some men and all politicians appear to suffer. And well did the pretty Mrs. Rhand appear to understand the force of the subtle flattery implicit in her attitude towards him. She

was so appealing in her ignorance, so simple, so attractively awkward in her attempts to make a cast.

Laughing at herself, she got him to laugh too; and when he laid
his line on the water as lightly as if it had been a spider's thread,
her little cry of admiration made him swell with self-satisfaction. I
took it as a tribute to the woodenness of my attitude that neither of
them seemed to be aware of my existence. Indeed, for all the notice
they took of me I might have been no more than a mechanical figure
constructed for working boats.

But we caught no fish. I took the most likely reaches, hovering
about where any burn entered the loch to give them a chance with
fish which might be feeding there. Not a rise did we get. They got
tired of it after a couple of hours, and Sir Charles told me to turn
round and make for home. While he was reeling in his line the lady's
eyes wandered to the island and she began to question him about
the ruined castle standing on it. This was exactly the sort of thing
that interested him, and he told her it had been burned down by the
Duke of Cumberland after the Rebellion of 1745. Although I doubted
if Mrs. Rhand had ever before heard of that event, she declared she
must see the ruins, and so at a signal from Wridgley I ran the nose
of the boat ashore and they stepped out. A couple of heron flapped
clumsily away as Sir Charles and Mrs. Rhand disappeared among
the trees.

Resting on my oars I ceased for the time to puzzle my head over
what Mrs. Rhand's game with Sir Charles could be, and lighting the
long-desired cigarette, had a look at the castle. Even on that sunny
afternoon its crumbled grey masonry had a grim and almost sinister
appearance. Little more than the square tower rising above the trees
was visible, but not much more than that had been left undestroyed.
Standing on that small island, about a hundred yards from the nearest side of the loch, that castle must have been a pretty secure refuge
in the days of the old clan feuds. Now the island was tenanted only
by the herons, the shy birds who would fully appreciate its security.

Suddenly a voice hailed me, and looking about I saw Sir Charles
standing clear of the bushes, beckoning to me. Hastily dropping my
surreptitious cigarette into the water, I jumped ashore and hurried
over.

"Oh—er—Martin," he said, "I want your help to lift a heavy stone."

Inside the four bare walls abutting the tower, Mrs. Rhand stood waiting. At her feet I saw what I judged to be the stone we had to raise. It looked like the cover to a well and it took a lot of lifting. When we got it up Sir Charles stood back, wiping his hands with his handkerchief.

"Yes," he remarked, "as I explained, this was the dining hall, but perhaps you cannot guess what that was."

"A well, isn't it?" the lady suggested.

"No; with so much fresh water all around they hardly needed a well in their dining hall."

In the hasty glance I had taken into the interior I saw a small square chamber about twelve feet deep, the interstices of its roughly hewn walls filled with fungoid growths. Sir Charles, unbending under the influence of his show-man mood, turned to me.

"And what do you make of it, Martin?" he inquired.

"The wine cellar, sir," I suggested.

"Oh, of course," Mrs. Rhand laughed. "How stupid of me not to see that."

But Wridgley shook his head.

"No, it was for something that gave them more pleasure than wine." Mrs. Rhand, in the act of bending forward to peer into the interior, was startled and turned to stare at him.

"Prisoners!" he explained. "Prisoners beyond a doubt. There's a place exactly like this in Donvega Castle in Skye. They liked to feel their enemies under their feet, you know, and to let them have a smell, but only a smell, of the banquets."

She clutched his arm.

"Come away," she cried. "I don't like this. It reminds me of how my poor father once nearly starved to death in Africa. I can't bear to look at it."

"But—in Africa? When was that?" Wridgley asked, staring.

"Oh, it wasn't quite the same. It happened when he was out prospecting. He fell into one of those deep pits the natives dig as a trap for lions. He broke a leg when he fell in and his servant had to carry him on his back for nearly a hundred miles before he could get help."

They moved out of hearing towards the other side of the island. After taking a rather prolonged look into this horrible annex to a clan dining-room, I replaced the stone, suddenly revolted by the thought of the tortured wretches who had once starved down in that gloom. The world must have been just as fair to look on in those brutal days as it was on that afternoon. Through a jagged gap in the masonry I saw the line of blue hills, the loch shimmering in the heat and the long belt of cool-looking dark green pines stretching up from the water's edge.

After having a look at the tower I moved away, thinking it time to see that the others did not return to the boat ahead of me. I soon saw them at a distance, seated by the water in what seemed to be earnest talk. At least the lady seemed to have a good deal to say, and the cigarette she held between her fingers appeared to be used more to wave in the air to emphasize her arguments than to smoke. I turned and went back to the boat where I filled in time by taking down the rods and replacing the tackle. We had caught no fish. At least no fish of the sort for which these lines were made, I thought. But I now felt pretty sure that it was to catch something much bigger than trout that Mrs. Rhand had come out that afternoon. And though I knew she was playing him then at the end of her line, I wondered not only whether she would land him but also what she wanted him for. For something in connection with the Katangana plot perhaps, but what it could be was beyond my guessing. The last glimpse I had taken at them did not seem to promise success anyway. He had been sitting with hunched-up shoulders and down-bent head, warding off, as it were, the pretty lady's coaxing blandishments much as a man crouches in a storm of rain or hail from which there is no immediate escape.

But half an hour or so later I saw them arm in arm coming down the bank on which the castle stood. Had she landed her big fish or not? As they took their places in the boat I was not sure. She spoke gaily and even gave me a smile; but then women are born actresses, and with them you can never tell. And he did seem rather like a man who had escaped; his manner not exactly sprightly, but uplifted and relieved. At any rate he condescended to take note of my existence. Both of them were sitting in the stern facing me as I began to pull.

"Well, Martin," he said, with heavy jocularity, "so we go home clean—isn't that the correct term on these occasions?"

"Yes, sir."

Mrs. Rhand sat up suddenly as if she had been shot. "*Clean?*" she repeated, her eyes passing swiftly from his face to mine.

He laid his hand lightly on her arm with a queer little laugh.

"Oh," he said, "it's only the angler's term for a complete failure—when he lands no fish, you understand."

Whether he meant more by this than appeared on the surface I could not really tell; but she seemed to think he did, for after a moment she laughed oddly.

"Oh, I see. But it's a funny way of putting it, surely—to catch nothing and then call yourself clean, I mean. Looks like—like laying some flattery to your disappointed soul."

"Perhaps, dear lady, perhaps," he lightly agreed. "Many of these sporting terms do seem odd to non-sporting people."

Was this another thrust? I kept a wooden face and rowed on, waiting for more. But Mrs. Rhand appeared to be too intent on staring at the shoe on her extended foot to think of anything else. It was a very nice, strong, square-toed brogue shoe, of brown leather that looked as if it ought to be clumsy and yet was nothing of the kind, though it did make her ankle look even more delicately neat than it actually was. Suddenly she looked up with a pretended pout.

"I don't believe there are any fish to catch," she declared.

Up went his eyebrows.

"No fish to catch!"

"No," she asserted. "You were fooling me all the time, I think."

He waved his hand at me.

"Ask Martin there. He knows."

This somehow got me in the wind. I very nearly stopped working the oars. Of course he couldn't possibly know—well—for what I had come to fish. All the same it gave me rather a knock to see his words might imply that he did know. On looking up I found his eyes fixed on me.

"Well, Martin, what have you to say about it?" he inquired.

"Well, madam, there's plenty of fish about. But there's too much light and it's too hot for them just now. They lie out of sight all day, madam, and will only take in the dark. Night fishing is the only thing for it at this season of the year really."

Then I shivered on perceiving my words were as ambiguous and double edged as Wridgley's had been. The next moment I was glad they were, for I saw that he had no suspicion of me whatever. His eyes were on the woman, not me. And she clapped her hands in delight.

"Night fishing," she cried. "What fun!" After a moment she turned to me. "Do you think we should be more successful if we came out at night, Martin?"

"Not a doubt of it, madam. This heat makes the big fish dull and sluggish. At this season they only feed at night."

At that she looked straight at Sir Charles and asked him if he knew this. When he admitted that he did she demanded to be told why he had led her on such a wild goose chase. By this time I was quite sure of two things: that there was a deliberate and not an accidentally veiled meaning in their words they used to each other, and that neither of them suspected me of being able to detect the fact. Wridgley, in his own element at this sort of verbal fencing, laughingly inquired if it wasn't a big fish rather than a goose she had hoped to catch that afternoon, and then reminded her that as a novice she must first learn in daylight how to throw her line "even though for night fishing," he added, "you need *quite* a different kind of tackle."

At that thrust the lady bit her pretty lip, her eyes again thoughtfully on her shoes. For a brief space the silence was filled by the creaking of the oars in the rowlocks.

"What sort of tackle?" she asked at length.

"Ask Martin: he's an expert on fishing by night," came the prompt reply.

It was a reply that would certainly have reawakened my uneasy feeling that he was playing with me as well as Mrs. Rhand had I not recalled the terms in which Wentworth had testified to my sporting qualifications in the testimonial he had given me. So when the lady raised her eyes to mine I was ready with my answer.

"At night, madam, you need to use rather a longer hook and it has to be rather differently dressed."

"Dressed?" she echoed.

"Another of these odd sporting terms," Wridgley explained. "He means the tinsel and fluff with which your hook is hidden."

It has been said of Sir Charles Wridgley that he was a clever man who failed because he was not clever enough to know when to stop. I agreed with that judgment of the man when I read it afterwards, for it brought back to my mind this baiting of Mrs. Rhand. No doubt she had tried to fool him on the island and he had led her on. Now in my presence he was in his own way fooling her. I felt sorry for her. That last thrust of his as we reached the boat-house, did it. Whatever she had been trying to get him to do, or not to do, he had already made it plain enough that he saw what her game was. I did not again look at her till they stepped ashore. Her eyes were glittering, but not with any tears, and on her otherwise white face two spots of hectic red stood out like burns. She looked almost ugly. After that I began to feel rather sorry for Sir Charles Wridgley.

On getting back to the house I heard a bit of news that gave me something else to think about. While putting away the rods and tackle George strolled in to inquire about the fish we hadn't caught. Then in reply to some clumsy banter from me in which I advised him to practice better manners in view of the approaching visit of a Portuguese nobleman, he electrified me by saying that the count's visit had been put off.

"Put off?" I cried. "When? How?"

Darby was perhaps a little surprised at my tone.

"Oh, don't worry, Martin. You'll not lose much by it, I can tell you. These foreigners never tip you much. Anyway, his visit is only postponed, Barker says."

So Fernandez *had* been detained. It was enormously cheering, this sign of activity at, so to speak, the other end of the line. Biddulph had not failed me. I must not let him down. There were two questions to which I would have liked to know the answers, but I risked only the one of real importance to me, and learned that Count Fernandez was supposed to have merely deferred his visit for just a couple of days. So the atmosphere of disquiet and restlessness I had discerned in Rhand and Elliott as well as in Wridgley, was accounted for. They did not like the news.

My chance to get at the drawer in Rhand's room came during dinner that night. And as things turned out, it was a better chance than I expected. Long before eight o'clock I had finished my preparations for getting safely away. Awake to the fact that the distance I had to travel in order to reach Keppoch Bridge was my chief danger, I had even provided myself with a parcel of food so that I could hold out for a night and a day on the road. Not that I intended to keep to the road all the time. I should be too easily seen and overtaken if I did. Indeed, in these Northern parts the night of real darkness is so brief that I could count on but an hour or two in which I could use the high road with any safety. And for my operation on the drawer I had filled my pockets with a great variety of keys collected from every piece of furniture that had a lock to it in all the empty bedrooms.

So when the dinner gong began its thunder I knew that now my only source of danger left was Bantok. Had he been an English servant I could have counted on his methodical habits to know where he would be at any given time. Already, however, I had seen and heard enough of Bantok to know that he might be anywhere at any time. He was always snuffing and hovering about, like a dog waiting for his master.

But luck certainly was with me that night, at least it was when the night began. For just when I was myself snuffing and hovering about in and out of Elliott's room, and all on edge for my chance, there rose from the terrace the sudden shrill blast of the pipes. Then I remembered that George had told me young McPhee had after all been taken on at Lady Wridgley's request as house piper, though Sir Charles, as George put it, refused to have any of the alarm clock business in the early morning. So McPhee was making his debut. Lucky for me, too, since the novelty would certainly attract everyone's attention. But as I stood behind Elliott's bedroom door, listening to hear Bantok leave his master's bedroom, I did not realize just how lucky it was till I heard Bantok go padding quickly down the corridor.

Wondering what had happened, I went to the window, and there was McPhee marching along the terrace in all the glory of his red tartan kilt, feather bonnet and skirling bagpipes. The next moment

Bantok appeared on the terrace. But not, as my first thought was, to stop McPhee. On the contrary, Bantok stood still as the piper passed him, and if ever I saw surprise and admiration on any face it was on Bantok's as he gazed after McPhee. I am not well enough up in pipe music to say what he was playing, but it was probably some war march, a wild and barbaric riot of sound that appealed to Bantok's savage ear.

You may be sure, however, I didn't linger to wonder over this; it was enough for me to feel certain that Bantok would take neither eye nor ear off McPhee till he had gone. Without hesitation I went into Rhand's room, and on my knees got quickly to work with my keys. For a time I had no success. It was not that they were too big or too small, but that the lock in this drawer appeared to be of a more complicated pattern. Then just when, getting anxious, I began to hurry over the keys, I found one that went home. It wasn't quite a fit, but it did turn, and after a little pressure and coaxing I heard the click of the lock as the tongue fell back. So great was my excitement as I pulled at the drawer that I jammed it. But I got it far enough open to see all I needed: the drawer was quite empty. No, that is not quite exact. There was something in it. For as I stooped down to squint inside, a large brown moth fluttered out, and as if blinded by the light, blundered up to hit me in the face.

Well, at that I could have sat down on the floor and laughed at myself in sheer self-derision. I had been so sure that the small black box with the two red and white stripes must be in that drawer! Outside the bagpipes sounded still, though the tune had changed. No, there was no danger, but it was proving itself a difficult job, rather more difficult, perhaps, than even Biddulph himself had guessed.

There would be no get-away for me that night. In a properly crestfallen spirit I gathered up the dozen or so keys from the carpet, shut and relocked the drawer, and after a careful look to make sure no traces of my presence remained, I left the room, feeling very cheap.

CHAPTER XIII

Later that evening I went to the gun room. I went there because it was the quietest part of the house. The gun-room key was in my charge, and at that hour nobody would come there. Indeed, that end of the house was deserted at that time. It was a lovely evening, and the declining sun flooded in through the windows, filling the room with a soft yellow light. Drawing up a chair to the gable window which I had opened, I sat down and lit a cigarette.

After all, I told myself, there was no real cause for depression in the fact that I had failed to get my hands on the black box that evening. It was my first real try for it. Now it simply remained to try somewhere else. And upheld by the thought that I was engaged in a highly patriotic duty, I set myself to consider where I must next search. Where else except in his own room could Rhand keep it in a house in which he was a guest? But I had searched the room and seen that the one locked receptacle in it was the empty drawer of his dressing table. Elliott certainly had not got it in his room. Of that I had made sure. Sir Charles? Possibly. He was certainly involved in the business. But I did not quite see how he could come to have letters sent out from a department of which he was the head at the time they were written.

As I understood it these were letters addressed to Rhand by some unknown official in the department of which Sir Charles was former-ly the head. How could he have them now—unless—! I sat up at the sudden possibility that here flashed into my mind. Had Sir Charles Wridgley also, like myself, been after that black box? The possibility that the documents might be wanted by his political enemies for use

against him was, I recalled, one of the first things I thought of when
Biddulph was talking to me in his room that first night. That suspicion I had dismissed as really too far-fetched. But with Rhand in the
business it was another matter. Rhand at least was capable of using
any means that gave him a pull on anyone. If these letters gave him
a hold over the ex-Chief Secretary, he would not scruple to use them.

That set me off considering what evidence there was of pressure being put on Sir Charles. Unfortunately I soon found the evidence contradictory. That Rhand should be a guest at Glengyle at all
seemed to me strong evidence that he had a pull on Wridgley. And
Wridgley's whole aspect and attitude when I had seen him looking
out of the billiard room window at Rhand and Elliott on the terrace
seemed to be those of a man who was feeling the squeeze.

But, as against all that, there rose up the remembrance of that
afternoon on the loch. That the fishing expedition had been suggested by Mrs. Rhand for an ulterior purpose I could not doubt, but
whatever the purpose might be, she had certainly not tried to compel
him to it. On the contrary, all that passed between them after they
returned to the boat indicated that she had been trying unsuccess-
fully to wheedle and cajole him into something; and when I recalled
her face, scarlet with rage, when they left the boat, I felt sure that
if she had had the power to compel him to do the thing, whatever it
might be, she would not have stooped to persuade.

So the difference between the Wridgley in the billiard room and
the Wridgley in the boat took my attention. Had something happened
in the interval? Had Rhand lost his squeeze? Had Sir Charles, as the
empty drawer suggested, got possession of the incriminating letters?

But before I could explore this new possibility further the door
opened softly and the face of Gracie Turton peeped round. Seeing
me, she stepped inside and carefully closing the door, came over to
my window. Miss Turton had several times let it be seen that she was
not unwilling to find herself with me. In fact I was quite aware, so
often had she been hovering around when I was about my duties,
that I had to be quite as much on the alert against her as against
Bantok himself when I entered Rhand's room. And this did not pre-
dispose me to welcome her advances now.

"Hullo, Mr. Martin, are you all alone?" she greeted me.

"Till you came, Miss Turton," I replied in the manner prevalent among such a high-class staff as ourselves.

"Meaning you wish I 'adn't?"

"Well—yes," I said bluntly, but with the thought in my head that a little plain speaking now might save worse later on. The girl winced at my rudeness.

"Maybe you'll say different when you hear what I've got to say," she said, nodding significantly.

Already I regretted hurting her. After all, it was through what she had told Jim Peters that I had got into Glengyle.

"Then sit down and tell me about it, Gracie," I said, dropping the high-class manner. She melted to it instantly.

"It's about Bantok, Martin. You don't mind if I do call you Martin, like as if it was your first name, do you?" she added, pleadingly.

Telling her I did not mind in the least, I asked her what she meant about Bantok.

"You watch him, Martin. He means no good by you. And I'd be sorry if anything happened to you, even if it 'adn't been through what you did to him for me."

The notion that the Kaffir would retaliate on me had hardly entered my head. He had seemed so thoroughly cowed.

"He wouldn't dare, Gracie," I said. "Why, when I meet him he goes by with his eyes on the ground."

"Don't you believe it, Martin, don't you believe it, for God's sake," she repeated excitedly. "I've seen him. He's only pretending. I've seen him when he didn't know I was there. He mayn't look you in the face as you pass, Martin, but if you could see the look he gives you *after* you've passed, you'd know what you might expect from that black savidge."

Gracie's earnestness compelled me to consider Bantok. Perhaps my thoughts had been too much concentrated on the one object which had brought me to Glengyle. In thinking almost exclusively on that black box, had I overlooked the black man rather too much? Gracie, mistaking my silence for unbelief, laid her hand impulsively on my shoulder.

"He's watching you, Martin, I tell you. He's always watching you. He'll have a knife in you yet. Don't trust him, I tell you, and for my sake lock your door every night. Tell me you will. I couldn't a-bear it if you was to come to any harm through what you done to him for me."

It was easy to reassure her on this last point, since as a matter of fact I always did lock my bedroom door. But what troubled me was the doubt as to whether Bantok could be watching me on account of her. That he had been watching me I did not now doubt. Gracie ought to know, if anyone. She herself had so persistently hovered about in her attempts to strike up a friendship with me. Possibly I owed more to this girl than I had guessed, if Bantok meant mischief. But it was a new idea to me. Up to then I had looked upon him as a nuisance; never as a danger. The truth is I began to be rather perturbed by what Gracie had said. She was no doubt right in saying the beastly Kaffir was watching me, but quite likely wrong as to his motive. What if he had been set to watch me because I came under suspicion already? There were those pointed words Sir Charles had used in the boat about my being an expert at fishing by night, and so on. I had been startled at the moment he spoke, but had dismissed them as being mere coincidences due to the fact that Mrs. Rhand was like myself, "fishing" for something other than she affected to be. Yes, and like a fool I had been sure that Sir Charles had seen through her but not through me. Gracie heard the soft curse I breathed out at this point.

"Don't you go and get fighting with him any more," she pleaded, her face clouded with anxiety and distress.

"Has he tried to kiss you again?" I asked.

"Kiss me!" she cried. "Not 'im! He'd sooner knife me than kiss me now." This change caught my ear: had Bantok found the girl as much a nuisance as I had done myself? Thinking it well to probe into this, I asked her, little anticipating to what the question would lead, what had made him change like that.

Gracie shook her head.

"I dunno. Not as I'm complaining about it, Martin. Only I won't go near his room again. I've not been used to such language, that's all."

I didn't think it was all by any means, and pressed her for particulars. She needed pressing, evidently dreading another fracas between Bantok and myself. Finally she yielded.

"Well, it was like this. This morning I was doing the brasses and the door knobs on the upper floor where his room is. I didn't know he was in his room but 'ardly had I begun to use the brasso when he bounces out on me all of a sudden and soon as he sees me he starts in cursing and swearing something shocking."

"What for?"

"All on account of the noise I was making, he said. But I weren't. I 'adn't even reached his door by then. I'd got no further than the box-room door at the end of the passage."

The indignant and half tearful Gracie was either too preoccupied with her wrongs or too blinded by tears to notice the sudden joy her story brought me. But, impelled by a rush of gratitude to her I jumped up and, throwing an arm about her, planted a smacking kiss on her cheek. She promptly relaxed, laying her head on my shoulder.

"Oh, that 'as made me feel nice again," she breathed. "Sort of quite blots out the one he gave me, it do."

"Mean to say nobody's kissed you since then?" I laughed.

"Nobody as counts 'as. Only George who took me unawares when my hands was full."

And then while she was anxiously begging me to beware of Bantok, I was thrilling over the revelation she had all unconsciously made to me. I knew it was there. I felt it in my bones that there it was. The little black box with the two red and white stripes was in the empty case in the box-room. In the box-room among all the empty trunks and cases and bags where no thief would go unless he had a strange, abnormal taste for stealing empty cases. Yes, it would be in the biggest and shabbiest of trunks right at the top of the house where none but a housemaid went, where Bantok slept, the watchful Bantok who took alarm at the slightest touch on the handle of the box-room door.

Long after Gracie's duties had taken her off I sat considering how I could get at the box-room. The psychology which lay behind that choice of a hiding place for the documents did not escape me; and I wondered what unexpected defense I might have to overcome even after I contrived to get inside the box-room. Who but Otto Rhand would have thought of a box-room, a room which suggests nothing to one's mind but empty receptacles, a room which never enters one's thoughts till the time comes when those same trunks and cases are once more needed. I had a great respect for Rhand's astuteness, and saw the possibility that there might be some dangerous monkey-like trap, some piece of malicious trickery lying in wait for anyone who got into that room. But I pushed the unwelcome possibility out of my thoughts. After all, I hadn't got as far as the room yet. First I had to get Bantok out of the way.

For a long time I pondered over possible ways of getting round Bantok. Even after I was in bed I lay awake scratching my head over the problem. The night seemed the least promising time, for Bantok had that upper floor to himself, and one had to pass his door to reach the box-room, and I knew how his race sleep. It was in his blood, an inheritance from his savage ancestors, accustomed to sleep in the open, surrounded by hostile forces, that he should wake up instantly wide-eyed and alert, as if by instinct.

Short of getting him drugged at supper I did not believe it possible to pass his door unheard, much less to unlock or force the box-room. And I had nothing in the way of dope either. For a time I even toyed with the idea of getting McPhee to give Bantok lessons on the bagpipes. Bantok loved the pipes and never missed getting as close as he could when he heard them. But it was doubtful if anyone else would allow him to play near enough the house to be serviceable to me as a notice of his whereabouts. No; I'd have to chance a flying visit to the upper floor some time when he was occupied with Rhand during the day. Perhaps I might have to go up to the room more than once if the job took any time.

The risk was greater since I had much further to go and no occasion to go up there at all. And the worst of it was that that Kaffir's want of regular habits doubled the risk, since you never could tell where or at what moment you might hear his feet come padding up behind you, if you heard them at all. There was this one fact, however, which counted for a lot: neither Bantok nor his master would dream that anyone yet knew where the box was kept.

I went to sleep with the thought that given any luck, this would be my last night in Glengyle.

On getting down to my first duties next morning I found the Captain's room empty. This was unusual. After setting the room in order

I learned from George that Captain Elliott and Mr. Rhand had hurriedly breakfasted together and had gone off in the car half an hour ago. Just as I got ready with a question or two, Lady Wridgley appeared at the top of the stairs, and George passed into the breakfast room with the hot dish he was carrying.

I resumed my work of polishing up one of the weapons which together with various trophies of the chase formed part of the lounge hall's decorations. Lady Wridgley, however, did not pass into the breakfast room. After hanging about a few moments she went over to the table by the door on which the letters were put which Postie would collect about nine, and began to glance over them rather rapidly, in a way that struck me, since it contrasted so much with her previous leisurely movements. And George made her almost jump when he suddenly emerged from the breakfast room.

"Oh—er—Sir Charles not yet down?" she said to him, quite clumsily for her. And George replied in his respectful negative as she passed through the door he held open. All this somehow set me wondering. Of course at this time my ears and eyes were keyed up to the highest pitch, and when one's senses are strung up like that, it is easy to read significance into trifles. But it was certainly clear that morning that Lady Wridgley had lost some of her poise. Her nerves were on edge. Intent on seeing the letters on the table, she had in passing omitted to give me her usual smiling "Good morning" bow. She had lost that self-possessed, almost queenly condescension of manner which I had never seen her without; which, in fact, most big political hostesses seem to acquire for life, however brief their husband's tenure of office may have been.

I replaced the long, bright-bladed assegai on the wall, and then when Sir Charles came quickly down with a letter in his hand, I guessed how it was that Lady Wridgley knew her husband had not yet left his room. She knew that letter would be on the table if he had come down. It was for that letter she had searched on the table. I took down the antique arkquebus, wondering if anything would happen before Postie called for the Glengyle letters, as he was due to do inside the next half hour. Presently, his work done, George sauntered along, and I stopped him by pointing the ancient weapon at his head.

"Here, how d'ye know it ain't loaded?" he cried.

"It hasn't been, not for hundreds of years," I reassured him. I pointed the arquebus at the assegai. "Now, that is the thing to make you tremble if it got loose."

"What is it?" George inquired.

I told him it was a Zulu assegai, the weapon Bantok's ancestors handled so magnificently.

"Oh," said George nodding, "so that's why I saw him looking at it so close."

Then I got out, with an air of naturalness, the question for which I had stopped him with the old gun. "Has he gone with them?"

"In the car? Oh, no, it's the Captain's car they're using."

This was a two-seater *Invicta*. But the news disappointed me.

"Where were they off to?" I next asked, in the casual manner of the servant mildly interested in the master's doings.

"They forgot to mention it to me, but just now I heard 'er tell 'im they've gone to Keppoch Bridge to ring up the missing Count, who seems to 'ave got himself lost in the delights of naughty old London town, which is what I'd like to be," George added with a sigh, as he passed on.

A few minutes later Lady Wridgley hurriedly appeared with a letter in her hand. She made straight for the table by the door just as the bell rang. She had timed her trick perfectly. She must have been able to see Postie on his cycle as he reached the terrace. I saw her put down her own letter, and though I did not see her lift one with the other hand, I knew she had got it in her pocket, and that it could only be the letter which Sir Charles had placed on the pile before he went in to breakfast.

Now all this pointed to a split having taken place among these plotters. And Lady Wridgley's trick with the letter revealed another line of cleavage among them. That helped me. For when such people became distrustful or unsure among themselves they are apt to have eyes only for each other and become more or less blind to what is going on outside their own circle. But I had no idea of how serious the split had become till Darby came in to call me to lunch. I happened at the moment to have one of Elliott's express rifles in my hands.

"Good job it was only a billiard cue and not that thing he had in his 'ands last night," he murmured.

I asked him what he was talking about. Then it came out that going in to the billiard room rather late in response to a call for more whisky, he had found Sir Charles standing on the hearthrug and Rhand, who had been playing with Elliott, facing him, brandishing his cue, just as if he wanted to do in the other on the spot, as George put it. The sight made Darby pull up inside the door, and at first no one noticed him. "And there was the master," George ran on, "looking mighty white but standing very straight, and Mr. Rhand facing up to him like a screeching little devil, his face near black with rage."

"What was he saying?" I asked.

"Oh, I don't know. I was too much struck of a heap, you know. Just 'eard a lot o' names flying—Fernandez' and Lady Wridgley's and some others I don't know, and then Sir Charles twigged me by the door. 'You'll cut the cloth if you don't take care,' he said, all calm and soft like. And Mr. Rhand, who was drawing back the cue, threatening him, like as if it was that Zulu spear I saw you shining up, wheeled round and twigged me. That cooled him down mighty quick. He bent over the table, pretending to see if he'd cut the cloth, but looking all the same as if he'd rather cut the master's throat."

Piecing this with other things George told me, and adding to it what I already knew, little doubt remained that the trouble had some connection with the holding up of Fernandez in London.

Mr. Barker had assigned that afternoon as my afternoon off, but hoping to glean some news when the car returned from Keppoch Bridge, I did not stray far from the house. Neither, unfortunately for me, did Bantok. After hanging about for a chance to go up and examine the box-room door, I went round to the garage to see what I could find there. Of course I had prepared myself for the attempt on the door in the same way as I had prepared for my attempt on the drawer in Rhand's bedroom. I had, that is, filled my pockets with the keys of all the doors in the empty north wing of the house. But I was determined not to be beaten, even if the keys failed, and to that end searched in the garage till I came on a tire lever big enough to burst the box-room lock if all else failed. This I carried to my room in my sleeve. After secreting it under the fender, however, a new idea came. It held just the possibility of a better way into the box-room. Had I not, I asked myself, concentrated too much on the door of that room? Rooms have windows as well as doors. And surely even a box-room must have a window for light and ventilation. That is why I went out again and mounted the hill behind the house to look for the position of the window.

The slope was clad with tall pines, but the undergrowth of close-set Douglas firs made it rather difficult to reach the edge under which Glengyle sat, on its terrace below. After some scrambling among the little Douglases, which were scenting the whole wood on that warm afternoon, I reached a point immediately above the east wing, where under the roof at the end nearest me were both the box-room and Bantok's bedroom. No window showed in the gable, but there was something much more promising on the roof, and that was a skylight. At once my eye ran along the whole line of roof. There was no break between this wing and the main frontage; but a skylight in the box-room was no good to me unless I could get on to the roof somewhere else.

I plumped down among the bracken to consider. There was another skylight on the corresponding room on the west wing, but even if I got into that room and out at its skylight, it would mean a tremendous clamber right along the entire length of all the roofs before I reached my objective. In fact the two skylights were at the two extreme ends of the house.

The idea of fixing a rope to one of the trees and swinging myself down to the roof did cross my mind. But that was impracticable, for the house, close as it stood against the hillside, was not close enough for that, and in any case such an attempt to land on the roof, as I must make, in the dark, would be almost certain to end in a broken neck.

Then I seemed to remember there was a light at the top of the main staircase. I tried to think where it was exactly. The staircase opening out of the hall was lit at each landing by tall windows, deeply recessed and filled with stained glass. But on the top floor there was no scope for such a window, and I felt almost certain the only light there was was one on the roof.

Then just when I saw that this would shorten my climb by half, a succession of blasts on a motor horn ascended from below. I recognized the horn, it was the *Invicta's*, and something about the way it was being sounded, where there could be no need to blow at all, suggested that Rhand and Elliott were returning in much better spirits than they had left. Pushing a way through the undergrowth I slid down the slope at some distance and got back to the house by the drive.

But it was not till an hour or two later that any news leaked down to me, and then I heard from George that Count Fernandez was arriving next night. So, I said to myself as George was speaking, the London people consider they have given me enough time to do the job. In that they were mistaken. But I had still one night left, and with what I now knew, it might be enough. By tomorrow I might be well on the way to London.

My only danger lay in the chance of getting caught on those thirty-six miles to Keppoch Bridge. But for that stretch there was a bicycle, belonging to the forester, which was kept in the wood-shed, and this I intended to borrow. I ought to reach Keppoch in time to catch the seven-twenty in the morning. And for the remainder of the journey I still had those four precious notes stitched in the lining of my waistcoat.

CHAPTER XIV

It was just after half past seven on that eventful night that I met Mrs. Rhand at the top of the stairs on the first floor. The second dinner gong had sounded and I thought they had all descended. I was making my way to the Captain's room for the last time, as I thought, when I saw her. My idea now is that she had been waiting for me. Anyhow, when I caught sight of her she was standing still a yard or two inside the dimly lit corridor and just out of sight till one turned off from the staircase landing. Her ankle-length black dress, of some lusterless material that took no light on its surface, made her look like a very dark shadow. But she moved forward when she saw me. I stood aside to let her pass, but she did not pass.

"Oh, by the way, Martin," she said, "we thought of trying for the fish tonight. Can you arrange about the bait?"

The question brought my eyes up again. She looked very beautiful and I did not reply for a moment. Perhaps she read admiration in my eyes, for the ghost of a frown appeared in her own. Then mechanically she lifted a slim white arm to smooth down or arrange, quite needlessly, the masses of red hair above her left ear, while I looked down at the scarlet shoe that peeped out below her dress.

"Bait, madam? We don't use bait in night fishing on the loch," I said.

"Of course not," she smiled. "What on earth was I thinking of? It's a fly, a specially dressed fly, isn't it, that's needed?"

"Yes, madam, the best kind is one with a black body and some white so as to make it easily seen, and just a touch of red," I said.

She shot a quick glance to see, I suppose, if I was aware that this was rather like a description of herself, but by this time I was well schooled in how to show an impassive face.

"You can provide the right sort then?" she suggested.

On that I had to explain we had no such flies in the house, but if I were given an hour or two I could have the fly dressed to pattern.

"All right. We won't be starting out till about eleven," she said as she moved for the stairs. Then, as my heart sank to my boots at the prospect of being taken away to row the boat, she turned to thrill me by saying they did not propose to rob me of my night's sleep and would take Bantok with them; it would be enough if I provided the flies.

This, as can be imagined, made good hearing for me. I hurried off to get my work finished, all the time aware that I knew where to get the best possible dressing for a night-fly. While we had landed on the island I had noticed the heronry there, and it would be queer if I didn't find among the trees a few of the black breast feathers of the cock heron which every knowing night fisher prefers to all others for this kind of sport. There was just one snag: I had tried my hand at making up a fly, but that was a long time ago when I was a boy and spent my days on the Teith river above Callander, and I doubted whether this was a knack that had survived. Still, I wasn't going to let that stop me. Too much hung on it. Somehow or other I must contrive to dress that night fly well enough to pass muster and to get these people away on the loch, whether the trout turned up their noses at my flies or not. Anyway, I didn't intend to be there to hear what might be said about the flies when they returned.

It was getting on for nine before I was free to go to island to search for the cock heron's feathers. Most of the way I ran to the boat-house, since I would need all the light that was left for a search among the trees, though in case of failure I had a notion that the McPhees might have picked up a few for their own use at nights when no keepers were about.

As soon as the boat was heading up the loch I took a look about me to judge how much daylight was left for my search. I was struck by the stillness and the calm, clear beauty of the evening. The day had been hot and cloudless, with never a breath of wind, and though

as yet the air was still motionless, it felt cool enough to the face, now
that the sun had disappeared behind the Duich hills. There should
be good fishing later on, on such a night.

Abreast of the island I turned the boat's head, and after a few vig-
orous strokes let her ripple through the smooth water shorewards.
Resting on my oars I saw the color had quite faded out of things
except on the distant mountain tops which were still pink tipped.
Down below, however, everything was grey and dark, the trees a vel-
vety black mass sloping down to the edge of the grey water. As the
boat slid with a sharp rustle into the shingle, I thought it likely that
if I was to find those cock heron feathers it would have to be more
by feel than by sight.

For some time I scouted about around the spot where I remembered seeing the feathers, along the foot of the dismantled tower
and under the pines whose fallen needles left the ground dry and
springy. It was quite dark there now, and rather eerie in the absolute
stillness, a place full of deep shadows even in daylight. For perhaps
twenty minutes I peered about, in that time coming across several
specimens, only to discard them as being either too old or not the
kind needed. I had to go down on hands and knees to it at last, but
I did come on a couple which felt like what I wanted. Putting them
into my pocket, I was about to resume my dog-like search along the
foot of the wall when a strange sound pulled me short, like a pointer
who has come on his quarry.

Still on hands and knees, I listened. It was a dull, heavy, thudding sound, and it came at regular intervals. For quite a time I stayed
listening, rather awed, if the truth be told, for there was something
unearthly about such a sound in such a place, and its muffled quality
made it almost impossible to tell the direction from which it came.
The one thing of which I was certain was that the sound came from
somewhere on the island itself. For, muffled as the thudding sounded, it was yet far too near to be something that came across the water
from even the nearest side of the loch.

That was what kept me motionless so long. It was simply an infernally eerie sound to hear at such a time and in such a place when
I had good reason for thinking I was alone on that island. For so far
as I knew there was but the one boat I had myself used on the loch.

I didn't like it at all. You see, though I knew the sound to come from somewhere on the island, yet I felt that since the island was so small I ought to have been able to hear it much more distinctly, ever so much more distinctly than was in fact actually the case.

At last I was able to describe it to myself: the sound was somehow *buried*. And at that discovery it is still a puzzle to me why I didn't rise and make a bolt for the boat. For the next instant I remembered the bottle-necked dungeon in the courtyard and all the horrors of the starved prisoners it had held in the old savage days. And no one except myself could be on the island. It was impossible. There was no other boat. Just in time I got back a grip on myself. "Look here," I said, and in my striving said it aloud, "you don't believe in ghosts or fairies or any such cattle. Very well, there must be a natural explanation for this sound, which a little investigation would reveal, if you had guts to get on with it."

And get on with it I did, though in a funk all the time as I tiptoed on, my hands feeling along the rough masonry of that crumbling tower. I did not stop, I did not dare stop, till I arrived at a point where the shattered walls of the burnt-out old stronghold opened out on the courtyard. But there I did pull up, for right in the center of the open space I saw a shaft of faint light rising out of the ground. And that sight sent me clean back into my right senses. It explained everything in one flash. There was someone in the dungeon, at work hammering, with the help of a lantern. No, not quite everything perhaps. It did not explain how he had got on to the island. And that was odd, unless, I suggested to myself, he had swum across. But that would in itself be an odd thing for anyone to do.

Curiosity soon sent me creeping across the courtyard towards that shaft of light. I had to know who was there and what he was doing. Whoever he was he was working hard, for the sound never stopped and I had little danger of being overheard. For all that, I could not help making my approach as stealthy and cautious as possible. Once I got near the man-hole I went down on hands and knees, and creeping up to its lip, I craned over and peered down into the interior.

To this day it is a wonder to me that seeing what I did, I yet did not cry aloud. Not so much at the unexpected identity of the man, as at his occupation. He was not hammering, he was digging, hard at work digging what was obviously, from its shape and depth, intended to be a grave. That grave took the eye in the first flash as I blinked down into the light, but almost simultaneously I saw that the man was Bantok. He stood up to his knees in the grave, naked, his skin glistening with the sweat.

I recall withdrawing my head and resting my forehead on the cool dew-drenched turf to think. Who was to occupy this nice little hole? That it was a grave admitted of no doubt. A swarm of bewildering possibilities floated across my mind. But even then I could not think that this secret preparation in that old dungeon had anything to do with me. The secret service work on which I was engaged could, at the worst, only put me in an awkward situation if I got caught at it. The old phrase Biddulph had used that night once again came back. "Difficult but not dangerous," I could hear his voice drawling. And that was exactly what I had found it. For if I had come up against tragedy in what happened to the Irishman Martin, that was entirely accidental and had no direct connection with this affair. Besides, as I told myself, even if it was known why I was in Glengyle, it was incredible that they would risk their necks by putting me away unless those same necks were already in jeopardy. This plotting of theirs was no life and death affair, but merely a scheme to make great personal gain at the expense of the country. And after all, I had no reason to imagine that I had awakened any suspicion.

But, having decided that Bantok could not be laboring down there to provide me with my last resting place, the question remained: for whom was it intended?

I took another peep down at Bantok. He had laid aside the spade and was now busy with the pickax, the gleaming muscles of his great shoulders rippling, relaxing and tightening to the rhythm of his mighty strokes. He had set the lantern on the heaped-up earth at one side of the pit, and the rise and fall of his body, the violent swinging arms and the pickax were being grotesquely repeated by the magnified and distorted shadows thus cast on the wall beyond him. It was curious how these multiplied movements gave me the impression of great haste. But anyway, there was no doubt that Bantok was in a hurry. An idea came to me.

Already I had noticed the ladder Bantok had used to get down
to the floor of the dungeon. For a moment I hesitated, just not quite
sure it might not be too heavy for me. If it turned out to be beyond
my strength to do it quickly enough, then I'd be lucky if I got away
without being discovered spying on him, lucky perhaps if I got away
at all. Still, another glimpse at him going at it hammer and tongs,
beyond any doubt for some infernal purpose, made me throw aside
all hesitation. I got to my feet, seized the end of the ladder and pulled
like blazes with all my weight.

He must have heard something, the squeak of the dry wood on
the edge of the hole, probably, as I got it up a bit. Anyhow, I heard
his startled cry and the rattle of stones and earth as he leaped out
of his trench. I did feel a momentary grip on the other end that
knocked me off my balance. But he must have had to leap for it, and
before he could make another grab I had got the ladder not only sufficiently far outside to prevent him from seeing who I was, but also
far enough out to get my whole weight on it, and so to lever it up
beyond his reach. After that, when I'd got it more on the balance and
so made it far less of a dead lift, it was easy enough to slide it clean
out of the pit altogether. Then I dropped it and ran.

It was with a feeling of delight that I rowed down the loch again:
No need now for a climb along the roof to reach that room. Bantok
was safely out of the way for—well—it was hard to say for how long.
The floor of the dungeon was not less than twelve feet below, and I
could not guess how long it would take him to shovel a pile of earth
and stones high enough for him to reach the manhole. The plight
in which I had left him did not trouble me in the least. In fact, so
moved was I by the certainty that he had been digging a grave for
someone in that place that it would have pleased me to know he
must now occupy it himself.

But as I ran the boat back into the boat-house a thought came
which sent me sprinting hard along the road to Glengyle. Of course
I'd been rather an ass not to see it before. It was, I suppose, because
I was blinded by the feeling of a petty personal triumph over Bantok.
Seeing him so much in a hurry to get his work done, I was moved
to stop him. But now it occurred to me to ask why he was in such a
hurry. The first answer that suggested itself was that he was anxious

to get back to keep an eye on me. But that did not convince me, since I had no reason whatever to believe that he had the slightest suspicion of me. That opened my eyes rather. Opened them, I mean, to the possibility that I might have been just too exclusively concerned, indeed, egotistically obsessed with the importance of my own job for which I had come to Glengyle, to see the significance of anything else, even when it was going on under my nose.

There was the trick of Lady Wridgley's with the letter. What did that mean? And what was Mrs. Rhand's game with Sir Charles? I had seen it fail, but without guessing what her game was. And now there was this island grave secretly and hastily got ready. It was intended for somebody. That seemed certain. And I saw that this was a matter too serious to be ignored, even for the sake of getting clear away with the papers that night. No, assuredly it was not to relieve the tedium of his idle hours in the house by a little physical exercise that Bantok had gone to dig in that place.

All this I was now seeing as I ran. Bantok had been sent to dig that grave in a hurry. And Bantok was to go out with the fishing party that night. But what would happen when Bantok did not turn up? I slackened down to a walk to consider the answer. And I had not walked more than a yard or two before I found an answer that set me off at redoubled speed. This time, however, I was not making for the house. Presently the glow among the trees showed me I was getting close to the McPhees' encampment, and on reaching the entrance into the quarry I saw to my great relief the old man and his son squatting by the fire. A pile of pots and pans between them showed me they had been putting in a busy evening with the soldering iron. Apparently, however, their work was finished, for both, with rather smoke-begrimed faces, sat in relaxed attitudes, the old man cutting up tobacco for the clay pipe on his knees.

A snapping twig under my foot made them look up. I produced the three feathers and told them my trouble. Flies were needed for night fishing in something less than half an hour, and I wasn't sure I could dress them at all, but quite sure I couldn't do them in time.

The old man emptied the tobacco carefully into his dirty clay pipe and then extended a hoary hand to take the feathers. The next instant he had dropped them in the fire.

"No good, far too old," he said.

Then, when I was about to protest, he nodded to his son and Murdo jumping up, disappeared inside the tent. The old man with a pair of his pincers lifted a red ember from the fire and lit his pipe.

"I'm rather in a hurry," I said.

"You've been to the island; it's the only place here-away for these birds," he remarked as Murdo emerged from the tent with what looked like a dirty well-stuffed pillow slip. Well stuffed indeed it proved to be, when he shook half its contents into one of the pots by his side. A sight of the contents made me less impatient, for it was filled with all kinds of feathers. As Murdo turned them over the variety of birds from which they had been collected astonished me, for I recognized plumage from ptarmigan, teal, grouse, woodcock, duck and plover. Then when the young man picked out a few of the curly black breast feathers from the cock heron I perceived that he too had been to the island, though I could not imagine how he had got there. Murdo saw my surprise.

"We gather them here and there," he explained, "and sell them to Mackay, the fishing tackle maker in Inverness. Just to turn an extra penny or two, you understand."

I did understand. This was Jim Peters and his little side lines over again. But the fact that they collected plumage used for making flies did not prove that they could dress a fly. When, however, I put the question, a smile hovered for a moment on the elder man's lips.

"Och, yes," he said, "it's lots of queer things you have to turn your hand to when you're born on the road like us. Murdo there now is as good at turning out a fly as any you'll find between here and Inverness, except maybe myself," he added with conscious pride.

So it was the old man I hurried to the house to make up the flies. And I soon had cause to regret it. It was close on half past ten when I set him to work at the table in the gun-room. At any minute now Mrs. Rhand might be sending for the night flies. As the minutes passed, in spite of myself I got more and more on edge with impatience. Old McPhee's deliberation as he sat at the table laying out the naked hooks, snipping the feathers, adjusting the red heckle, binding it with the silk, was too much to stand still and watch. Deft as he was, it became maddening when I asked for speed, to see him cock

his head on one side to appraise his handiwork and then unwind
the thread to remove the feather so that he could snip an almost
microscopic fraction from its inner edge. Maddening indeed it was
when one suspected the vain old fellow was only doing this to exhibit
his skill, while I was only anxious to get the work finished, to see the
fishing party off on their expedition so that I could have the free run
of the house for the job I had in hand. All the same, I didn't want any
of the party to stay behind because of a scarcity of flies.

However, my good luck of all that day held out. McPhee had
scarcely gone when Mrs. Rhand herself entered in search of me.
While I was showing her the flies Sir Charles and Captain Elliott
came in together, the former, like Mrs. Rhand, wearing a heavy coat.
Elliott did not seem to be going. That, however, did not worry me
much. For though he would be a tougher customer to deal with at
close quarters than Rhand, I knew his habits so well already that I
thought it would be easy to avoid him at the critical moments.

Mrs. Rhand had one of the flies in her hand and was examining
it curiously as the others came in. Sir Charles took it up.

"Ah, that's the stuff," he nodded.

McPhee had built up the fly as I directed, the body of black heron with a touch of white from a duck's wing, and near the bend of
the hook I had added a tag of red, not because it was necessary but
simply because I had said it was when I saw Mrs. Rhand's red shoes
peeping out beneath her black frock.

"A sure killer. We ought to have good sport tonight," Sir Charles
added, looking at her pleasantly. Mrs. Rhand looked at me.

"Very clever of you, Martin," she said. "Thank you very much."

Elliott picked up one of the flies on hearing this, and asked what
the plumage was. He did not seem to be as well up in fishing as Sir
Charles who suggested heron and teal. Elliott looked at me for con-
firmation.

"Heron?" he questioned. "Then you must have gone to the island
to get it."

That unexpected assertion made it a queer moment for me.

"Well, sir," I replied, "as a matter of fact I got all the plumage
from the McPhees. In fact it was the old man who made up these for
me."

"Ah," Sir Charles cut in, "poachers, both of them. They know all about it. Many a good fish they no doubt pull out of the loch when the gamekeeper is snoring between the blankets."

Elliott somehow seemed to be as much on edge as myself by this time. He put one question that was in my own mind.

"Well, what are we waiting for?" he inquired, fidgeting with his cigarette case.

"Otto; he's gone to look for Bantok," Mrs. Rhand replied.

Sir Charles began to button up his overcoat.

"Is he—essential?" he inquired.

"Well, he is to be our boatman," she replied. "Funny where he can have got to. Usually he's rather too much in one's way, you know."

Sir Charles laughed.

"Yes, I've noticed that. He's here, there and everywhere in the most unexpected places. Rather like a dog, isn't he?"

"In his devotion to Otto, yes," Mrs. Rhand agreed.

A minute or two passed in silence while they hung about waiting. Elliott then said he would go and hurry them up. When he had gone, Sir Charles suggested it would save time if I put the rods, the rugs and tackle into the car at once. I then gathered that Elliott was to drive them to the boat-house. Outside on the terrace it was so dark that I found the low hum of the throttled down engine a help in discovering where the car was standing. The moon was in its last quarter and would not rise till much later.

I stood beside the car for a little while listening. Nothing seemed to stir, not even the air, and except for the faint rustle of the river down below not a sound reached my ear. It would be a good night for fishing, but not so good for finding one's way over the moors and hills if one had to leave the road—at any rate till the moon came up. On re-entering the gun room I got a shock.

"We shall have to take Martin instead, that's all," Sir Charles was saying.

My heart stood still. Better far to have left Bantok at large than this! The irony of the situation so struck me that I could have laughed aloud. To have made so sure of Bantok's absence in order that I might get at the papers, only to find myself taken away on account of his absence—safely removed from my last chance of getting at those papers! I was brought to my senses by some words from the woman.

"I don't think he's quite well," she was saying.

Sir Charles too was staring at me.

"Anything wrong, Martin?" he asked sharply.

An inspiration came to me from his question.

"Well, sir, not really. Only—"

"Well?"

"Only it's so dark outside I missed my footing on the steps and came down rather badly on my right wrist, sir."

"H'm. You do look rather white. Sure it's not broken?"

Before I could do anything Mrs. Rhand had come across and taken my hand. She put it gently upon the palm of one hand and began to feel it tenderly with the fingers of the other, her eyes on my face all the time. Her touch was almost like a caress.

It made me forget to exhibit any sign of pain or distress. Then a queer thing happened. Sir Charles was standing a little way apart, his back to the window, watching while she manipulated my wrist. With her eyes on my face like that she made me feel such a humbug that I had to look away. As it happened I looked beyond them both to the window behind them. And there I saw a thing which gave me a big enough shock not only to make me wince, but actually jump.

"Ah," she said, "it's a badly strained tendon. Better hold it like this till you get it bound up." While speaking, she buttoned my coat so as to give support to the injured hand, which she inserted and placed over my heart. It was indeed the right position in which to place it. For if the strain on the tendons of the wrist had been a fake, the strain on the tendons of the heart was real enough. Staring in at the window, his eyes bulbous and distended, his huge teeth gleaming white against the glass, like a beast snarling with rage, was the shadowy face of Bantok.

Then the door opened and Otto Rhand strolled in just as Sir Charles remarked that they might as well go to bed as the fates seemed set against any fishing that night. I remained at the door until they decided what to do, since it was my duty to lock up and take away the key of the gun room every night. I imagine they must have discussed the situation among themselves, but for a time nothing that passed entered my conscious mind. Other things indeed went flashing through my head. How had Bantok contrived to escape? It was incredible that he could have shoveled enough material in the time to build up a pile high enough for him to reach the top. It was a task not to be done under a day at the least. Had there been someone else on the island whom I had not seen? That would solve the mystery. The ladder could be lowered again just as quickly as I had pulled it out. That, in fact, was the only explanation which could account for the rapidity with which Bantok got back to the house.

But it seemed quite as hard to account for the presence of another on the island at that time. Who could it be who had got there without the boat? If this supposed third party had taken Bantok over in the boat, it would be easy to imagine him strolling about the island till Bantok had finished his work. But the boat could not have been so used, since I myself had found it tied up in the boat-house. Bantok, of course, swam across from the further bank to which the island stood much closer. That had been my first belief when I saw him down below, naked, his black hide still shining with moisture. In fact, so incredible did all this seem to me that I began to wonder whether that vision of the black face staring through the window was not pure imagination. After all, I had seen no more than what I took to be the whites of his eyes and teeth.

They were in the act of leaving the room when I came to myself and held the door open. Sir Charles laid his hand on Rhand's shoulder.

"Well, anyhow, it can't be helped now," he was saying. "We must put it off till some other night."

He and Rhand seemed on excellent terms with each other. In fact they were going out arm in arm. Mrs. Rhand looked at me, hanging back momentarily and making the others pull up.

"I hope it feels better now," she said.

Rhand turned.

"Does what feel better now?" he demanded.

"Martin, here. He sprained his wrist."

"Oh, sprained his wrist, has he?" he repeated, giving me an odd kind of smile. "How unfortunate." Then, as he looked up at me, the whole expression of his face changed. The smile of affected commiseration vanished and was suddenly replaced by a flashing glare of malignity so intense that I knew the man had found that hatred beyond his control to hide. And in that brief second I read murder in his eyes.

CHAPTER XV

I locked up the gun room and put the key in my pocket. That blaze of uncontrollable hate told me two things good for me to know. I now knew that the trick I had played on Bantok had knocked the bottom out of some scheme of Rhand's, which, whatever it was, seemed to involve putting somebody away into that vacant grave on the island. It could have no tenant now, at any rate so long as I remained alive and able, from what I had witnessed on the island, to suggest where anyone who had suddenly disappeared might be found.

The second thing I now knew was that my attempt on the papers must be made that night or not at all. The conviction was borne in upon me that I should get no second chance. I had seen too much and am willing to admit that I was horribly frightened.

While making for the service staircase I ran into George Darby, who was laden with bottles for the butler's pantry.

"Hullo, off to bed?" he greeted me.

"Yes. I've got cold feet," I said.

"What, a young feller like you! There must be something wrong with your heart then."

"There is, George. It's in the wrong place."

His eyebrows went up.

"Well, I once knew a chap who'd his on the wrong side of his chest. Yours there too?"

"No, mine's in my mouth," I said.

"Meaning," George laughed, "that only a drink would put it back to its normal situation. Well, laddie, come and have one."

That had not been my meaning; but all the same, after getting that good stiff drink I felt much better.

It wanted only a few minutes to one when I got off the bed and opened my window cautiously to have a look at the night. The moon would not be up for another two hours or so, and I calculated to be an hour on the road before it rose, so that I could have the darkness in the country more or less known to me, and some light as a guide to direction where it was up. So, as I allowed an hour for getting along the roof, breaking in the skylight and finding out where that black box with the red and white lines was hidden in the box-room, the moment for action had come.

It was a fine night, the air dry and almost cold. So much of the sky as was visible seemed cloudless, and from the trees on the slope there came an occasional faint rustle of foliage stirred by the fitful little night breeze. Not a light showed at any window.

Peeling off jacket and waistcoat and locking my door behind me, I crept barefoot along the passage and up the service staircase to emerge on the front corridor, and so reach the top main staircase which alone gave access to the top floor of the house. I had little to fear except in getting past the occupied bedrooms in the front corridor. I had nothing to fear from creaking floor boards, I knew that; the house was too well built and the floor itself too well carpeted; but in the dark where I had to feel my way, there was always the danger of tripping over something and stumbling against a door. Foot by foot I crept along, and though once I stirred a pair of shoes which appeared to have been tossed out rather than set down, I reached the staircase at last and once more began to breathe without discomfort. In fact, till I got out on to the roof it was all easy, for as I have said, the upper front floor was unoccupied, and though the rooms below were not, there was no need for me to make any noise overhead, since the fanlight opening on the roof was in the corridor at the top of the stairs. And having used the short ladder put there for that purpose, I was out on the roof in less time than I had taken to traverse the second floor corridor.

I had still a long way to go, but now with no fear that I should be overheard, though in some dread that I might overbalance, I crept along the leaden gutter, getting the illusion of safety from the six inches of stone parapet between me and the eighty-foot or so drop to the earth. At first I thought it was going to be easy, and I thought how right I had been to take that way rather than make an attempt on the box-room door from inside the house. That I had shirked after seeing Bantok's face at the window. I didn't consider there was a chance of passing his door unheard, neither did I now fancy a rough and tumble with him in the dark.

But I hadn't reached far on the roof before I began to doubt whether I hadn't taken on something far more dangerous. Things went quite well along the front of the house. With my knees in the lead gutter, one hand on the stone parapet and the other on the slates, I reached the angle where I had to turn along the wing that went backwards towards the hill behind the house. Once round this very awkward angle, my troubles began.

On emerging from the fanlight I had found the slates were wet. That of course was from the heavy night dew following the hot, cloudless day. But the real handicap this made for me I did not discover till I began to crawl along the wing. There, probably because of the more or less overhanging hill at the rear, the slates were green with slime, and in consequence my now wet left hand slipped whenever I put any weight on it. The first time this happened I nearly went over the parapet, for the slip brought my left shoulder down with a bump so hard that I overbalanced and would have slithered right over the parapet but for an instinctive straightening out of my legs which kept me low in the gutter. For all that, I believe I must have gone over but for the tire lever sticking out of my trouser pocket, which jammed against the parapet.

It was just as well that there could be no turning back, or I might have given up there and then. But to get back would have involved rising to my feet, in order to turn round, and the roof was one of those steeply pitched affairs characteristic of Scots baronial architecture. To stand erect there was beyond me, I had a dread of heights. My nightmares, whenever I have one, invariably put me on the edge of an abyss from which I look down on tree tops and the roofs of houses and people moving about like little black flies just before I topple over. So I just had to crawl on.

But presently I had something else than the height to think about. Bantok's room, it will be remembered, adjoined the box-room. Bantok, in fact, had been relegated to this otherwise unoccupied corner under the roof because none of the other servants cared to have him near them. And Bantok, it seemed, rather preferred to be by himself. He had all the idiosyncrasies of the colored man, and it flattered his vanity, I fancy, to be given a room apart from the servants' quarters. It was the roof of that room I had now to cross before I could reach the skylight in the box-room. By the time I reached the danger spot, however, practice had made me more expert in my movements, and with my attention now turned another way, I ceased to think of the height at which I was crawling, and in consequence my head got much steadier. I think that last fifteen feet or so of the gutter was traversed with less noise than a hopping sparrow would have made.

But having reached the skylight, I sat up to take breath and wipe the slime from my icy cold hands and rest my knees which now felt just raw flesh. From the lofty altitude on which I was perched the whole expanse of sky was within my view. As yet no sign of the moon appeared, and the stars, glittering as they do on a cold Northern night even in summer, showed there was not so much as a wisp of cloud on that vast expanse. It certainly would be clear enough once I got well away on the road.

Then, taking hold of my tire lever, I set to work on the skylight. I had chosen the lever for operating against the door should none of my keys fit; but a better implement for lifting a skylight could hardly be made. Inserting the sharpened and rounded end, I used the leverage afforded by its strength and began to prise gently. I was prepared to risk some noise in breaking the usually flimsy inside catch such windows have, but to my delight the edge lifted without a sound. The catch had not been fastened at all. And why should it, at such a height and with such an approach? In next to no time I had the skylight lying back against the slates, and after swinging my legs through the aperture, I dropped lightly onto the box-room floor.

Had Gracie been right about the box-room? Or rather had my inference from her story been right? The next quarter of an hour would show. Having without much splutter lit the end of candle I had carried in my other trouser pocket, I got to work. There were all types and sizes of cabin trunks and cases in that room. But I knew the ones into which there was no need to look. For it was very certain the little black box would not be kept in any trunk which belonged to anyone but Rhand, since that trunk might at some unforeseen moment be wanted by its owner. And it was quite a simple matter to identify Rhand's cases by the numerous labels with which they were bespattered. First of all I tried for one that was locked, and it was easy to feel the lock without having to displace or dig out any of the trunks from the piled up heap. But I did not find one. On all Rhand's cases the hasp was free.

This discovery irritated me slightly, for I had thought my idea astute enough to enable me to pick out the right trunk straight away. There was no help for it after that. I had to lift down or pull out every one of the eight which bore his name and open each in turn. And that job took a much longer time than might be supposed owing to the need for doing everything in silence. With laborious care I got out and explored seven of the cases, and when I got to the eighth I had reached that pitch of disgusted irritation where one says to oneself that the thing sought for would be sure to be in the very last possible place. But it wasn't. The last trunk was as empty as the first.

That discovery made me sit up and look around. My petty annoyance vanished. If the small black japanned box was not in one of Rhand's own cases, it might be in any one of all that big pile. But suddenly as the hopelessness of that search loomed up, there came the thought of a false bottom to one of Rhand's cases. He was just the man to use that sort of device. Confidently I began a minute re-examination of the eight cases. It took up, with the measurements I had to make, much more time; but in the end I was satisfied that not one of the eight had a false bottom to it. That brought me to the verge of despair. Had the inference I had drawn from Grace Turton's story been quite erroneous? Was the box not kept there at all?

As I looked around my thought was that it might still be there for all the chance I now had of getting my hands on it. Even if there had been time to explore them all, it was now evident that the stump of candle I had brought would not last the time. With the feeling of one sent out on a forlorn hope, I picked up the candle and went over once more to examine the stack of baggage. I would try Mrs. Rhand's

first, then Elliott's, and after that, if I got so far, anybody's. Of course
the first case bearing Mrs. Rhand's name that took my eye was one
at the very bottom of the pile. Almost savagely I began to lay hands
on the half dozen stacked above it when I noticed a peculiarity that
made me lay the trunk I had snatched up very gently on the floor.
Had I seen aright? Going down on my knees I examined the end of
that brown case bearing Mrs. Rhand's name. Yes, I was right. It was
far from being so inaccessible as it seemed. For the trunks on each
side and on its top were so built up as not actually to rest upon it at
all. It looked as if it could be pulled out without disturbing any of
them. It looked like it. Gingerly I slipped my fingers into the heavy
leather hand-hold and pulled. The moment it began to move I knew
I had found the place where the black box lay hidden.

And this time I was right. As soon as I got the lid up and my hand
went down to touch a cold hard, smooth surface, I knew that, here
and at last, I had come to the end of my search.

CHAPTER XVI

It was while I was squatting on the floor, almost lovingly handling the little box on my knees, that I noticed the patch of light high up on the door. The box was locked and I was casting a look about me to see where I had put the tire lever. I had been considering what an awkward bit of baggage that box would make for a man clad only in shirt and trousers who had to crawl his way along a roof. The tire lever would burst it open all right, but certainly not without a good deal of noise. It would be safer to perform that operation on the roof. If overheard, it would be taken as some external night noise belonging to the outside world. In that small room it would be quite another matter. But there was a certain danger of losing the contents if the box were violently burst open out there in the dark.

Then it was I noticed the light at the top of the door which told me how much longer the hunt had taken than I had bargained for. The moon had risen, and risen high enough to enter by the skylight and lay a distorted square of light half on the ceiling and half on the door. That set me on the move for the return journey. With the help of a big trunk I was out on the roof again with my tire lever and the box. And I didn't dally over breaking the box open. Jamming it sideways against the parapet, and with one foot on either side of the lock, I inserted the lever under the edge of the lid and pulled with both hands. The lid gave at once, but the noise in the middle of that death-like silence seemed terrific—a rending of metal that ended in a loud report. It started off an echo that seemed to keep rebounding from the steep roof to the face of the hill behind and back again.

Hastily and blindly I stuffed the contents of the box into both my trouser pockets and moved off back along the gutter.

I had not gone far, however, before a noise from the box-room made me stop, and looking back round my shoulder, I saw a shaft of light rising from the skylight. Someone had entered the box-room with a light. I hung on without movement for a little. It could only be Bantok who had entered. No one else slept close enough to get there so quickly after the noise I had made with that infernal box. And he would see instantly that the booty had been taken. But as I had shut down the skylight window when I left, there was just a chance that in his haste he would think I had come and gone by the door. Anyhow, I breathed a fervent prayer that he would, for I had no fancy for a tussle with Bantok just there.

When the window crashed upward and back against the slates I knew my hopes were vain. To say I was afraid is to flatter me. I was for the moment rendered motionless with fear. I knew he would see me quite plainly in the moonlight, and see me he did the moment his head and shoulders came through the aperture. I could myself see even his teeth when he grinned with delight to see me so close. With a curious feeling of fascination I watched his black torso rise in sight as he heaved himself up. He was quite naked. It was whispered among the servants that he slept like that. But in his hand and somewhat hindering him as he got his knee on the sill, he held the Zulu assegai, and its long blade glittered wickedly in the moonlight.

I believe it was the sight of that blade that set me scurrying like blazes along the gutter again. I had been polishing the weapon that very morning and I knew how infernally sharp it was.

At the start I had the advantage of Bantok, for I had been that way before and knew how to adapt myself to the conditions. I think too he soon found his nakedness a handicap, for his bare knees must have done some slipping on the greasy leaden gutter. But I heard him coming on. And then he must have seen and copied the style of moving which I had found to be best, for before I had reached the corner where the wing of the roof joined the main front, I knew from the noise that he was catching me up.

It was a ghastly feeling to know the gap between us was closing up. I was in a hopeless position, quite defenseless, crawling on like that with him coming up behind me. A distinct sensation developed in my ankles, as I foresaw the moment when that long black arm would stretch out, and I wondered which of them would first feel the clutch. That sent me forging ahead faster than ever. But I had to slow down where the two roofs met and made a very ticklish corner, as I knew. One had to get off the leads there and almost slide over the angle on the slates from the one roof to the other. I prayed he would take it too fast and pay the certain penalty in an eighty-foot drop on to the terrace below. But he didn't. The astute devil must have watched to see how I negotiated that cursed angle, for he was still coming on. My one hope now was to reach the staircase man-hole on to the roof far enough ahead to pull away the ladder I had left there.

For I did not believe that even Bantok would risk that drop to the floor. Inside the house it would be quite too dark for him to calculate the depth he would have to drop, and the fact that anyone dropping straight down must land perilously near the well of the staircase, would almost certainly stop such an attempt. And apparently Ban-tok knew this. For just as I got near the manhole in the roof, I was surprised by a silence which told me he had stopped. The next instant something sharp ran along my right shoulder, and before I felt any pain I saw the assegai rattle clumsily on the slates ahead of me and then skid sideways into the gutter. He must have got upon his knees to make the throw. But either he had not the skill of his fore-fathers with that weapon, or the awkwardness of his attitude put his eye out, for he had almost missed me.

Having now not much more than the length of the weapon to go, I took it with me as I went through the open manhole, and just sim-ply slid down the ladder on to the landing. And my feet were not well on the floor before I pulled the ladder clear. Then I stood watching the oblong of sky above my head. Almost at once it was darkened by the head and shoulders of Bantok. He was looking down, trying to see me, and to calculate the depth of the drop. I knew it was too dark for him to do either. For, as in the box-room, the moon was not yet high enough to do more than lay a diagonal square of light on the wall of the staircase opposite me. And even this he himself obscured by his own head and shoulders.

So we stayed for quite a time, I without movement, while his head went this way and that, his eyes striving to pierce the interior blackness. I felt the blood trickling warmly down under my shirt from the wound on my shoulder, but I held the weapon in my own hands now, and regaining my breath by degrees, felt quite master of the situation.

But I had to know just how Bantok would decide to face it. And at last, after what seemed an eternity, although it could not have been more than a minute, he made up his mind. He was going to risk that drop into the darkness. The head disappeared but was instantly replaced by a pair of legs which began to lower themselves through the opening. I imagine he made sure I had gone. And it was for that exactly that I had kept quiet. But I admit his pluck amazed me. He must have gone raving mad with hate to take the risk of such a fall, for it was just about an even chance that he would come down on the wrong side of the banister and go crashing to certain death. Not that I minded if he did. Still, he might land close to where I stood without much damage, and though I did not think so, I could not be sure. That is why I stopped him. And it was an almost comically easy thing to do. Just as his legs began to swing, I let off a little cough into which I put a great deal of significance. That was enough for the good Bantok. He might not know the well of the staircase yawned below his feet: he did know I had his weapon. And gladly would I have hastened his retreat by a prod or two on his hinder parts, but the height was much too great; and, in any case, he got back nimbly enough.

As soon as I saw the overhead square of light clear of him, I slipped quickly down the stairs and made for my room, recklessly, at the double, even when passing all the bedroom doors.

It can be imagined how hardly I was pressed for time. I had to get back to my room and change, since I could not take the road in the state to which I was now reduced. And it was exactly this chance to change and get the parcel of food I had prepared, that I had won by that few minutes' watch on Bantok at the top of the stairs. Had I allowed him to take that risk of a broken neck I would have been compelled to take to the road straight away, in shirt and trousers. Now, having forced him to retrace his way back over the roofs and in by the box-room whence he came, I had gained—well—ten minutes for certain. And as soon as I saw my condition in the light of my room I fully recognized how precious these ten minutes were. Ten yards in daylight would have made me a marked man. My shirt was sticky with green slime and blood, and the trousers were in rags with my raw and bleeding knees visible through the tears.

But I didn't stop to wash and dress then. Tumbling on a fresh shirt and jumping into the trousers of my best suit, whipping on waistcoat and jacket and stuffing one pocket with my packet of sand-wiches and the other with the bundle of letters for which I had risked so much, I cleared out, shoes in hand. But just in time I had the fore-sight to lock my door and pocket the key. A locked door would keep Bantok guessing when he had worked his way round to this wing. He might even sit down to watch it for the remainder of the night. At the end of the passage I stopped for a moment, straining my ears. Everything was still, so still that had I heard the ticking of a clock I might have taken it for the distant sound of running feet. But the house was as quiet as the grave and almost as dark.

Stealing further on, I reached the end of the passage, slid the window up, squeezed through and dropped on to the soft earth of the flower bed underneath.

CHAPTER XVII

I remember being rather pleased with myself as I stepped out of that flower bed. So far things had gone according to plan. For though that encounter with Bantok on the roof had not been anticipated, still I had got clear away with the swag safe in my pocket. The rest should go like clock-work. So I was thinking as I shoved my feet into hurriedly laced-up shoes, and ran for the wood-shed where the young forester kept the bicycle I meant to borrow.

Everything seemed motionless and asleep; all soft moonlight and sharply cut shadows, the great house itself, as I rounded the corner, silhouetted in one great black mass on the hillside against which it stood. On such a night the road over the moors and up the hills would lie like a white ribbon ahead of me. On such a road I would be miles away before it was discovered I had left the house. Yes, and even when that happened, and the chase was taken up, I could certainly see the car in time to hide myself and the cycle in the gorse or heather by the roadside till they had passed.

In my exhilaration I laughed softly as I ran, foreseeing what a game of hide and seek might be played along the moorland road before morning. Even if they ran the car without lights they could not keep the engine noiseless, and on these empty moors the beat of an engine carried for miles. So, in fancy I saw myself hiding till the car passed, then remounting and following till I heard them returning, and then myself getting clear away. I simply did not mind how often they ran up and down the road, for cover abounded on it, and I knew there would always be time for me to hear them before they could see me.

But a check was put to this frolicsome fancy when I reached the wood-shed; there was no bicycle there. It had gone; removed by its owner, no doubt. But when I realized its absence I could not have cursed with more vindictive heartiness had the bicycle been mine and not his. I felt wronged, aggrieved, and quite at a loss about my next move till I saw a window in the house leap into light. That brought me to my senses. I ran out of the wood-shed, along the back of the house in the shadows till I reached a point where I could scramble up the hill and take cover among the trees. To reach the shelter of the trees one had to climb a slope on which there was nothing but the rough, white-bleached grass through which here and there the hill projected its ribs of dark mossy stone.

Clutching at the tufts of grass and digging in my toes, I was doing quite well when a shot rang out behind me. A second report followed before I could turn, and almost before I could see from where the firing came a third shot brought me down. Indeed, it did more than that: it almost brought me back to the house. For it got me on the left leg which doubled up under me so that, losing my balance, I went rolling down, to end up where my climb had started. But nothing could have served me better, for before I was hit I saw the shots were being fired by a man who was leaning as far as he could out of a second-floor window, and a yard or two of downward rolling took me out of his sight. He must have begun his fusillade just too soon; in fact as soon as I had come into view. With the moon straight in my eyes I could not see who fired; but it wasn't Bantok—unless indeed Bantok had just gone to put on a suit of nice clean pyjamas.

But that I thought of afterwards. At the moment when I bumped down to the gravel my one thought was to get away. I did not even think about my wound beyond one flash of wonder as to whether it would let me run. But I soon discovered it would not—not, at least, as I wanted to then! It stung like hell just above the ankle, but I could feel no warm flow of blood as I had earlier on when Bantok sent his spear ploughing across my shoulder.

So in less time than it takes to tell, I was making along the end of the house for the face of the terrace which I reached after doing a fine variety of steps, from a hobbling run to a hop and skip and the slower "dot and carry one" style of the lame duck. Then, more or less sliding down the face of the terrace, I reached the shelter of the bushes which lined the river bank. There I rested to draw breath, to have a look at my leg, and to decide on my next move.

A wound on the leg was a serious matter. To one in my situation a hit almost anywhere else would have been less deadly. But on pulling down my hose I was amazed to find no puncture. I could not understand it, for my leg felt as if it had been drilled right through by something not smaller than half a crown. It was thick-witted of me, I suppose, not to see at once that I had been hit by a bullet which had ricocheted off a boulder. But when I did see that I plucked up spirit again. That was a bit of good luck long overdue. All the same, as I soon discovered, there would be no long trek for me that night. And, as I should certainly be discovered by daylight if I remained there among the bushes, I was steeling myself to hobble on a mile or so to lie in the woods, when I thought of the McPhees. Would they shelter me? Very little reflection let me see I had no other hope. I could not get away that night. And whoever fired that shot at me knew I had been hit. The probability was, indeed, that I had been able to reach those bushes only because I had first been looked for where I came down. Knowing me to be wounded, it was around there, and the out-houses and sheds of the back premises which they would scour for me first.

But the circle of search would widen presently, and then I would be for it if I were taken there. That would be to make it easy for them. A day or two later a body with a bruise on the head from contact with a rock, would be found in the river. Though why in heaven's name they should consider it necessary to put me out of the way I could not imagine. Biddulph had said that if caught I might expect six months' jail for it. And I thought it more than enough! It made me both angry and perplexed to think of the danger to which I was now exposed. In fact I felt rather like a small boy who was being grossly over-punished for a minor offence. And like the small boy I wanted to hit back and damn the consequences. But, luckily for myself, I did exactly what the boy does on these occasions. I resisted the temptation and was content to bide my time.

As I hobbled along the river bed, looking for a good place to cross, the snapping of twigs further back hinted that my move had not been a single minute too soon. The river fortunately was slow, and yet had enough water running among the stones to drown any noise I made in wading across. Once across I was in the shadowed side of the glen, with the dark firs for cover and the McPhees' encampment only a step or two along the road.

The quarry looked as black as a cave when at last I reached the entrance. At first I could not even discern the tents, and I might have thought them gone but for seeing the dull red embers of the dying fire. It must then have been something after three o'clock. As I stepped gingerly over the ruts at the entrance, my approach was notified by a low growl from the dog, who had seen me before I could see him. He had been asleep by the fire, and when his warning did not stop me, he jumped up and began to bark in a sudden rage that simply rent the still night with fury.

I pulled up short, feeling, as the dog began to circle round me, like a shrinking man who has been thrust unexpectedly into public notice, appalled to think of the distance that rending noise must be carrying.

"For God's sake stop him," I cried.

A shout came in reply.

"Bran, ye brute, lie down, will you!"

Something heavy hurtled past me and hit the dog somewhere and drove him away from me, but merely changing his barking into a higher pitched yelping of vastly increased traveling power.

"Who's there?" old McPhee challenged me.

He was standing outside the largest tent beside the upturned cart.

"I've got into trouble," I said, getting over to him.

"Have you so? That's bad," he said, peering at me.

"As bad as it can be. They were on my heels just now. And that dog will tell them just where I am."

He whistled softly to the dog, which ceased yelping and came over to lick his hand. But my fear was that the harm had already been done. The one remaining chance for me was to get a yard or two into the wood above the quarry.

"You won't tell them you've seen me?" I begged.

"Is it hurt you are?" he questioned, as I began to hobble off.

"I'd be far from here now if I wasn't," I said, in quick bitterness, noting that he had given no promise of silence.

In the next breath something caught my eye which indicated that such a promise would now be useless. For out through the quarry's narrow entrance I saw the road and the foliage of the pines which overhung it, brilliantly lit up by the head-lights of an approaching car. McPhee coming over, quickly took my arm.

"Come in here. We'll hide you so they'll not get you," he said in quite a matter of fact way. He had asked no question as to what the trouble was or who sought me. And from that I gathered the McPhees were not unfamiliar with trouble themselves. They knew, like other gentry of the road, what it was to have authority on their heels, and like all who suffer in that way, their sympathy went to the law breaker and not to the law. He lifted the flap of the tent.

"Go you in there and lie down," he said, pushing me inside.

It was pitch dark inside. When I moved my head brushed against the tent. I got down on my hands and knees and felt about till I touched something.

"Go you over to the other side," a woman whispered. "There's his own bed there."

I had never before spoken to old Mrs. McPhee. On the few brief visits I had made to their camp she was either away on her rounds of the outlying cottages or busy at her own domestic concerns. With a murmured apology I crept across and found the bed, no more than a waterproof sheet on the ground and a blanket or two. I covered myself with the blankets just as I heard the car pull up. In another second came the sound of several feet, more or less stumbling on the rough track. The dog began to bark again.

"Call off that dog or I'll shoot," came a voice I recognized as Elliott's.

"Bran, ye devil, be quiet," McPhee shouted angrily. The dog, growling dislike, seemed to move round to its master as the others came up.

"Can't think what's got him at all, barking at nothing the way he's been this night," McPhee explained.

"At nothing, eh? We're not so sure of that," came crisply from Rhand.

"Ask your honor's pardon for that word. But the dog's not used to seeing gentry folk come here, nor anybody at this hour of the night," McPhee explained.

"A man came in here not ten minutes ago," Rhand declared. "We want him and we're going to get him."

Elliott's voice joined in contemptuously.

"Of course that's why your dog barked. Dogs don't bark at nothing."

"Dogs have a custom of barking at the moon," McPhee said mildly.

"Which isn't in sight from here," Rhand snapped. "Don't you try and shield the man or it will be the worse for you. We're going to search every damned hole and corner till we get him."

"Search away," McPhee replied. "He might have slipped in for all I know. It was the dog barking that got me from my bed."

There came a murmur of voices among them, too low for me to catch what passed, but apparently Bantok was sent to scour the quarry, for I heard his padding feet near the tent, and then Elliott said he would watch the entrance. Evidently Rhand remained to keep an eye on McPhee.

"Poachers are very plentiful when it gets so close to the Twelfth, your honor," the old man remarked.

"Are they?" Rhand replied in a tone suggesting that his real attention was elsewhere engaged.

"They're out every night just now."

A grunt from Rhand.

"Is that where your son is?"

McPhee laughed.

"Och, your honor, no. More likely it's some lass. That's the kind of game a young fellow like him goes after. Now this poacher you're after—"

"He's wanted for theft, not poaching," Rhand cut in.

"O-h, theft!" McPhee's voice came in a tone of dismay, almost of disgust. Then there was silence. I lay quaking more with indignation than fright. That McPhee should not consider poaching a form of theft was perhaps natural enough; but that Rhand should get his sympathy, as he evidently had, by branding one who was acting in the interests of his country as a thief, that got me on the raw. Almost at once, however, I heard sounds of routing about that warned me

Bantok's search was drawing nearer. Rhand called out to him to look in this other tent.

"I been there. Nobody there, baas," Bantok called back, in his guttural voice that brought Elliott away from his post. They seemed to be conferring together. McPhee's continued silence kept me on edge. I doubted whether, since hearing my crime, he cared if they found me or not.

"Well," Elliott said, "take a look into that other tent just to make sure."

Then I thought my number was up. McPhee's voice came at last and very emphatically.

"You can't go in there. My wife's asleep in there."

Someone called to shove him out of the way, but he stood firm.

"He can't be there. It's myself came out when Bran started barking, and I have not been further away than where I am since then," he protested. "You can't break in on her like this."

"Break in!" Rhand laughed.

McPhee, however, like every vagrant, was well up in such law as touched his own life.

"It's no different from the castle itself," he cried warmly. "Only the police have the right, and then only if they have a warrant."

"Look here," Elliott said, "you know this man we want. For all we know you may be in it too. You've been seen talking to him."

"What of that? Haven't I been seen talking to Sir Charles himself? If it was him you were after, would you be coming here to look for him in my wife's bed? It's losing your time you are," he laughed.

"What do you mean by that?" Elliott inquired.

"Why, isn't it clear enough now you know he's not here? The dog barked when he heard the man passing the mouth of the quarry. He'll be half way to Duich by now."

They appeared to consider this. Finally Elliott admitted the possibility.

"You can't have hit him at all," he suggested.

"I brought him down," Rhand asserted.

"With fright or surprise, perhaps. Come, let's hop off."

I heard their feet, hurrying away. Then the engine began to beat and presently its throbbing faded out in the distance.

"It's safe you are now," the woman whispered across to me.

"I can hardly walk," I said, my mind on my next move.

"We'll see to that when himself comes in," she reassured me.

Himself seemed in no hurry. I heard him call the dog and walk away.

"He's seeing to it that none of them stayed behind. If there is, Bran will find him," she explained.

Half an hour later I was in the other tent and McPhee, by the aid of a lighted candle, was attending to my damaged ankle. Apart from the bruise caused by the ricocheting bullet, it appeared that I had overstrained a ligament by keeping my foot in a stiff position while blundering among the boulders in the river. McPhee shook his head when he saw the swelling.

"That's bad for you, and for us as well," he said.

"You mean they'll come back?"

"Tomorrow if not tonight," he replied. "They only half believed what I said."

He got busy with a cold-water compress on my ankle. His tone was not cordial; though he handled my foot gently enough. After watching him for a time I had to speak.

"You seemed to have believed all they said," I burst out.

He stopped his work to look up at me and ask what I meant.

"They told you I was wanted for theft, did they not? Yes, well now, it's only my word against theirs, unless you heard the shots fired," I added.

He sat back to consider.

"I heard some shooting a little while before you came here. I noticed it because I took it for poachers and I was thinking they were bold fellows to be at their work so near to the house itself."

On that I told him the shots were fired from the house itself, and that I myself had been the game fired at. Pulling away the compress I showed him the circular bruise in the center of the swelling, and told him that it came not through my hitting my leg against a rock but from a bullet which glanced off a rock and then hit me.

"You don't shoot a man for theft," I declared, seeing the horror that had overspread his face as I spoke.

"No," he agreed, "it must be something worse than that, God help us."

After a moment I saw nothing for it but to take him into my confidence and tell him just as much of the story as he could follow. The resolute way in which he had stood by me, even when he supposed me to be guilty of the kind of theft he did not approve, made me sure he was safe. And if there was any risk it was a risk I was forced to take, since it was now almost a certainty that without the help of the McPhees I could not hope to get away.

The story was one which it was easy to make impressive. And McPhee listened open-mouthed and still on his knees beside me while I told him of my secret service work and of how I had been sent there to get possession of documents wanted by the Government in the interests of a British Colony. Having at the risk of my life succeeded in finding out where the letters were concealed, and got possession of them, it was his duty and the duty of every honest citizen to do everything possible to assist me.

It made quite a good story. In fact in the act of rolling it off I was struck with it myself; and as I did not suppose McPhee did much in the way of reading romances, it must have been something absolutely new to him. But though the old fellow liked the story as a story, he was soon glowing with pride and something like awe to find himself working in the interests of the State. And he had not quite recovered before young McPhee slipped into the tent. Murdo had approached unheard and the astute Bran had himself been silent. Murdo revealed no surprise at sight of me, as he laid down some half dozen good-sized trout he had taken on night line in the loch.

"I knew something was up when I saw Bran posted out bye," he said.

A quick interchange of what seemed questions and answers in the Gaelic tongue followed, and I gathered that Donald was re-telling my story. At least so I judged from the round-eyed wonder with which the young piper listened. Finally he turned to me.

"It's true what my father says. You are not safe here beyond another hour," he nodded gravely.

I indicated the foot on which the old man had resumed operations. Another rapid interchange of Gaelic followed, and while waiting, I drew out from my pocket the packet of letters and papers which I had got at the risk of my life. Not till then had there been a chance to examine them, and a shabby enough lot they appeared for which to hazard one's life. In all there were five letters and an assortment of odd papers, most of which appeared to be in code. The letters were all in envelopes addressed to Lady Wridgley. On looking up I found both the McPhees had stopped talking to stare at the papers in my hands.

"If only these were safe," I said. "Hidden till my foot is better."

"Och, that's easy. We have a place where we hide things," Murdo said. "It's where to hide yourself we were talking about."

"This comes first," I said, holding up the packet.

Father and son exchanged a glance. At a nod Murdo went across and picking up his bagpipes handed them over to the old man. With a knife he slit the sewing of the bag's tartan covering.

"Here," he said with a chuckle, "is where we hide our things, and for all the place has been searched, there's never a policeman yet has had thought of it."

I handed over my packet in complete confidence, and when it was inserted between the outer tartan covering and the inner lining, McPhee, with a needle and thread he produced from somewhere under his armpit, sewed the opening up once more.

"You see," he slyly explained, "it's only on nights like this and when there's a loch nearby that Murdo and his pipes get parted."

But though the McPhees had found the right place to conceal the letters, it was I who thought of the right place to get myself concealed. That was after the old man had scratched his head for quite a time over the problem. It was when my eye fell on the trout, silvery in the candlelight, that the inspiration came to me.

"If only I could get to the island. It's the very last place they would think of looking for me," I said.

Both their heads went up at that.

"It's true you would spy anyone coming at ye from there," Murdo said. "There'd be no call for ye to be always on the watch, as ye would when lying among trees."

"Yes," old McPhee admitted, "and with a little meat you could stop safe there till your leg's rested."

But besides all that I knew other reasons that made the island the place for me. Just because they knew I had seen the newly-made grave there—which I now thought *might* have been intended for me—I knew the island to be the last place they would think of. And that alone made it as safe for me as the bagpipes were for the letters. If only I could get there! Murdo looked at his father.

"I've carried heavier than him," he said.

"That thought came to me too. But it's more than a mile it is."

"I'm about twelve stone," I said hastily. They took no notice of me.

"There'd be no cause for hurry if we kept to the woods and never touched the road," Murdo said.

"Well, he can't stop here. It's my belief they'll call in the lot of the Duich men."

I knew what he meant. These Duich men were fishermen from the village seven miles to the west, who had been engaged to beat up the game. They were accustomed to do such work for the shooting tenant of Glengyle, but would probably enjoy a man hunt best of all.

Soon after that, mounted on Murdo's back, I was well away among the woods. The going was not so difficult as I had expected from the steepness of the ground, for Murdo knew how to utilize the rabbit runs that crossed the slope, and had there been a little more light our progress would have been astonishing. But the sunrise was not due till well after five o'clock and we dared not wait, since daylight must not catch us on the open waters of the loch. Knowing the boathouse to be locked up I had wondered how I was to get across to the island, and once when I was off Murdo's back to give him a rest, I put the question.

"Oh man," he said, laughing between heavy breaths, "ever since the Flood the McPhees have taken care to have a boat of their own."

Later, when we reached the foot of the loch and still kept on among the woods fringing its south side, I knew the McPhees must have a boat, since the Glengyle boat-house stood a little way along the northern shore. Stops for breath became more frequent and the ground more difficult on account of the steepness of the slope above the loch. I wondered how much further the boat could be, for we were almost abreast of the narrow strip of water separating the

island from the southern shore. It was then, after we had been resting for what seemed a very long time, I put the question.

"We're there," he replied.

But there was no boat that I could see. When I said so his answer
was that it was not meant to be seen. Murdo, I fancy, was so pleased
with his achievement that he enjoyed seeing me at a loss. And I was
at a loss, not only about the boat but as to why we should rest so long
when he had to carry me no further. And I myself was so satisfied
with his achievement that I did not bother him with further questions for quite a time, till, in fact, I became afraid we must be caught
by daylight where we sat.

"What are we waiting for?" I asked in the end.

"Maybe you'll notice it's growing darker," he replied.

It was quite true. I had been too impatient to notice that or anything else.

"There's just a wee while, a matter of half an hour maybe, after
the moon goes in behind Ben Va'ar and afore sunrise."

So, on the bank about the loch, with the penetrating scent of the
dewy pines and the heavier earth smell about us, we sat and waited
for that half hour of darkness.

CHAPTER XVIII

The boat which Murdo pulled out from the hazel bush might well have been in the possession of his clan since the Flood. Indeed, it might have been modelled on the Ark itself. For it was nothing but a square wooden box framed with four pieces of heavy timber to keep it stable in the water. And there was certainly not room for both of us in it. Even in the darkness that had now fallen Murdo perceived my doubts.

"I'll show you how she works," he said, and with a rudely shaped oar he embarked and pushed off. Then on hands and knees, he used the oar in the manner of one paddling a canoe, with results which settled my qualms. After all, I had not much more than a hundred yards of water to cross. He saw my doubts were satisfied.

"And after all," he said, "it's no' that far to swim. I've done it often."

So I didn't tell him the distance was far beyond me—in fresh water hopelessly beyond me.

"It's leaving you alone on the island I dinna like," he went on. "I'll tell you what. I'll be up here tomorrow night after a fish or two. Then you'll be able to signal me."

When I inquired how, he put his fingers to his mouth and startled me with a perfect imitation of a hooting owl. So, as this was beyond my power to imitate, we fixed it up that if circumstances did not force me to leave the island before then, I was to show a light when I heard his cry.

Then I took over his ark, and after he had handed in the provisions they had got together for me, I pushed off.

It is not likely I shall ever forget that night on the loch. I had no sensation of fear, either from the loch or from my enemies. In fact, once out a little way, the first sensation I had was that of being in complete safety. But after that and when, having gone far enough to get fatigued from using an oar in such an attitude, I stopped for a rest, quite a strange feeling followed.

I must have been about half-way across. Anyhow I could see almost nothing on either hand beyond a vast darkness, and within a foot or two of me the clear black ripples of the water. And not a sound reached me except the low lapping of the water on the sides of my primitive canoe. It made the loneliest moment in all my life. Kneeling in that box in the midst of these waters, for one queer moment I looked around and knew what the first man must have felt—or the last. Anyhow, it frightened me enough to set me off again, and ere long the mass of the island loomed up ahead. I knew where I wanted to come ashore, and pushed round to the overhanging clump of hazel bushes I remembered. There, having so disposed of the branches as to cover my ferry boat, I crept in among them to hide myself, and in a second or two, half dead with fatigue and reaction, fell fast asleep.

It was broad daylight when I awoke. I had no means of telling the time, but lying on my back and looking up through the screen of translucent green leaves, I saw it was still early, the sun not yet overhead. My first concern was with my foot. As the bandages had worked rather slack I removed them, and then unexpectedly discovered that the reason for the slackness was a distinct reduction in the swelling.

After that discovery I slid down the bank and sat with my foot in the water, taking care, however, to keep still well screened by the bushes which hid my boat. And had I had anything to smoke I might have been almost happy for hours like that. After keeping my foot submerged in the shadowed water for perhaps an hour, at any rate till I began to feel cold myself, I replaced the bandages, and while eating some of my own rather stale sandwiches, began to consider how I would put in the day. For, well as my foot had done, I knew there was no question of putting any weight on it yet. So, as I was still in arrears with sleep, and had the fact borne in on me in the usual way, I decided I must find a warmer place than the damp turf among the bushes on which I had tumbled.

The trouble was that a warmer place would of necessity be a more exposed place. But it was still very early and I was on the side of the island not open to view from the road on the northern shore. Eventually I decided that I could crawl up towards the southern wall of the castle and try for a quiet sun-lit corner among the ruins. However, as I got among them I came on something that gave me quite another notion. To be frank, though there were many nice corners which promised to be sun-baked presently, I did not like the idea of lying there, in what I knew would be a dead sleep, fully exposed and deaf to the approach of anyone who might chance to land. Then it was I saw the ladder. I knew that ladder. It was not exactly where I had thrown it down, for it had been lowered since I drew it out of the dungeon, lowered by someone who had come to Bantok's rescue.

It was my turn once again with that ladder. Not that I proposed to lower myself into that sinister place. I was going higher, not lower. That's where my notion came in. But I owed it to seeing the ladder there. The very safe place needed was, I saw, the one remaining segment of the outer battlemented wall. Of the stone platform behind the battlement there remained only a section about ten feet long. It was to this I climbed with the help of the ladder. To my joy I found that I could stretch myself on the platform, the stones of which were already warm with the sun, and completely concealed by the parapet from being seen by anyone below, go to sleep in perfect security. And that is what I did, when I had pulled the ladder up after me.

When I awoke again it was with a start, and I thought I had only been asleep for a few minutes. But a glance at the sun showed me my sleep must have lasted many hours. The next thing I noticed was a small stone lying on my chest. How had that got there? I puzzled drowsily over the question. But not for long. My drowsiness vanished as if by a sudden gust of wind the next instant when a second stone struck me smartly. Someone down below was throwing the stones. How I resisted the first quick impulse to look over the parapet I do not know. When it passed I lay still and listened.

For a long time nothing happened. But just as I was beginning to breathe once more my eye was caught by a tree, a young chestnut, which stood well outside the old wall. One of its branches seemed to be blown about by a violent squall from which I was sheltered. Then

the black face of Bantok appeared among the foliage. He saw me at
once and let off a hoarse shout of triumph.

"Better come down now," a voice called quietly from below.

So Rhand was also there! I lay prostrate, motionless, quite inca-
pable of doing anything except wonder how in heaven's name they
had found me. But I wasn't allowed to indulge in any prolonged
meditation on that or any other subject. A rude interruption in the
form of a shot rang out, and a bullet sent some of the ancient mortar flying quite close to my head. Then another flattened itself out
against the parapet before it dropped on to my shoulder. Bantok was
enjoying himself in his tree. He was in a position to rake me with
bullets, for the tree overtopped the wall, and in spite of his precari-
ous foothold his shooting had been good. I crawled to the edge and
looked over. Rhand had a nasty looking blue automatic in his hand.
A decision was easy.

"All right," I said. "I'll come down."

"Quick about it then," he snapped.

I don't think he could complain about my speed. As hurriedly
as if my life depended on it—as indeed at that moment I thought
it did—I slipped the ladder down and was myself on the ground in
a trice. Then, as naturally as I could, I lifted the ladder away from
the wall, got it first on the balance, but just as I was about to swing
it round he saw my intention. Stepping out of range he lifted his
weapon.

"Drop it," he cried. "Drop it, damn you."

I let it fall. And with it went what looked like my best chance.
A poor enough chance it might have been; but if only I could have
knocked him off his feet and got possession of his gun, I'd have
risked an exchange with Bantok, good shot though he had shown
himself to be.

Now we stood looking at each other, waiting for his black hench-
man to get off his perch. I noticed he did not order me to put up my
hands, or follow any of the routine that seems to be observed in such
situations. I suppose he knew that I had no weapon or I'd never have
tried that clumsy trick with the ladder.

Then Bantok came bounding round the corner, eager to slake his
thirst for vengeance. In what gods he believed I do not know, but

he must have thought they were showing their best form in putting me under his thumb in that particular spot.

Rhand, finger on trigger, began by ordering me to back till I found myself right in the angle formed by the west and south walls. With the two facing me in that position there was no hope, even had I been fit, of making bolt and chancing it. But knowing what was coming next, I did not despair.

"And now," said Rhand, "now, my friend, disgorge."

It was exactly the sort of moment I had foreseen before I handed over the letters to young McPhee. My hands went behind my back and stayed there.

"Quick now, hand them over. This is no time for dallying," he cried.

"I have nothing to hand over," I said

He did dally a bit though. For a few seconds I saw from the way he eyed me that he wondered which would be more convenient: to shoot me first and search me afterwards, or to search me first and shoot me afterwards. And for those few seconds I stood just stiff with fear. It would be so easy for them. With that ready-made grave not twenty yards away, the temptation to provide it with an occupant must be overwhelming. I could see his finger toying with the trigger.

"You don't think me such a fool as to have them on me," I said.

That decided him. His arm came down.

"That I don't know yet. Only that you were fool enough to get caught," he said. At his nod Bantok advanced to search me. I held out my bandaged foot.

"But for the bullet in that," I said, "they'd be in London now."

Meanwhile Bantok had begun to feel about me for the bundle of letters. He felt the packet of sandwiches almost at once and, grinning with malice, drew it out and held it up in triumph. Rhand was wary and kept his distance, gun still at the ready.

"Count them," he ordered. "There ought to be five."

"There ought to be six," I said. "I had eight and I've only eaten two."

With an oath the six sandwiches were flung against the wall, to scatter and disappear among a bed of nettles. After that it became more of an attack on me than a search. I fell to the ground and while prostrate, Bantok astride my body soon had his filthy fingers all over me. Of course he discovered the four pounds pinned in the waistcoat pocket, very promptly transferring them to his own. Even my shoes were removed and examined. But I took good care to cry out and writhe a lot when the left one was pulled off.

When in the end Rhand was satisfied the documents were not on me, I fancy he was glad he had not shot me first and searched afterwards. I sat up, nursing my injured foot, while he and Bantok conferred together. After a little Rhand, watch in hand, came over to me, leaving Bantok squatting on the turf, nursing his pistol.

"You've got three minutes to say where they're hidden," he said, for all the world as if he was only giving me a friendly warning that I'd only got three minutes left to catch a train.

"I can't tell you that," I said.

There was a pause.

"One," said Rhand.

"I was sent here to get the documents."

With his eyes on the watch he had no comment to make. I took a glance around, looking for help from any quarter. But I only saw a blue sky empty of everything save the white clouds whose lower edges were gilded by the setting sun, and down below within the four ruined, weather-worn walls, there was only Bantok, squatted on the fresh green turf, with his chin resting on his updrawn knees, and eyes glittering watchfully.

"Two," Rhand counted.

"Hang it all, I was only doing my duty," I blurted out.

But to be quite open, I really was in a fine state of funk at that moment. I had banked on being fairly safe when I got the things hidden by young Murdo. My argument was that Rhand was too clever and cool-headed a rascal to sacrifice his own interests to gratify his passion for mere vengeance. But now I wasn't so sure. And it was this uncertainty which made the third minute just hell. Had it lasted two seconds longer I think I would have given way. But just in what must have been the last split second Bantok intervened.

"Ba'as," he called softly.

That broke the tension somehow. Rhand had not said what he would do at the three minutes' end. But when he went over in answer to Bantok's call I saw my gamble had come right: he was not prepared to bump me off and lose the documents. He wanted to get them back too much. Afterwards—yes! But not till then.

I fancy they were at their wits' end about what to do next. Bantok, to judge by his gesticulations, was quite fertile in the way of suggestions. It was impossible to overhear what they were. And perhaps that was just as well, since even Rhand appeared to shrink from them. But of course Rhand wanted to get the papers, while Bantok was merely out after blood. And when at last Rhand got up, it was from the disappointment on Bantok's face that I drew a crumb of hope for myself.

"I'm going to be kind to you," Rhand announced.

"Thank you," I said.

"We're going to leave you here tonight in the hope you'll think better of it by tomorrow. It will be quite safe for me to do that, of course."

"I suppose so," I said, hope dawning again. "Certainly it will, after we've taken away that cockle shell you crossed in."

He laughed when he saw how my face fell. "You didn't think we were such fools as not to ask ourselves how you got here," he said reproachfully. "We'll take away the ladder too," he went on.

"The ladder!" I said, surprised.

"Why yes, the ladder," he repeated. "The ladder which gave you away to us. It was so prominent, sticking over the edge of the parapet, it told us someone was up there out of sight. And if by a long chance anyone else should visit this lonely island, it might suggest someone was *down* there out of sight."

"In the dungeon?" I gasped.

"Exactly," said Rhand.

"You call that being kind?" I cried.

"Certainly. Compared to what may happen to you tomorrow I'd call it petting you."

He must have thought I was weakening.

"After all," he went on, "Bantok might, like yourself, have starved to death down there, if I hadn't seen the ladder when I came to look for him. I'm giving you a better chance than you gave him. You have only to speak. But," he nodded, "let me warm, you that, if it's a better chance, it's also your last."

That I did not believe. He was much too anxious to get the papers. What I did believe was that my last chance would be gone the moment he got them. I didn't need Rhand to tell me what my last chance was. My last chance, indeed my only one, was to temporize.

"Look here," I said, "I can't surrender the papers to you like this. I'd be sacked if I didn't make a better fight of it."

He eyed me narrowly.

"All right," he said at length. "We'll see to it that the fight is quite real. Up you get!"

A sign to Bantok brought him over. Before I realized it I was being marched across the courtyard, and with their two pistols at the small of my back I was made to lift the stone slab, let down the ladder and descend into the hideous prison. Then the ladder was drawn up again, the stone replaced, and I was in darkness. Had I been a fool to let myself be put there so tamely?

I think it was the clapping down of that stone above my head that gave the feeling of finality to all my adventure. For at that moment, oddly enough, there came to me the memory of a boyish story-book I once possessed. Instead of the usual two words at the end which gave you the unnecessary information that it was the end of the story, this book had a tail piece: the picture of a candle with an extinguisher on top. That is what I felt when that stone was clapped down. I felt exactly as if an extinguisher had been put to my own story.

CHAPTER XIX

I am not going to describe the hours spent in that old prison house on Innisgarr. One hour was too much like all the others after the first half dozen. But I recall the thrill with which, when I started to feel about me in the dark, I came on the spade and pickax left behind and evidently forgotten by Bantok and Rhand. That was an oversight I began to put to my own advantage the moment I thought them out of hearing.

I started with the pickax on the wall under the opening, trying to chip away the mortar to make holes by which to climb to the top. But I soon gave that up. Even with light to see where to strike it would have been hardly possible. As it was, I struck the granite nine times out of ten, and the tenth, more often than not, just smashed one of the pulpy fungoid growths adhering to the wall, filling my nostrils with an odor of corruption and decay.

Then I tried to build up the earth as I had imagined Bantok would have to do when I pulled away the ladder. This promised better at first, for he had left me plenty of loose earth. But when I found it necessary to smite the earth I heaped up so as to consolidate the pile, there came the heartbreak. To make it solid enough to carry my weight would take days. And I had only hours. Besides, I soon became certain that even if I could build sufficiently high to get right under the opening, that soil could not be made solid enough to withstand the shove of the shoulder I must apply to that stone. I threw the shovel away.

Hours passed. The time came when I could discern by one dim streak of light deflected past one side of the stone overhead that a new day had come. I sat on my heap of earth waiting for Rhand's return. Hours again must have gone by. Then I ceased listening for him, telling myself he had never meant to come. Another mockery was not wanting. I discovered that though my ankle still pained me a little where it had been struck by the bullet, the effects of the strain had passed away. Of course it needed only that discovery to cap things. The irony of it! Now that I could no longer use my foot it was well again!

Then the light from the overhead chink grew more dim. But just when I was thinking it made no difference to me to know whether it was day or night up there, a faint hope returned. Murdo, finding no response to his repeated signal, might do something. What he could do I did not know, but I clung to the fact that he did tell me he had often swum across to this island. At first he would think I must have gone away; but when I did not turn up as arranged to take over my packet again, he must think something had happened, and would perhaps then come to investigate. But would he know about this old prison pit? The answer came a little later when I heard the stone over my head being pushed away. I looked up and incoherently shouted my joy. Someone laughed. "So you've had enough of it, eh?"

The voice was Rhand's.

"Yes," I said after a little. "Oh yes, I've had enough. For God's sake just give me a drink."

"That's good. Now we'll get to business. But no tricks, or God help you."

To be candid, I never thought of tricks till I learned he proposed that I should tell them where the papers were hidden and remain where I was while they went off to get them. Fairly certain that in that event I was likely to remain there forever, I told him the papers were in a place where no one could find them but myself. That got me once more into the blessed fresh air. It went to my head like wine so that I could hardly stand.

"Sure you can walk?" Rhand said. "Your foot seems worse."

There was mighty little sympathy in his tone, only fear I might not be able to lead them to the papers. But I took the hint, and did a lot of limping before we reached the boat. How little sympathy he felt was made evident enough when they made me carry the ladder while they followed close behind. But I think Rhand put away his pistol when he saw how crippled I was.

In the boat things seemed just as hopeless at first. For to keep an eye on me I was made to row, with Rhand in the stern, the ladder across the boat in front of him, and Bantok in the bow with his gun pointing at my back. I had no chance to use the oars for any other purpose except that for which oars are intended. So I went on using them as oars yet thinking hard all the time. We had nearly reached the boat-house before I found anything. Even then it seemed to me desperate enough, but it was the only trick I could think of, and I resolved that when we were not much more than fifty feet from shore I would try it on.

You see, I knew their whole attention went to the oars in my hands. These were possible weapons of offence, and no doubt it was thought I might try to use them much in the same way as I had tried to use the ladder against Rhand on the previous day. Rhand, I saw, was nervous of the oar, for he watched it. Of course they were forced to let me have the oars, otherwise I would have had to sit either in the bow or in the stern with whichever of them did the rowing between me and whoever had the pistol.

Now I knew it was useless to attempt to knock both of them overboard by a sudden swing of an oar. But they were by no means sure I wouldn't try. So, counting on their attention being fixed on that possibility, I took my one last chance. It was very simple. Having reached a safe distance from the shore I threw my legs over the right-hand oar at a moment when my arms were extended forward for the pull, and then with the oar handles coming towards me, I dropped them and slithered over the right oar on to the edge of the boat, my feet going into the water as the boat heeled over. Instinctively they jumped up and made the grab at me on which I had reckoned. Bantok got me, but as I had again reckoned, let go as the boat was capsizing. I went right under. How cold that water was! I struck out for the shore, Rhand at my heels. He was a pretty good swimmer, twice as fast as I am. Fortunately a cry from Bantok made him turn back.

Only when I reached the shore did I pause to look. The boat was quite visible, a black blob drifting bottom upwards. Some way off I could discern what looked like two footballs bobbing in the water:

the heads of Rhand and Bantok clinging apparently to the ladder and trying to propel it shorewards. I watched only long enough to see they were making sure headway, and then ran for it.

Aware that I now had the best chance I was ever likely to get, I made straight for the McPhees' camp in the quarry. My plan of operation became instantly clear. I had to pick up my papers, get some food and be over the hills and far away before morning. The camp was little more than a mile distant, but I soon had to slacken the pace. Not, thank heaven, on account of my foot. The ample rest and the massage treatment I passed the time in applying to it in that pit, had set it right again. But though my work with the oars had taken the stiffness out of me, I was too exhausted by hunger and thirst to be capable of any more fatigue. Yet during the last half mile when my walk was little more than a tottering advance, I comforted myself with the thought that even so I was forging ahead much faster than Rhand and Bantok could swim.

Old McPhee, reclining by his wood fire alone, sat up as if he had seen a ghost when I dropped down opposite him. Murdo, he told me, had swum over to the island that afternoon, and not finding trace of me or the boat, had gone off to find me and give me a warning that all the beaters from Duich were scouring the hills for miles around.

"He hasn't taken his pipes with him?" I cried in sudden fear.

"He has that. It was in his mind he could play a note or two now and then so's you'd know he was seeking you."

That made it sound not so hopeless. Anyhow, I had to make the best of it. While McPhee got out what was left of their supper, I did my best to wring out and dry my water-logged clothes. So they had had the searchers out on the hills all that day! Though all that day they knew just exactly where I was, they had kept that knowledge to themselves. That was eloquent indeed. It told me that whoever had been their first choice, I at least had been the second-choice tenant for that grave. But there would be no fooling when the Duich beaters were sent out tomorrow. However, it put me in good heart to hear, while busy with a mug of very hot toddy, how the McPhees' baggage had been searched for the articles said to have been stolen by me, even while Murdo was actually playing his pipes on the terrace.

McPhee accompanied me through the wood to the point where the hill began. In all I had not been much more than twenty minutes at the quarry, and I was sure it would take Rhand quite as long to get the bulky Bantok safely ashore. Following the directions given me as to where I was most likely to come on Murdo, I cut away diagonally over the face of the hill among the clumps of whin bushes and bracken. It was not easy going in the dark, but I had plenty of time before me to get into safe cover among the heather on the high moors before dawn. So I rested pretty often, stopping to listen for a note or two from Murdo's pipes. I knew he would think it safe at that hour to let me know where he was.

For a couple of hours I moved on in that way till I reached a position so high up above the loch and the glen that I began to meet the light wind coming off the moors. There I sat down against a bush, afraid that if I went further I might get out of earshot of Murdo's piping. I was now hot and blown besides being a trifle uneasy to have come so far without getting into touch with him, and sat very still, intent to catch any sound that would mount up to me from below.

It was a quiet and lovely night; the soft air from off the heather touched my cheek like a caress, and after the night in the musty prison pit the fresh smell of the gorse and bracken was as wine to me. Nobody except Murdo would think of looking for me there. When last seen, I had been running on the north side of the loch towards the eastern exit from the glen. But from the quarry I had doubled back up the hills on the southern side of the loch towards the west. I felt very secure. That night bird Murdo would be sure to find me. Then I must have fallen asleep.

I sat up with a jerk, the last echo of the shot which had awakened me still in my ears. The bushes around me stood pale yet distinct in the grey of dawn. But no one was within sight. Lying back again, with ears intent for another shot, a breaking twig or a sniffing dog, I could not guess from what direction the shot had been fired. And though of course I had been there at least an hour too long, I dared not move until I knew. And without hearing more than the sleepy twitter of a bird in some neighboring bush, I waited till the mist began to roll like smoke along the flanks of mighty Ben Clova opposite me, and a rosy red like fire on its naked peak, began to eat its way downward.

The shot must have come from the woods below. There could be, I told myself, no guns on the moors for a couple of days to come. On hands and knees I peeped down at the wood. It was still dark down there and would be silent till the growing light reached it and the birds awoke.

Suddenly I saw something. First one shadowy figure getting through the fence at the wood's edge, then another fifty yards further along. I did not wait for any more. Crouching till I was nearly double, I ran dodging through the whins till I reached the bare heather slopes. Then, aware that I was well out of sight, I straightened out and went hard for the nearest little hill to put it behind me before the men got high enough to see me.

Almost at the little hill's foot I put up a couple of grouse who went off with that loud and startling cackle which is so like mad laughter. A shot rang out, then another, and even as I ran I saw the birds one after the other sail stiffly to the ground. In another minute I was up the little hill and face to face with a man, gun in hand, who stared at me with down-dropped jaw.

"I'm being chased," I gasped out. "There's beaters behind me."

The poacher wasted no words.

"Follow me," he cried, turning, and making off down the further side of the slope.

For about a mile I followed him, hell for leather, till he reached the summit of a small knoll or hillock where he pulled up.

"Inside with you," he gasped as I came up.

I could not see what he meant till he stooped and tore up about a square yard of heather fastened on lengths of hazen boughs. Then I saw this covered part of a deep basin-shaped dip in the ground otherwise invisible. Tumbling in after me he pulled the heather screen back into place, and I found myself lying flat among a fine collection of grouse with the poacher panting beside me.

"Did I hear ye say they were beaters?" he asked, as soon as he could speak.

"You did," I replied.

"But it's breaking the law to kill before the Twelfth," he objected.

I thought it prudent not to tell him it was not to shoot grouse they had come. He was a little, wiry man of about forty, with a weather-beaten face, rather red, though I couldn't say how much of that color was due to our fast sprint through the heather.

"Ye must have been hard pressed to drop your gun," he remarked. "D'ye think they'll come on it?"

Seeing what he meant, I told him I was no poacher. He turned in surprise.

"But it's you they're after, isn't it?"

When I admitted this he lay for a time with his hands clasped behind his head. We were both on our backs.

"It'll no be for nothing they want ye," he remarked at length.

This I again admitted.

"Well, there are worse things than being a poacher, as ye called it."

The name I had used evidently rankled the little man, and I was beginning an apology when he laid his arm on me.

"*Wheest*, they're just on us," he whispered.

Presently my pulses quickened again as I heard the swish, swish of feet going through heather. My friend lay apparently undisturbed, like a hare in its form. I took courage from his placidity. He was more annoyed than frightened. The footsteps died gradually away. Twisting round, he crept to the end of our nest, and shoving up a tuft of heather, peeped out. When he beckoned me I crept forward and he yielded his place to me. I saw a line of men, each about fifty feet apart, methodically scouring the ground over which they were passing.

"Must have caught sight of you," my friend murmured. "They're going so slow."

It was then I recognized the artfulness of his hiding place. Apart from the cleverness with which he had taken advantage of the dip in the ground at the top of this little knoll, the knoll itself was just steep enough to make a searcher pass it by when he could, as he would think, see all that was to be seen on it from below. When at last the line of men disappeared in a distant undulation on the moor's purple surface, I thought it time for me to make off in another direction. The little poacher, however, would not hear of it.

"The heather," he declared, "is the safest and the most dangerous place a man can hide in. Lie close in it and an army couldn't find ye. Stand up in it for a second and ye can be seen for miles. Na, na, laddie, ye'll bide where ye are, for my sake if no' for your own."

Of course I could do no less, since it was I who had brought the beaters out on the moors two days before he expected to see them there. So, as neither of us dared show our noses above ground with so many men on the *qui vive*, we made the best of it in the heather-clad lair, which, as it turned out later, was well stocked with food and drink as well as game. He himself, I learned, did most of his sleeping in the daylight, and both of us did a good deal of sleeping throughout that long summer day; but when not sleeping I heard much from him about poachers and their tricks with keepers. Though he bore me no grudge for being the cause of his imprisonment there, I roused his indignation once by asking if he were a native of these parts.

"Ye surely never took me for a Mackenzie?" he demanded, with outstretched neck.

I hadn't taken him for anyone, but feeling his indignation without being able to divine its cause, I remarked that all the land around was Mackenzie country.

"That's just it," he said. "And if my name was Mackenzie, it's no' in Mackenzie country I'd be collecting the birds."

"You come from a distance then?" I ventured.

"Och ay; but it's all quite fair because, ye see, I've no further to go than the Mackenzies themselves."

"You mean you each poach the other's birds," I said in my surprise.

This made things worse.

"What's all this talk about poaching? 'The earth is the Lord's and the fulness thereof.' That's Scripture, isn't it?" he cried argumentatively. "And does it not go on to say 'He hath given it all unto the sons of men'?"

I could not resist asking him why, in that case, he and the Mackenzies didn't take the game at home and so avoid these long journeys. This moved his contempt.

"Man, d'ye no' see but here I'm only a law breaker in taking the birds. But if I was to take Sir Alexander's in the Fraser country, I'd be making myself a moral offender, since I'm a tenant of his, and forbye that he'd turn me out if I got caught on his moors."

There was nothing to be said to this, and I think we both fell asleep for a time. At any rate the last thing I remember was that he had as good as told me his name was Fraser.

Much later, before it got dark, he nudged me awake to give him a hand in stringing the grouse together. I don't know how many brace he had, but there were certainly far too many for him to carry alone. They were all, he told me, for the London market, to be kept for sale there on the afternoon of the Twelfth. For the past ten days he had been sending on grouse for that purpose.

"Ye see," he explained, "by a merciful dispensation of Providence, they like game to be high in London."

"But how do you get them there?" I inquired, adding as I saw him hesitate, "You see it's where I want to get to myself, only I've been robbed of my money."

"Have ye so!" he said, smiling. "Well, I doubt ye'll no' be able to travel as one o' the birds. That canna be contrived, but," he went on after some hesitation, "ye might earn a *lend* o' the money by lending me a little help this same night."

Then it came out he was himself in trouble. His trouble was that he had more game than he could get down to the point on the road where it was collected by a man in a cart for transport to the railway station. He had, in fact, two other caches full of game at different points on the moor, and it was essential to get all the game to the road-side by midnight when the collecting cart would pass. And the game must be in London before the market got glutted by birds actually killed on the day the shooting opened. I jumped at his offer. To get away with the birds that night was no good to me. But to have the money in my pocket meant that I could hang around there, especially as I now had such a perfect hiding place, until I got into touch with McPhee and recovered the papers.

As soon as it was quite dark our tramp began. It proved to be pretty hard going, for though few could have known the ground so well as the poacher, he was compelled to take a course the least likely to be used by anyone else. And, laden as we were, it made about the roughest journey I had known. After a bit I just followed blindly, fearing all the time for my ankle. At last we came to a road, and there under a little bridge deposited our burdens. But that was all

of the road we saw. Without rest we headed up the hill once more to
another of Fraser's caches, where we took up another load of birds.
The little man's nimbleness in threading his way amazed me, especially when I saw how he loaded himself. He seemed to dance his
way among the whins.

By the time we got down to the bridge again I was so dog tired
that I flung myself down on the grass. The distance we had covered
was possibly not more than four miles, but I was so blown with the
pace, so shaken and bruised with my many falls and stumbles, that
I felt I had already done much more than earn the *lend*, as he had
put it, of my full fare to London. Wiping the sweat from my face, I
groaned aloud to think there was yet another journey to make.

"*Wheest*," Fraser commanded. "There's somebody on the road."

He was standing rigid, bending his ear. No sound except the tinkle of the little burn water among the stones reached me. In another
moment he had gripped my arm. "Slip in here," he whispered. "He's
walking this way."

Under the culvert among the heaped-up birds, we stood waiting.
In a little I heard footsteps on the road. They were those of a man
who walked leisurely. Fraser, who maintained his grip on my arm,
was obviously both puzzled and alarmed. On the bridge above our
heads the footsteps ceased. The suspense that followed must have
been, though for a different reason, ghastly to Fraser as well.

Then at the sound which broke the silence, he must have had the
surprise of his life, for it sent me scrambling to my feet, all fatigue
gone from me, for what we heard was the groaning bagpipes make
before the tune begins. And before the tune had time to begin I was
out from under the bridge and scrambling up the bank. In fact the
tune never did begin. The mouthpiece dropped from Murdo's lips as
I leaped before him on to the road.

"*Creag Dbhu!*" cried Murdo, "it's yourself."

He seemed overjoyed to have found me, to judge by his face and
hand-clasp.

"You've got it safe?" I asked.

"I have that. You feel that," he laughed, offering me his pipes.
"It's been safe like a child in arms all the time."

"All right, Murdo," I cried, laughing too, "I'll take on the nursing myself now."

We soon had the stitches out and I was transferring the packet of papers to my pocket just as McPhee caught sight of the poacher's head peeping at us over the parapet of the little bridge.

"Who the divil have you got there?" he said.

Fraser scrambled up.

"And who the divil is it that's blowing his noise here at this hour?" he cried wrathfully. "Is your music so bad that only the wild deer or the mountain hares will stand it?"

In another second the two fiery Celts were at it hammer and tongs. Heaven knows what insults they hurled at each other, for they lapsed into their native Gaelic, which for all I know may be richer in terms of abuse. Prudence compelled me to interfere in the duet. Stepping in between the pair I told them they were both friends whose help I could never forget, even though their quarrel now should make that help useless.

Fraser first came to his senses. He had as little desire as myself to attract notice. And though Murdo at first declared he had nothing to fear from any since there was no harm in a man playing himself home on the road, he knew well enough now in what fear I went. Presently I had them shaking hands. Indeed, in another ten minutes Murdo was offering to go instead of me to carry in the remaining load of birds. I was glad to let him go, as glad as Fraser was to have him, for time had been lost, and Murdo would be far quicker on the job than I could be.

Then just when Fraser went under the bridge to get the carrying poles on which the grouse were slung, Murdo seized my arm.

"I doubt you'll no' get through," he whispered. "There's too many out after ye."

"Where?" I asked.

"Everywhere. They're dotted about everywhere—thick enough to stop even a rabbit from getting through. At least that's what it looked like to me."

"You've seen them?" I asked.

"Ay. But no' before they saw me. You'll never do it. Better come back with me."

Before I could reply Fraser reappeared, and they left me sitting alone on the bridge with Murdo's bagpipes on my knees.

For the next half hour the only sound I heard was the tinkle of the burn. The country was wild and lonely, just great rolling hills and empty glens. In the next twenty miles there were but two houses on the road. I looked at the great darkness into which those endless wilderness of moors stretched, and it was impressed on me that only in daylight could I hope to travel there. But in daylight on the moors a man can be seen for miles. Things seemed pretty hopeless.

A minute or two later they were made to look a little more hopeless when I was abruptly wakened out of my reverie by a sound on the road. Up till then I had sat on the parapet, confident that I could hear footsteps at a long distance, and the beat of a car's engine several miles away. But it was none of these I heard then, only a slight whirring sound, rather close at hand.

Without waiting to see what it might be, I slung my feet over, dropped on to the bank behind the parapet, and lay still. The next instant I detected the whirring of rubber on the gritty road as a bicycle crossed the bridge. It had no light. But that proved nothing, since in that unfrequented road lights were hardly necessary. Still, after that I got right under the bridge among the birds and stayed there, listening. For a long time the only sound that came out of the blackness was one far-away cry from a hill sheep. Then the feeling of loneliness which that thin cry seemed to intensify was broken by another sound. The distant throbbing of a motor engine, waxing and waning to every dip and bend of the road. It, too, appeared to have no lights, but I felt quite secure under the bridge, and waited till it passed overhead.

That sense of security, however, vanished with lightning abruptness when I heard it stop on the bridge. Then someone got down. I heard his heavy feet on the gritty road. He moved about a little and I distinctly heard a muttered curse. Something had gone wrong with the engine. He moved over to the parapet and I heard a match struck and saw a dim light that bobbed up and down once or twice and then went out. He had lit his pipe and was sitting on the parapet waiting. This, I thought, must be the game collector, as Fraser had called him. It relieved me to think so. But I let him wait. It was no time for me to take a risk. And as it turned out he had not long to wait. Presently, from out of the darkness, I overheard the now familiar swishing of feet in the heather, then a snap or two of branches, and breathing audibly, two laden figures hove into sight to be greeted with whispered curses by the man on the bridge.

When I in turn got up on the road my interest concentrated on the vehicle that stood there. I hoped for a covered van in which I could lie concealed. It was a bitter disappointment to see an open lorry, laden with herring barrels and fish boxes. Obviously this was the fish carrier who carried the fish from Duich to the railway at Keppoch Bridge. But, like my friend Jim Peters, he evidently believed in having a side line to his regular business.

"Fish!" I said in my disappointment.

Murdo laughed.

"Ay," he said, "fish wi' feathers on them."

Murdo was right. There may have been a box or two of fish to give the right smell, but from all I saw I fancy the side line was in fish, not in game. Anyhow, in double quick time the boxes and barrels were loaded up with the birds and then Fraser and the carrier drew apart and the chink of money punctuated the whispered colloquy that followed.

"Ye might get through in one o' the empty barrels," Murdo whispered.

"It's what I mean to do," I replied.

"It'll be sair riding though, even if he'll take ye."

"I'll split on him if he doesn't," I declared.

"Oh, surely no!" Murdo cried, horrified.

But no such threat was necessary. Fraser, having evidently explained the situation, introduced me to the carrier, McAndrew, at the same time, with McAndrew as a witness, handing me over the four pounds which he was so trustfully lending me. I say trustfully, for if Fraser looked on the loan as a kind of blackmail, his farewells would hardly have been as kindly as those given me by Murdo himself.

McAndrew, an expert at concealment, did his best to make me as little uncomfortable as possible. Having now his lights on, he told me to keep at his back and be ready to lift the barrel over my head whenever he might sound his horn. So for mile on mile we bumped along, I behind his shadowy shoulders, the road all lit up to a micro-scopic distinctness in the glare of his head lamps, and my spirits rising with every milestone we left behind.

Then there came a blast from McAndrew's horn. We must then have been passing the lonely Corry Inn. I dived for my barrel, tipped it against the side of the lorry and somehow got it over my head just as a voice hailed us to stop. The brakes screamed and we pulled up.

"Where do you come from?" the voice demanded. "Duich wi' fish," McAndrew replied. "Is it a lift ye want?"

At first no answer came, but when it did I knew the man was on tiptoe peering into the lorry.

"Have you given a lift to anyone on the way?"

The carriers' answer froze my blood at first.

"Oh yes," he said, "a man stopped me a couple of miles out of Glengyle, and I took him as far as the Gart burn. Said he was going over the moor into Glen Doyne and would follow the burn."

"What was he like?" a new voice demanded. I knew this voice: it was Captain Elliott's, the big game hunter.

"A young fellow, in a blue suit wi' no hat. I was quite glad to get rid of him. But maybe he wouldna' have been so bad looking if he hadn't looked so hunted and frightened."

"Gart burn is nine miles back," the first voice remarked.

"Damn!" said Elliott.

"Oh, we've as good as got him, sir. He'll not get far up Glen Doyne till it's daylight."

"An ill-doer, is he?" McAndrew cut in. "Well, I must say he looked it."

I caught a murmur of voices as the others conferred together. The engine began to accelerate.

"Well, I must be getting on," McAndrew continued. "Fish will no keep, ye understand."

But just as the clutch was let in and we began to move, Elliott's voice came again.

"One moment," he called. "This man has got away with the pro-ceeds of a burglary. There are several watching for him on the road. I want you to tell them to get back to the Gart burn."

McAndrew expressed his willingness. I heard him thank the Captain, for something passed to him as he asked where he was to look out for these others. The voice that replied was that of the young forester on whose bicycle I had had designs.

"At Invererity. Then on the bridge before Mamoch. And you can look out at the Tom dhu corner as well," he said.

McAndrew laughed when we were beyond earshot. "You might as well come and sit beside me," he said, "now I know the danger points."

But I stayed on the floor. It was enough for me to be out of the barrel except when we were approaching the danger points, at each of which McAndrew was stopped and questioned.

Whether they had other pickets out at Keppoch Bridge itself, or at the railway station, I do not know, for I parted from McAndrew a mile or two short of the village. Then following his directions, I took the bye road to Ardberg, a wayside station further on where, at eight o'clock, I boarded the almost empty morning train for the south.

By twelve I was in Glasgow, seated in a Union Street barber's chair. For once in a way the barber was unloquacious, though the shop was empty. It was while looking in his glass with approval at the improvement he had made to my appearance that I saw him looking around for my hat.

"I've lost my hat," I explained.

"Have ye so? Ah well, a little bit of jollification does nae harm now and then," he remarked, laying down the brush.

"Jollification?" I said. "You think I've been enjoying myself, just because I've lost my hat?"

"Hoch, no; it's not by the hat by itsel' I'd judge," said he briskly. "But when a man comes here wi' three days' growth on his chin, and in clothes he's slept out in, forbye throwing himself back in the chair so weary that he starts yawning his head off right away, I ken he's been on the spree."

"You should have been a detective," I said.

"Och, we all enjoy a spree till it's over," he said, adding as he eyed me thoughtfully. "If you're as hungry as ye look there's a verra good place up the street."

It was only when my spree seemed over that I began to enjoy it. I went to the place up the street, and over the meal savored the sweets of my achievement. I had done my job. That very night I would be at Biddulph's door with the goods, as he had called them, in my hands. I wanted to wire him the great news there and then; but recalling his strict injunction forbidding any communication, I wired Jim Peters instead to expect me at St. Pancras by the ten o'clock that night.

And at ten that night when the train glided into the terminus, Peters was there. I caught his eye just as I was handing over my ticket. He met me with outstretched hand. But just as I felt his grasp, another hand fell on my shoulder.

"Alexander Maitland, I believe."

Before I could reply, another hand had taken my arm and I was propelled gently away from the throng of hurrying people.

"Alexander Maitland, you are wanted in connection with the death of Francis Martin. We are taking you to Scotland Yard where the warrant will be read to you. Meanwhile it is my duty to caution you that anything you now say may be . . ."

"Well I'm . . . *damned!*" Peters' voice came penetratingly in the intensity of its horror and surprise.

My so-called *spree* was not quite over yet.

CHAPTER XX

At Scotland Yard they put me through it all right. After the warrant was read to me I was searched and all I had on me, not much more than the packet of letters and a few coppers, taken away, and I was removed to another room for interrogation.

At first it amazed me to see how wide of the mark they were.

"It was on the 18th of May you left Dublin, wasn't it?" the Chief Inspector briskly began, while the other fellow just watched me.

"Never been in Dublin in my life," I asserted.

"You crossed to Holyhead the same night. On the boat you met Francis Martin in the bar."

"No."

"You deny all knowledge of Francis Martin then?"

This took me aback rather.

"Well, I did meet him," I admitted.

"That's better. You had a few drinks together on board, hadn't you?"

"No; I first met him in London," I declared.

"When? Where?"

"Oh, I just met him casually. We got into talk in the street," I replied, wondering how much they knew.

His eyebrows went up.

"On the day you met him, then, you each changed to another address?"

"We did."

"At the same time exchanging your names?"

"Quite so."

"Why?"

I hesitated. To answer that softly put question would have meant telling the whole story. And it was not my story but Biddulph's. I was now exactly in the position I had foreseen, though as a wild possibility only, that first night in Biddulph's room. And Biddulph had forbidden me to speak even in such circumstances.

"This is what you call the third degree, isn't it?" I tried to temporize.

The Chief Inspector held up a shocked hand.

"Didn't you hear me say you needn't answer a single question—unless, of course, you wanted to clear yourself?" he added.

"It's all a ghastly mistake," I said. "I had nothing to do with his death."

The Chief Inspector sat back. He was actually twiddling his thumbs while he stared at me. Not for a moment did he believe me. I saw it in his eye. Suddenly he bent forward and tapped my knee.

"Look here," he began in a new tone, "let's drop this trifling. We *know* you're the wanted man. We got at you through James Peters. When he came to the mortuary to identify the man murdered under the name of Maitland, he thought at first we had shown him the wrong body. So did Mr. Lucius. But whereas Lucius obviously was frank, Peters as clearly wasn't telling us all he knew. That is why we took steps to have a look at his correspondence before it reached him, and so got a sight of your telegram from Glasgow this morning. Your connection with the man murdered in the Café Sorrento we established as soon as the replies to the circulars sent out to hotels and boarding houses began to come in. We fastened on to Papini's description of the man who had stayed at his place for one night only, because it explained the mystery as to the change of clothes which had taken place in the dead man's rooms. For the suit in which Martin had arrived at Papini's was that found in the dead man's room, while that in which he left Papini's tallied exactly with the description of the suit worn by the man who registered as Maitland at the Café Sorrento. That," he concluded, "is how we knew the man at Papini's had been in the dead man's room."

It took no more than a breath or two to see the significance of all this. But I wasn't done yet.

"And did Papini tell you about a big red-faced man who had called to ask for a Mr. Martin when he was out?" I asked.

"Papini told us everything. And we did not overlook the possibility that the man might have come seeking the sham Martin and afterwards found the one he was really looking for. But that possibility faded when we found only one man's fingerprints in the room."

"On the match-box," I cried involuntarily.

"And the knife," the Chief Inspector nodded.

There was a long silence after that. He was quite sure he had me cornered. And cornered I was. Unless I called in Biddulph. There simply was no other way out. Biddulph had warned me that I must keep my mouth shut even if I got into the hands of the police. But what he had in his mind then, surely, was not Scotland Yard but some provincial police court where there would be local newspaper reporters eager for news items acceptable to the big London press agencies. And even then he had only the possibility of a six months' sentence for me in his mind: not the sort of charge with which I was now faced.

"Want to make a clean breast of it?" the Chief Inspector suggested.

I stared at him. He was once more twiddling his thumbs.

"Will you let me 'phone someone up first?" I asked doubtfully.

Rather to my surprise he consented, himself looking up the number and putting through the call. I knew, as we waited, it was only a chance Biddulph would be at home. The younger officer who had been writing, left the room as soon as we got our call taken up. Alas, I thought to myself, it was not in this fashion I had seen myself speaking to Biddulph again!

"Hullo!" came his voice.

"Maitland speaking," I called back.

"Who?" It was almost a cry.

"Maitland speaking. Look here, I'm in trouble. Will you please come and answer for me? It's late, I know, but—"

"Where are you speaking from?" he cut in.

"Scotland Yard."

There was a pause. Then his voice came almost angrily in a rush.

"I'll see you damned first. You ought not to have rung me up. You know what our understanding was. If you've got into trouble it's your funeral, not mine."

"But, Biddulph—"

The jar of the replaced receiver came through from the other end.

Since that night I have often wondered what course Biddulph would have taken had I begun by telling him I had succeeded. I may be wrong, but I believe that if I had put that great news first and my own need second, he would have acted differently. For of course he could not but think I had failed and got caught. That was bad luck for me. But it was Biddulph's bad luck too that he was now to be robbed of the honor of presenting to his chief the prize for which he and I had schemed and worked so hard.

So I turned to the Chief Inspector. He was reading some papers which had just been laid before him by his subordinate who had returned.

"Look here," I began, "I must see Mr. Wynne Chatsworth at once."

He looked up quickly to stare at me. He seemed almost frightened. Whether he thought his interrogation had sent me crazy—and there had been some talk lately about third degree at Scotland Yard—I don't know, but for a few moments he just gazed fixedly at me.

"Mr. Chatsworth must be in bed long ago," he said slowly.

"Never mind, he'll sleep better when he's seen me," I said very confidently, for I recalled Biddulph's telling me how Chatsworth's anxiety over this business robbed him of sleep.

Instead of replying the Chief Inspector indicated the slip of paper which had been laid on his desk.

"What understanding did you have with this man Biddulph?" he asked.

Then I perceived that my brief talk with Biddulph on the 'phone had been tapped. That, no doubt, was why he had so readily agreed to let me 'phone. The record of the talk was now on his desk.

"Mr. Biddulph is an official in Mr. Chatsworth's department," I explained.

He waved a hand at the paper before him.

"We know that already. What I want to know is what connection Mr. Chatsworth can have with the Café Sorrento murder. Come, Mr. Maitland," he went on when he saw me smile at this notion, "there's no doubt more behind all this than I thought; but surely you can see it's no light matter to get a Cabinet Minister out of his bed at this hour of the night."

His complete change of tone gave me confidence.

"He'll be the last to complain," I asserted, "if you give him what you took from me."

"You mean those letters to Lady Wridgley? What can they have to do with the case?"

"That's for Mr. Wynne Chatsworth, not me, to tell you, if he likes," I said.

There was some further parleying. But finally the Chief Inspector, after being away for some time possibly consulting greater men than himself, returned to tell me with obvious trepidation, that Mr. Chatsworth had been summoned to the Yard.

We had a long time to wait. I was left in charge of the younger officer who did his best to make me comfortable. About one o'clock coffee and sandwiches were brought me, and glad I was to break my long fast. Cigarettes were even provided, and it was over one of these that Inspector Mellor planked a photograph before me.

"What d'ye make of that?" he inquired. "It came in from Dublin tonight."

One glance was enough. At once I recognized the heavy face.

"Why, that's the very man who followed me," I cried—"the red-faced man I spoke of."

"Good!" cried Mellor. "That's good. But lucky you were he didn't get you. No wonder Martin wanted to get to Canada with Jim Mc-Cabe after him."

"What was it—political?" I inquired.

"Oh, something of the sort. This man Martin blew the gaff on him and took a reward for it, in the matter of some shootings and burnings a year or two back. When McCabe served his sentence Martin cleared out of Ireland."

Then, just as he was beginning with further questions, after reminding me the Yard had still to fix the crime on McCabe, the door was flung open and Mr. Chatsworth was shown in, followed by the Assistant Commissioner of Police.

It was the first time I had seen Chatsworth in the flesh. But the press had made me too familiar with that round, almost cherubic face, whimsical mouth and smiling eyes for me not to know him. He ought to have been smiling then, for he carried my packet of letters in his hand. But not the hint of a smile appeared and his words were incisive.

"I want to hear your story," he said, waving me to be seated.

Chatsworth seated himself straight and stiff on a chair in the middle of the room, the Assistant Commissioner slipping into a chair against the wall. This wasn't in the least as I had pictured the moment. For I had seen him shaking my hand with heartiness and with gratitude in his eyes. And now my thought was that if I had robbed Biddulph of this moment I had not robbed him of much. Rather disconcerted, feeling small in the presence of such a great man, and possibly influenced by his use of the word "story," I began at the very beginning as a child might.

"Well, sir, when I got back from South Africa—"

"Never mind about South Africa," he cut in. "How did you get your hands on these?" he said, holding up the bundle of letters. A doubt assailed me at his tone.

"Aren't they what you wanted, sir?" I asked.

His face flushed up.

"Wanted!" he cried. "Wanted! Why, man, I've wanted these more than a miser wants gold or a saint wants God."

Well, after that outburst I thought I knew what he meant. He had got what he wanted so much; but, like the schoolboy some critics said he was, he now wished to hear and gloat over every detail and item of the story. So much was this so that he didn't stop me when I began with things he knew already such as my call to Biddulph's flat and his own telephone message. In fact I told him the story much as I have told it here, and not till I reached that morning when I saw Lady Wridgley steal her husband's letter did he interrupt me.

"How do you know it was his she took?" he asked.

"Because she had looked over the pile before he came down. And not finding what she was looking for, she hung about till Sir Charles put it there," I replied.

"Go on," he said, with the first smile I had seen since telling him how Rhand and Elliott had almost quarreled about the latter's surreptitious over-buying of the Katangana shares. But he laughed outright on hearing of the anxiety caused by the detention of Count

Fernandez in London through invitations from quarters too exalted to be declined. Indeed, he rubbed his hands over that with such delight that I fancy he himself had a hand in that bit of strategy. There was, however, no sign of amusement when I came to my discovery of Bantok digging the grave on the island. For, after hearing of this, he went back on my story to question me about that day when I went fishing with Mrs. Rhand and Sir Charles, and what I remembered of the curious talk between them.

At my discovery of the box-room and my journey along the roof, he sat forward to listen, as indeed did the Commissioner when I told how I had hidden the letters in McPhee's bagpipes and how I got trapped on the island and my escape from the boat. About the day on the hills with Fraser the poacher, however, and how I had got finally clear away through McAndrew, the game collector, I thought it safer to say nothing.

Yet at the end it rather disappointed me that Chatsworth sat so long silent. I fancy even the Assistant Commissioner, Sir Edward Beatson, was surprised that he had no word to say. But Chatsworth seemed far away in thought. When the silence became tense I had to break into it. After all, this was the end.

"I hope, sir, the Nerani railway is now safe," I said.

"Eh?"

His eyes gleamed life again as I repeated my question, for it was natural that I should wish to know my patriotic work had not been in vain.

"Oh yes, safe as houses now," he said. "Thanks to you," he added with real heartiness.

"And us," the Assistant Commissioner remarked with emphasis.

"Ye-s," Chatsworth agreed. "Thanks also to you. God knows what might have happened if you hadn't—"

"Quite so," said the Assistant Commissioner as he too accepted a fag.

After that I appeared to be forgotten.

"You see what happened, of course," said Chatsworth.

"Well, Wridgley must have got wind of what was afoot. Then Rhand tried to force his hand by threatening his political ruin through these letters to his wife."

"But," Chatsworth cut in, "like the honorable man he was, Wridgley wrote, probably to me, the letter his wife got hold of. He meant to expose the plot, whatever the cost. Good Lord, and then Mrs. Rhand tried to vamp him. Think of it! Of course she failed. So that same evening Rhand sent his man to dig a grave on the island, for that same night they were to have taken Sir Charles out fishing. Yet we can't touch them, Beatson, we've nothing to go on."

"These letters no help?" Beatson suggested.

"None at all. No use whatever," Chatsworth said.

Now that touched me up. To have risked one's life and then hear that, was too much. Had his thanks been a polite insincerity only?

"But, sir," I protested, greatly daring, "if they are useless, your thanks to me just now must have been a mockery."

Chatsworth's well-known look of half mocking raillery grinned back at me.

"I thanked Scotland Yard too," he said. "And I'm the last man to treat the Yard with mockery."

"Well, I did wonder what thanks you owed Scotland Yard in this matter," I said.

Like a shot the answer came.

"Because the Yard arrested you and so stopped you from taking the letters elsewhere." He held up a silencing hand when I was about to interrupt. "You misunderstand, Maitland. When I said to Beatson here that the letters were useless, he meant and I meant useless for the purpose of incriminating Rhand. We knew Rhand was behind this. We knew he had bought Elliott for the purpose of getting at Lady Wridgley. We knew Lady Wridgley got the information from someone in our office. But who that person in our office was I could not even guess till I read these letters here tonight."

All this I already knew from Biddulph. What I did not even yet see was what Scotland Yard had to do with it. Scotland Yard had hindered, not helped me.

"But, sir, if I hadn't been arrested you would probably have had the letters sooner, for I always thought of myself as engaged by yourself for this duty, even though it was through my friend Biddulph you engaged me."

Chatsworth sat forward again.

"Look here, Maitland," he began. "When I agreed with Beatson here that I owed thanks to the Yard, I was quite serious. Had you not been arrested, I never would have known the identity of the traitor in our office who was betraying us, since you would in all innocence have handed over the letters to the traitor himself. You see? That telephone call he let you overhear was a fake to take you in and make you think he was talking to me. He must have been half out of his mind when he knew that Rhand had not only got the information he was selling from Lady Wridgley, but the letters in which the information was contained. Lady Wridgley was a fool. But he soon would know how remorselessly Rhand would squeeze. Squeeze? I'll bet once Rhand had those letters in his hands he never paid another penny to any of them. Biddulph, by the time you met him, must have been doing his dirty work for nothing. That is why he was ready for any desperate attempt to recover his letter. Ready, Maitland, even for such a forlorn hope as you took on."

Wynne Chatsworth looked up suddenly, the elfish, whimsical light back again in his eyes, and his head cocked to one side.

"Devilish odd, isn't it, Beatson, to remember that if an Irish footman had not chanced to get murdered in an Italian café in Soho there would be no railway through Portuguese Africa to connect a British Crown Colony with the coast."

COACHWHIP PUBLICATIONS
CoachwhipBooks.com

THE INVISIBLE
BULLET

& Other Strange Cases of
Magnum, Scientific Consultant

MAX RITTENBERG

COACHWHIP PUBLICATIONS
CoachwhipBooks.com

THE HEX MURDER

Alexander Williams

COACHWHIP PUBLICATIONS
CoachwhipBooks.com

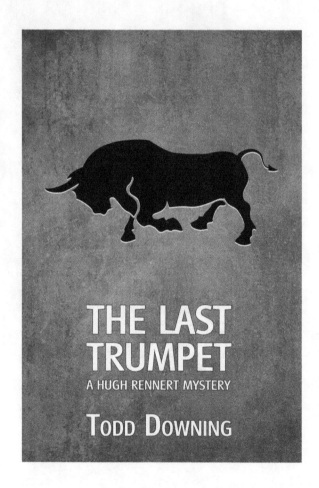

THE LAST
TRUMPET
A HUGH RENNERT MYSTERY

TODD DOWNING

THE CAT
SCREAMS
A HUGH RENNERT MYSTERY

TODD DOWNING

COACHWHIP PUBLICATIONS

CoachwhipBooks.com

PATTERN
IN BLACK
AND RED

FARADAY KEENE

COACHWHIP PUBLICATIONS
CoachwhipBooks.com

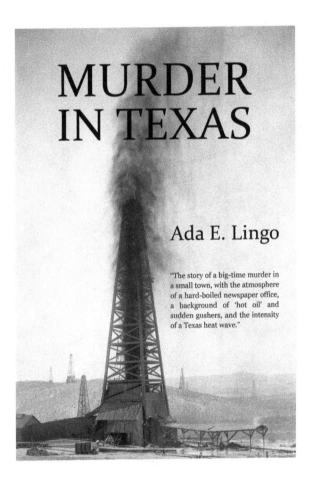

MURDER
IN TEXAS

Ada E. Lingo

"The story of a big-time murder in
a small town, with the atmosphere
of a hard-boiled newspaper office,
a background of 'hot oil' and
sudden gushers, and the intensity
of a Texas heat wave."

COACHWHIP PUBLICATIONS

CoachwhipBooks.com

THE GOLF CLUB MURDER | OWEN FOX JEROME

COACHWHIP PUBLICATIONS

CoachwhipBooks.com

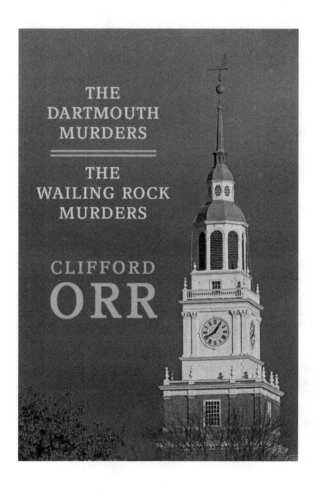

Printed in the USA
CPSIA information can be obtained
at www.ICGtesting.com
LVHW021926100524
779688LV00008B/839